The Mandrake Broom

The author welcomes inquiries from readers at JessWells.com.

Library of Congress cataloging data pending.

Printed in Canada

Also by Jess Wells

Fiction:

The Price of Passion

AfterShocks

Love Shook My Heart II

Lip Service

Two Willow Chairs

The Dress, The Cry, and a Shirt with No Seams

The Sharda Stories

Run

Non-fiction:

Home Fronts: Controversies in the Non-Traditional Parenting
Community

Lesbians Raising Sons

A Herstory of Prostitution in Western Europe

Dedicated to the nine million who perished in the witch-burnings.

Book One

Chapter One

Salerno, Italy, 1465

*T*he priests encircled the little girl, pressing her against the wall with the end of a cane. Like a chip of flint, a shard of a girl, she seemed as much *of* the stone wall as in front of it and she willed herself to seep through the mortar. To escape the priests'screaming questions and predictions of the Devil's presence in her, to run from their flapping black robes, their twisted faces with spittle on their beards and their eyes promising tortures that she had heard about. They couldn't burn her as a witch, Luccia thought, she was too young. But only too young by six months. She was nine. They could. They would. They would say that the Devil had sent her here with this big box in her arms, its lid flapping open and a vial broken on the cobblestones. Obstetric tools had clanged to the ground and lay across her tattered shoes. Soul snatcher, she heard them hiss. Stealer of body parts. The rack, the blades, they would strip a yard of her flesh for every soul she had taken.

Bells began tolling in the high tower and the great doors of the church creaked open. The priests turned in unison and Luccia ducked, ran along the wall, turned the corner and dove under the cape of a pie man, trotted sideways in the lane hearing the priests calling behind her. She folded herself into the twig bundles of an old man, darted out to be the swineherd, rolled under the wheels of a wagon, curled in the gutter was a bundle of rags. She tore her leg on the cobblestones, but saw that the priests were turning, befuddled. She sprinted up and grabbed a dirty cloth, became a tottering, cloaked old man, then pushed the rag into her pocket and joined a

1

gaggle of children. Within three blocks and down two narrow lanes she had become both genders, three ages, two professions and an inanimate object. Anything but be seen. Stealth, subterfuge: she would make her body as malleable as bread dough.

As a girl, Luccia Alimenti had heard the hem of her mother's skirt slap across the flagstones of the *piazza* as the sound of curtains being drawn to protect her from the dawn, of a sheet pulled over her young, sweat-chilled skin, of tea on a little plate being brought to her across the night-time room. It was the single note of sudden inspiration as her mother was driven from their rooms to the medical school across the square, and the sound of her mother's skirt was in harmony with the rustle of her students as they debated the merits of burdock root as a poultice.

This morning, with a lemony sun on her shoulders and her own skirts too short to make a sound, Luccia hurried to cross the *piazza* after her mother and the glory of her noisy skirts. Her mother, Giovanna, strode ahead to catch up with a wild-haired Irish woman, Fiona, who let her walking stick thud insistently on the stones and her cape flare out, displaying its deep blue lining. The women met without speaking, and Giovanna studied Fiona's eyes for some good news, but sighed over the anger she saw instead. Fiona put her walking stick under her arm and tried to collect her hair and her rage into its knot.

Fiona had a new gash on her arm and Giovanna reached for it, letting herbs in a flat basket she was carrying slip unnoticed onto the flagstones. Luccia gathered them as she approached—chamomile, St. John's Wort and tansy—clasp them like a bouquet in her fist, feeling their oils dampening her hand, their aroma filling her nostrils, and she crushed all but the tansy between her fingers, rubbed the heads of their flowers together until they coalesced into a gel that shone in the citrus sun. Luccia, nine years old and lanky for her age, threw her shoulders back and smeared the salve on Fiona's arm. The women, studying each other's faces in a silent conversation of disappointment, turned to Luccia, surprised. Her mother opened the girl's fist, inspected the basket, the stems that lay abandoned at her feet.

"How'd she know?" Fiona asked incredulously.

2

"More to the point, how did it gel without boiling?" Giovanna asked quietly.

Giovanna brightened with pride, standing tall behind her daughter and putting her hands on the girl's shoulders, but Fiona looked stealthily around them, then turned the clan by their shoulders and marched them quickly out of the square, leaving the scraps of the herbs on the cobblestones. As a priest crossed their path, Giovanna and Fiona averted their eyes and Luccia was gathered deeper into the folds of her mother's melodic skirt.

Luccia clung to her mother's hand and its messages but stomped across the square with irritation. Neither Fiona, nor even her mother, understood: they thought plants were just objects at the beck and call of the healer, but Luccia knew it was the other way around. Plants had will. They communicated. They didn't just grow together in each other's shadow by mistake, they chose each other to build community, they spoke on the wind, the breeze. They signaled their compatibility through color and smell. The plants in her mother's basket had made it clear that they belonged together. They had cast out the tansy. She knew. Not because she had heard Fiona's discomfort from across the square. Even when she was inches away from Fiona's arm with the salve in the palm of her hand, she didn't hear the pain of the torn skin. She heard the plants working together toward the salve. She had heard the cry of the rejected tansy, just as now that they were nearing their home, she heard the contented murmur of the moss growing thick on the fountain.

Fiona shut the door to their building as if they'd reached shore. After making a brief sign of the cross, Giovanna pleaded silently with the portraits of her family that hung down the hall of their flat — serious people in academic robes or the aprons of alchemists, holding mortars or herb sprays. Giovanna Alimenti was one of the few female medical professors at the University of Salerno, the last in a line of Alimenti doctors for whom babies had been named and cures had been dedicated, whose discoveries peppered the curricula. Now their paintings were hung with an attempt at ceremony and decorum, in a flat off a square they wouldn't have approved of, in a hallway much too short for the stretch of their grand history.

Fiona strode into the living room, tossing her walking stick to the floor where it hit with a violent thud, and Giovanna rustled in behind her.

"So they said no," Giovanna said quietly.

"Eve's sin," Fiona snarled, and Giovanna sighed, shook her head.

"We're down to just two copies," Giovanna said, pacing the room while Luccia pressed her back against the hallway wall, listening. Fiona threw her hands up in furious resignation.

That morning, Fiona had climbed to the abbey on the hill above town to plead once again with the monks to copy the works of Salerno's only woman master, Dame Trotula, who had held the master's chair in medicine at the university until her death in 1097 a.d. More important than Dame Bofana who brought mid-winter gifts, more cherished than anyone with a portrait in the hall, Trotula's name was invoked in the Alimenti household as if she were a dragon-slayer in a fairy tale. Giovanna told her daughter of Trotula as they baked, as they studied together. Trotula was perhaps the first to understand that there were three types of diseases, Giovanna explained, ticking them off on her floury fingers: inherited, contagious and self-generated. But Trotula wrote about women's bodies as well as men's, Giovanna said, pounding the dough with her fist. She documented childbirth and its diseases, gynecology and its intricacies. Trotula was the first to teach pediatrics as a separate branch of medicine. She had infuriated the medical world when she had suggested that the man was as easily at fault for sterility as the woman.

Fiona angrily muttered in the living room and Luccia hid within ear-shot: now there weren't enough copies of Trotula's work for the students, or the library, and they were receiving requests from other schools. The transcription of books was in the hands of just two groups, one of whom was the monks, who had recently taken to frightened refusal: it was against the monk's orders to write of female genitalia and of the ways to ease childbirth. Eve's sin, the monk who was head of the scribes had whispered fiercely, though it was his own fear of persecution that drove him. They wouldn't write on it, and the herbs to regulate menstruation and childbirth were outlawed. So Fiona had strode home furious, frustrated.

4

Luccia sat in the middle of the hall, her lanky legs tucked under her, staring at the portraits while eating a blood orange, the juice running down her chin, then her arm, to her sleeve. She licked at the juice nervously, troubled by the conversation and the sound of her mother's skirts as she paced the room. She searched the faces of her ancestors for an answer to her mother's dilemma, for a sign of herself, and as she did more frequently than she told her mother, for a sign of her father.

Luccia had been told perfunctorily that her father had died on the horns of an ox before she was born, that he had been a fine potter who had lived here on the square, but Luccia understood early on that he was not a man for whom portraits were painted. Luccia didn't remember meeting her father or any of the doctors honored on the wall. All that Luccia remembered of her family was the smell of lavender mixed with the wood of her aunt's funeral pyre, and the heaving of Giovanna's breasts.

Luccia sighed, and Giovanna turned to her, watching her scan the faces of her relatives again. Her daughter's search added to the abandoned feeling that hung through the flat. Usually, Giovanna, despite missing her people, treated her pain as unimportant. She and her daughter were Salernitas, she reminded herself, devoted to the town's cherished medical college. Unspoken and powerful for Salernitas was the knowledge that for most women, their pasts were something they were in flight from, a secret that made them feel unmoored at dusk. The medical school at Salerno was filled with women who had come from all over Europe and North Africa, cast out by their families, unsuccessful in their marriages, in contract with someone to avoid a worse contract with someone else. Muslims wouldn't let men provide medical attention to their wives so they educated women to be doctors in Salerno. Jews weren't allowed in universities anywhere else so Jewish women studied there. Christians wouldn't educate their women on any subject at all outside of the convent, so Salerno became the one place where a woman could congregate and study, could move through a city with a book in her arm without raising suspicion. So generations of women medical students became world-renowned doctors to kings, founders of hospitals, authors that schooled generations. There was a tenuous safety for them in Salerno, where women took each other at face value, in the present, no questions asked. So Luccia took her mother's word for it that her father had died on the horns of an ox and trusted her nose that her last relative had smelled of lavender and wood.

Salerno, just south of Naples, was perched between the Mediterranean and the crags of the Amalfi mountains. While up the coast, artisans fired kilns and made ceramics for the queen, the Salernitas sent up tiny curls of smoke from the fires of herbalists and received the stricken king, cured the maladies of Popes, diagnosed aristocrats who traveled far to find them, and healed the poor lucky enough to be in Salerno.

Luccia and her mother lived for a thin sinew of rosemary smoke, the aroma of hawthorn in the sun, the thick warm smell of marigolds being boiled for ointment. They were fleeting smells that caught Luccia as she walked around a corner, a thread of smoke that escaped out a window and quickly disappeared, experiments that wafted through a doorframe as a woman slipped out with the smoke clinging to her skirts. Next to shops filled with ropes and pulleys, buckets and nets for the ships, were windows filled with herbs drying upside down in little bouquets—Irish moss, witch hazel, stinging nettle, valerian, pellitory of the wall, comfrey, angelica, chervil. Barks were piled on the shelves, roots sent her their odor of rich dirt, twigs held their last clinging leaves, and—sitting in baskets prepared by the shopkeeper—hop pillows and vinegars for the bath. Bottles of blue liquid shimmered in front of her, and inside glass jars pickled animals showed their protruding teeth and their claws. Buckets of fetid smelling ooze made her hide her nose inside her sleeve while she studied the bird's nests and pickled eggs, vines that looked like nightmare spiders, the drying ears of unknown animals, little vials with tiny corks wrapped in tissue paper scratched with unknown languages. She was a little girl in a town of big smells, using her nose to navigate, too young to see the countertop but listening to the scraping sound of the mortar and pestle, the hiss of powders being poured into little linen bags.

Herbs and the ocean, they defined Luccia's Salerno, and as she walked with her hand safe within her mother's, comforted by the rustle of Giovanna's skirts, Luccia's mother recited the names of the plants they passed, each cluster in the window, each aroma that found them.

The herbs became street markers to Luccia. One narrow, twisting street housed the school for studies of the skin and the marigold and garlic to treat it. Winding away from the piazza in the lane behind the church was the avenue of the scholars of the bone smelling of comfrey and eggshells. The alley that held the butcher shop gave off an iron stench of blood, rosemary and dill.

Salerno was also a town filled with manuscripts—the texts of the great masters, of course, the *Passionario*—all 251 chapters of it—the *Antidotarium* as their pharmaceutical text. The Arabs brought their books of alchemy, their scrolls, and their spices. Books on the healing arts in many languages lay next to the stacks of bark, wedged between the bottles and the charts of the moon, the tides, the sunrise. In Salerno everyone carried notes: journals in boxes, disheveled studies with scribbles in the margin, extra papers stuck in a book, manuscripts carried through town like a suckling child. In Salerno, every vegetable basket had a folio stuck in the corner, every stack of washing had its study notes underneath. Papers jutted from pockets, from clammy, anxious fists, from bags, under capes.

They were a people who fervently believed in the power of a new idea, the remedy just invented, in collecting and comparing how it was done elsewhere. The scrap of paper and its cryptic note had more power in Salerno than the leather-bound volume, for the scrap was the hint of something new, and Salerno was a city in love with possibility, enamored of the shred of evidence, of chasing a thread toward discovery.

Giovanna Alimenti chased that thread, studying the medical texts of scholars from around the known world and the masters from the university. Master Ferrario taught the Salernitas to cure fevers. Engido taught them 20 types of urine color and the diseases they indicated. They learned to read the pulse, the color and feel of the skin. They could read the health of the body from the colors of the eye, they could differentiate between malaria and typhoid, calculate the height of the fever and the date of the recovery. Salernitas practiced surgery and da Parma documented its procedures, while Master Grafeo in the 1300s wrote on ocular surgery for cataracts. In Salerno, Luccia's mother proudly stated as she and her daughter wended their way through the streets, medicine was advanced, and the body revered.

Facing Fiona in their apartment, Giovanna placed her hands on the table and tried to change the subject, to diffuse the tension. "I've uncovered a new anesthetic," Giovanna offered. "In the *Antidotarium*. Opium henbane."

"Henbane?" Fiona asked.

"Combined with mandragora, hemlock, blackberry, lettuce and ivy," Giovanna continued. "I was astounded to read it."

"With mandragora? Mandrake?" Fiona repeated.

"From Palestine. To wake them up again," Giovanna said, "fennel juice poured down their nostrils."

Luccia, clutching the remnants of her orange, shuddered at the remembered smell of fennel. There was an additional secret in Salerno— conversations on painkillers and drugs for childbirth, more mysterious than all the scrolls and the notes in the city, Luccia thought. It was a whispered pharmaecopia shared among the women students and doctors.

This new remedy, startling and hopeful though it was, just exacerbated Fiona's anger. The women spoke the remedies but never wrote them, which made the information fragile and nearly impossible to disseminate, she grumbled to herself. With the work of Trotula threatened with obscurity, how many women would die in childbirth for lack of simple remedies that had been known for years?

The lemony day turned into a sultry evening, and after a bowl of broth, Giovanna and Fiona opened their doors to women students for conversation and study. The young women lay in their slips behind a tall fence of vines on Giovanna's balcony, listening to the splash of the fountain in the *piazza* and the hurried clop of donkeys crossing below. Luccia inhaled the smell of fresh anchovies grilling in the *tratorria* while Giovanna instructed her students.

As they spoke, Luccia could smell the barley remedy her mother described, remembered where it had been on the walks with her mother. She closed her eyes and let the visions of the leaves and the aromas wash over her.

The latest news was discussed that night by candlelight, the shadows of the little flames dancing across the women's faces like premonition, like doubt. Luccia twirled her thick black hair around her finger, inhaling the smell of lavender soap, the garlic of someone's lunch, the reassuring scent of her mother. Luccia curled onto a cotton rug staring at a map of Europe pinned to the wall just inside the balcony doors, and at a portrait of an old relative in a smock, while her mother flopped into a high-back chair, her books and papers spilling around her. She jotted notes to herself that had nothing to do with the discussion.

Despite the fact that it was hot, that dinner was over and they had been home for hours, Fiona O'Connor paced the floor still in her cape, half-listening, half-wrestling with the question of Trotula. Running her hand over her head, her sleeve button got caught in her hair and pulled the knot of it down around her shoulders, her long red hair brighter than flames. She had plain, indistinguishable dresses, but always wore a heavy pewter broach emblazoned with a Celtic knot that Luccia traced with her eyes. Fiona threw her cape back off her shoulders, as if she would jump out of her skin, the broach at the base of her neck.

"It's getting worse," she mumbled. "Much worse."

Luccia stared at the broach's outline to avoid Fiona's anger, and heard snatches of the student's responses. Another university closing their doors to women and Jews. "Salerno is nearly the only medical college left for women. Jobs denied even the best of them. This witch thing, an outrage."

Giovanna calmly turned the pages of a manuscript. "In this room, women are doctors. Surely it won't visit itself on us."

"A couple of shrews with angry husbands," one of the students laughed nervously as she circled the room offering lemon tea. "That's who gets caught in this witch thing."

Fiona whirled abruptly, waved the arguments away. "What about the mass burnings of midwives in Heidelberg and Cologne? What about Spain, in the Alpine regions? Have you forgotten those already?" she shouted back at Giovanna, fumbling in an interior pocket for a pouch. Fiona grabbed a pinch of it and stuck it between her lip and cheek, producing a stench on her breath that Luccia could hardly bear.

"There's still hope, Fiona," Giovanna said, raising her cup. "Several of the Queens of Europe have opened hospitals, have trained nurses by the hundreds. Scores of women students from Salerno are finding work there."

"To work beside the new doctors," a student sneered, "who've been taught that scorpions are born by rubbing basil between two stones."

"Exactly the reason this time will pass and these fools will fail," said Giovanna softly. "Not to put it crudely, but no people that stupid could triumph."

"Oh, not so," Fiona warned. "Can you imagine that they only teach now about the knife and bloodletting?"

"Well, we practice surgery as well," Giovanna said.

"But not surgery alone. Any peasant can walk into the forest and pick the herb to heal herself, but not if all she knows about is surgery. And these new so-called doctors, they refuse to attend to anything related to women's health. Anything at all. Even the teaching of the great Trotula will not be immune," Fiona shouted.

"In the dungeons I hear they use…"

"Not in front of the child," Giovanna snapped, turning to regard her daughter, then bending again over her papers to close the argument. It was a gesture Luccia most associated with her mother — whenever she worked, Giovanna's head would suddenly turn and she recognized that Luccia was there, as if encountering a species of animal that she knew she should know but couldn't quite place.

Fiona, pacing the room, turned to Luccia and her heart contracted. When she had moved in with the Alimenti family, Luccia was no bigger than an eggplant, and Fiona had tended her like a mother and watched her grow. Fiona's steely eyes looked at the girl, trying to find a safe path in medicine that could protect her. Fiona dug into a cloth bag for a brush, crossed the room, and knelt behind the girl, pulling Luccia into her lap. She struggled to get the brush through Luccia's hair while the girl leaned back against Fiona's torso. Fiona's glowing blue cape surrounded them like their own private world, but Luccia turned her head against the putrid smell of Fiona's chewing herbs.

"What made this blue?" Luccia asked her, beginning a private riddle between them.

"Woad," Fiona said with a smile as she had dozens of times before, her hands fighting to pull the brush through Luccia's hair.

"I think they used bilberry fruits as well," Luccia said, pulling the cape around her.

"Oh you do, do you? Giovanna, this child's hair!" Fiona admonished, and Giovanna sighed, exasperated, exchanging worried glances with Fiona, then jotting notes again. Fiona turned back to the girl.

Chapter Two

"Look at the map, child, and tell me all the countries of Europe," Fiona demanded.

Luccia curled her long legs underneath her, and stared at the map with flint gray eyes. Despite the downy child-soft skin that covered them, her high cheekbones and sharp chin, her nose that was unusually thin, gave her the appearance of one not so much born, as having been hammered out of rock like an arrowhead. Luccia had an arresting face, and fruit vendors and shopkeepers were held in mid-gesture as they offered her things, struck by the angularity of a girl so young. Not the pasty-faced, doughy anonymity of most children, Luccia cut her way into one's consciousness.

Giovanna's quill stopped when she heard Fiona mention the map, and the movement of the students halted in response. Giovanna had never ventured outside of Salerno, and there was no reason she should. This was the finest university in Europe, the best medicine in the world unless one speculated on the advances of the distant Chinese. Patients came to them. Knowledge, the latest developments in all that really mattered, came to Salerno. The world held no mystique for Giovanna. She saw no reason for her daughter's head to be filled with tales of travel. She did believe that her daughter should be taught geography, (at least to combat the foolish idea that the world held a ledge that one fell off if one ventured too far West) because geography had a lot to do with the potency of herbs, their specific purpose, and their remedial effects. But this didn't require that her daughter pack a bag and roam the world as Fiona seemed to hope. No member of the Alimenti family had ever emigrated, and she hoped they never would.

Her girl had a gift, she could tell. Today's example with the gel was just the latest she had seen. Whenever they stood at an apothecary counter, Luccia's hand in hers, she could feel Luccia's fingers twitch as if she were mixing a poultice. Luccia had learned to read in mere months, and when Giovanna told her bed-time tales of girls trudging through the forest, Luccia was never interested in the treasure at the end of the story, but which trees had grown in the forest, what the girl had eaten, how the trees, and the plants that grew beneath them, shared the light. Were the leaves broad or thin? She wanted to know, snuggled into her covers. Did the trees have resin? What did the forest smell like?

Luccia should stay in Salerno where she could nurture her talent and carry on the family name.

Fiona, on the other hand, knew all about the twisted geography of Europe. She knew first-hand the stow-away life, the slip-through-to-avoid life, the hiding-in-haystacks-until-the-horses-sped-by life, life in terrified flight. And before that, she knew the geography of Dublin, where life was supposed to be safe, where boat-loads of teachers and writers poured in from all parts of Europe, taking shelter in this last outpost of civilization, in the protection of the Celts. But Fiona's mother had been a midwife who had the misfortune of being chosen by the wife of the church council president, and of delivering her deformed child. They had strapped Fiona's mother into the dunking stool the very afternoon of the birth, the blood of the delivery still on her apron, and Fiona had run to get there in time, her old shoes pounding on the flagstones, shouting for her mother, her words ringing against the emptied houses. The townspeople were all crowded on the side of the quay, quietly weeping in meek protest as the Bishop stood beside the dripping dunking stool that held Fiona's mother. Fiona pushed forward and a woman whose legs she brushed turned to her. "No, Fiona," she said. "Go," she whispered as the Bishop's pointing finger swept over the crowd like a cloud over the sun. "You shouldn't be here."

Fiona had run, blind with grief and fear, down to the docks and onto a ship, to be close to the water, to dive in and save her mother, but she huddled behind bags of grain and after two days was dumped in London like another gunny sack. Too young to be logical, she stumbled through London, walking south, walking east, away from that quay and the Bishop's accusations until she was befriended by a group of old herbalists who were traveling to Salerno. Comforted by their talk of childbirths and remedies as in her own house, Fiona folded herself into their group, and arrived in the Salerno when she was 15. Oddly tall and fire-haired among the Italians, she was counted as a foreign guest and tolerated. Over the years, the clan of women who had befriended Fiona passed away just as Giovanna's clan had, and when the recently widowed Giovanna advertised for a boarder, the recently bereaved Fiona moved in.

While the two of them had much in common — both developing their medical knowledge — they did so from different perspectives. Giovanna considered her training part of a proud heritage, one of great things that made her a member of her ancestor's family. Fiona, on the other hand, regarded her medical knowledge as a dangerous flaw that made her vulnerable. It had been the cause of her mother's death. It trapped Fiona as an outsider, as a danger. Fiona was like a bird with beautiful plumage who knew her coveted feathers would be her downfall. Giovanna reveled in the beauty of the feathers, unaware of the hunter in the bush. Fiona attended to her studies with devotion to the subject and fear of the outcome. It was a tie to her mother that she both longed for and feared, and so she was a good student, but responded in classes as if the answers enraged her, reciting remedies through clenched teeth.

When Luccia demonstrated a love of herbs and a talent for medicine, the two women faced it with different reactions. Giovanna dismissed Fiona's warnings as the trauma of her past, not as an accurate assessment of a world that Giovanna had never seen and in which she maintained faith. Fiona watched Giovanna train her daughter, and regarded the instruction as lacking in an essential lesson: the consequences of holding the knowledge. Giovanna taught her daughter to walk boldly forward, ready to become a professor, while Fiona developed a nervous tendency to look furtively around all three of them, to watch the young girl with anxious eyes.

As a result, Fiona was reluctant to share her knowledge with Luccia, even when the girl asked her specific questions about the properties of an oil or the technique for roots. Instead, Fiona redirected her attention to cooking dinner or handling a knife, sewing (though the girl had no ability), making candles (though the child had no interest), and animal husbandry (though they had no animals).

Giovanna, on the other hand, worked hard at her daughter's schooling, beginning after a quick supper and continuing until the *trattoria* was shuttered in the square. She taught Luccia to strip the leaves and dry them, hanging them upside down if the stems had an essence that they would move to the leaves, or lay them flat on racks to keep the oils in their place. She taught her to preserve them, to grind them, to strip the bark mindful of the fibers, to cut the membrane from inside a stem, to grow a mold and scrape it, to boil herbs in syrup to make simples, to macerate leaves for a poultice.

Luccia stood at the table within the circle of her mother's arms, watching her hands work with the plants while her skirt brushed against Luccia's bare legs. Her mother brought each herb to her daughter's nose before adding it, giving her a sprig to roll between her fingers and memorize the texture of it. Luccia was inside the puzzle then, listening to the cluck of her mother's tongue as leaves proved to be stubborn or tough, the satisfied sounds she made as a mixture coalesced in the bowl. Luccia stood with her own mortar and pestle in front of her, a crude little wooden bowl that Giovanna had presented to her when she was eight, making a smaller version of the tincture Giovanna was creating.

Just last night, Fiona had put Luccia to bed after their lessons and turned in hours before Giovanna finally fell asleep over her papers, her hair tangling with the herb stems, and the quill silent in her hand. Luccia, unable to sleep through the night without accounting for her mother's whereabouts, climbed out of bed and saw Giovanna half sprawled on the table, fingertips just an inch from the herbs, cheek crushed onto the pages of work. Luccia climbed up the back of Giovanna's chair and draped herself across her mother's shoulders, stretching her long, thin hands down her mother's arms, her own fingers just inches from the plants. Under the herbs were diagrams of the body, drawings of the leaves accompanied by descriptions of their properties. They were a landscape to her, a magnificent other country where her mother journeyed, where she was teaching her daughter to go, so Luccia moved her hands over the paper. She touched the stalks of the plants and the ribs seemed to swell under her fingertips. Leaves quivered to meet her and pods fell open without provocation. In the shadow of the dying fire, baskets tipped their contents onto the table as if the plants considered her young hands a place of homecoming. Giovanna stirred in her sleep, without waking. Luccia's hands, picking up where her exhausted mother had left off, memorized the herb combinations. She clambered over the table, her nose learning, and her subconscious studying. Fiona had found them both in the morning, sleeping across the table.

Tonight, brushing Luccia's tangled black hair while the frightened chatter of the women swirled behind her and the memory of the monk's evil eyes was fresh in her memory, Fiona worried about Luccia's safety. But Fiona had seen the map, and was inspired with a simple plan. Rather than fighting against the girl's education, she would supplement it with an education of her own. In this age, it made sense to teach a girl the finer points of stealth. That could become Luccia's tactic — to belong through invisibility, to be safe by not being seen.

The next day, after Giovanna had gone off to the classroom, Fiona gave Luccia a small vial and told her to hide it on herself, to go through the city and deliver it to one of Fiona's friends, undetected. A secret game, she told Luccia. Luccia hid it in her waistband and encountered Fiona's friends along the way who tried to ferret out the object. When she returned home without her package being detected, Luccia was given hot buns and the sugar on her teeth was the taste of Fiona's pride.

"You're a good little shadow, my sweet," Fiona said, drawing Luccia to her.

In the evening, Giovanna gave her a lesson in Latin. Fiona brushed her hair and grilled her on geography, demanding the names of mountain ranges and rivers. And deep in the night, when neither adult was awake, Luccia would continue her conversation with the plants.

It was a hot summer day later that year when Fiona gave her the wooden box to carry. The box was wider than her chest and very heavy. Halfway to her destination, Luccia stood in a dank lane, facing a square in front of the church. She should cross it, but she stood frozen in indecision, looking at the priests that congregated on the steps. She couldn't hide the box on her and walk across the square with her head high like her mother. She stepped forward, then ducked into the lane again. She turned in confusion, her breathing heavy. Why couldn't she just stride across the piazza? She imagined her mother's wide, proud step as she made her way to the medical school. She stepped out, then ducked in again, pressed her face to the wall. Pride, stealth, what should she do? What would Fiona do? Luccia retreated inside herself, turning away from the square, unable to think. She didn't move, didn't hear the priests coming up behind her until they put their meaty hands on her shoulders and spun her around.

As she flew down a back alley, Luccia was pulled by Fiona into a dark corner of a lane that smelled of dead mice and melon rinds. She pressed Luccia into her legs and covered her with her cape, where Luccia clung and trembled, ashamed of her failure that had been born of her indecision, resolved to shape shift.

"The tools," Luccia said tearfully, and Fiona sighed. They were hard to come by, and their loss put children and their mothers at risk. But Fiona gripped Luccia's shoulders. Fiona had been following at a distance but didn't come upon the square until the priests had already swarmed on her. She couldn't even see Luccia for the cluster of black robes so when her little precious one darted out from between their legs, Fiona's heart had leapt into her mouth.

She gave chase, behind the priests, the fear shredding her insides, but each time Luccia transformed herself, Fiona brightened. When the priests stopped running and turned circles in one of the squares, confused and finally resigned, Fiona pretended to be examining fruit.

Fiona stumbled down the damp recesses of the streets, weeping into her hands. If she'd been more aware as a little girl, when she had been Luccia's age, maybe they wouldn't have taken her mother, there wouldn't have been the dunking stool and her mother a dead fish on the quay. If she had been smarter, more alert. If she had seen them coming. If she and her mother had known stealth and flight. Flight was the key.

That evening, Fiona came into Luccia's room with her hair loose and long, her face red from crying, and she seized Luccia as if the girl were about to fall.

"I'm so sorry," she whispered. "I don't want to teach you fear but you have to be smart."

Fiona took her post behind Luccia on the bed to brush her hair. Until this morning, Luccia had always listened to the litany of the world's dangers as just a list of facts, like recipes for the poisons that she should never concoct. Tragedy happened elsewhere, she had thought, but today she realized that she was the one who was elsewhere: hidden within childhood. The proximity of danger, the requirement that she dodge it, and the responsibility for her own safety was a very new feeling for her. She had been tested and she had failed. Failed to know which path, her mother's or Fiona's was the one to take.

"Close your eyes and name all the coastal towns from here to Marseilles," Fiona ordered softly, as Luccia's mother came in and held the girl's hands, curious over Fiona's tears. Luccia began the list as if it were the chant that would drain the red from Fiona's eyes, would lessen the crease in her mother's brow. The route from here to Marseilles.

Luccia doubled her resolve to become a shadow and make up for her loss of the medical equipment. Little leather pouches, tiny vials, bits of paper — Luccia learned to hide them in her hair, in her shoes. She became adept at disguises, developed a keen ability to disappear through the back alleys, the hidden portals, the empty barrels big enough to hide in, the ways to double-back and vanish. To drop the item, elude the imaginary interceptor, then return, collect and deliver. Fiona told stories of the complexity of Luccia's plans and her friends laughed with her as they pulled up the girl's collars and dug into her pockets, tried to guess the treasure's whereabouts, applauded her skill. A wily messenger was a valuable asset.

Fiona's friends trusted Luccia with money, and without Giovanna's or Fiona's knowledge, women asked her to ferry opiates for child-births that would land them on the pyre if found. Even in tolerant Salerno, pain killers were suspicious items, and more than one midwife had been apprehended and burnt when they ventured outside of town with opiates in their pockets.

The items grew larger as Luccia's skill increased, until she could run through the city in a summer slip, concealing a book in her clothes. She was a shape-shifter, an amorphous person, dressed like a boy, or a farmer with stinking bales. In a gunny-sack shawl and a filthy face, she moved about the city, now ten years old but stooped and tiny like an old man, delivering multiple bundles in an increasingly complex web of pick-ups, deliveries, triple-switch backs and evasion. Hot buns. Sweets. Smiling women with grateful hands.

In between parcels, Luccia followed the smell of herbs. She tracked basil through alleys to the back door of a restaurant. At the entrance of workshops, she deciphered who put honey in their tinctures and who used alcohol. She would stop in the middle of a square, spellbound, if they had cut the grasses on the hills outside of town. One summer day, for the fun of it, she ran through the city to smell herbs in alphabetical order.

That week, Giovanna set a big basket on the balcony and ordered Luccia to sit in front of it. She poured out tea for them — peppermint, echinacea, oat straw, the girl recited to her question. Then, Giovanna threw off the cloth covering the basket and lifted the plants out two at a time.

"Cowslip on the left, celandine on the right," Luccia said triumphantly, wiggling her legs on the rug. "Wild cherry on the left, Lady's mantle on the right," she retorted smugly.

"Luccia, you study well even without me at your elbow." Giovanna picked up an armload of plants and laid them out. Luccia jumped up onto her knees and inhaled deeply.

"Yellow dock, bistort, sorrel," she said, touching each one reverently. "This is peony and this old thing is just rhubarb."

Giovanna put her hands on her hips and they turned to see that Fiona had slipped onto the balcony.

"Behold the young doctor," her mother said as she took Luccia in her arms.

Fiona suddenly crumpled to the floor, and Giovanna moved around Luccia so fast that the girl toppled. Giovanna grabbed Fiona's arm, wrapped it over her shoulder, and struggled to get her into Fiona's bedchamber. She called over her shoulder for Luccia to put away the herbs but the girl followed instead and saw her mother pressing Fiona's arms to the bed while Fiona's body jerked violently. For nearly a half hour, her mother quietly counted aloud while Fiona shook, and Luccia sat at the threshold, shredding the leaves off the herbs and crying. It was the third episode this year and when Fiona

19

was still, Giovanna quietly crept out of the room and gathered up her daughter.

"Epilepsy is a malady, sweetheart, but it isn't catching," she said quietly. "It's her nerves, robbed of what they need. But best keep this to ourselves, Luccia. The unschooled consider it the mark of the Devil."

Later that year when the rains brought in the smell of the sea and the cobblestones were slick in the *piazza*, a midwife arrived from the north and sat in front of Giovanna's fire with a cup of broth. Trotula, she pleaded. The new doctors who straggled into the cities knew nothing but astrology. Death in childbirth had risen to one in three.

"One in three!" Fiona shouted, jumping up from her chair, while Giovanna twisted in her seat. "And the midwives?"

The northern woman bit her lip and looked at the floor. "The courts have been through," she said hesitantly, then raised her eyes to Fiona. "The midwives in the rural areas, all...burned. Jailed the doctors in Nice, Avignon. You can travel for days and not find anyone who can make a simple poultice. And those who can are too afraid. Nurses in the hospitals know nothing. They're like chambermaids. The sick just die around them."

"Maids and star-gazers," Fiona grumbled.

"The courts and the Church have burned all the copies of the texts," the midwife pleaded. "They saw off a man's legs but know nothing about how to stem the bleeding. Everyone's afraid of the hospital: it's a place to go to be killed now."

"Luccia go to your room please," Giovanna said, frightened.

"We want to train them," the woman said, setting aside her bowl of broth. "In the forests at night. But we can't without the texts."

"Schooling in secret, to be reduced to this," Fiona growled.

"We've been hiding the herbs, and we've been trying to spirit the women doctors away but..." the woman folded her hands to stop their shaking.

"And the trip here?" Fiona asked quietly.

20

"Marked by posts," the woman whispered. Giovanna watched Fiona and the northern midwife exchange knowing glances, but was afraid to ask what signposts she meant.

"We have precious few copies ourselves," Fiona said. "And the monks who used to copy it — begrudgingly — now flat out refuse."

Giovanna rose. "Then we must find a scribe to do it."

"And who's to pay for a scribe?" Fiona demanded, but Giovanna was resolute.

"We'll find a way," she said, as if the pronouncement might stop the midwife's trembling hands.

Chapter Three

Other than the monks who copied manuscripts while cloistered above the city, the scribes provided the laborious, word-for-word transcription of manuscript to paper, the last step between book and reader. The only step in the duplication of books. The scribes in Salerno were Jewish because of their multilingual education. In the offices of the scribes that were scattered throughout the city, men and women clustered and debated the accuracy of the translation, the ideas that emerged from a hidden language, the healing that might be wrought. But the final arbiter was always the scribe, who could shake his head and point at the original text, sometimes stand on tiptoes and gesture insistently in the faces of his client. If the argument grew too heated, with tall men crowding around the desk, the scribe would stand on the foot-rest of his stool to tower over the participants, dramatically slamming shut the text in progress. A hush would fall over the room and other customers would slouch slightly in their seats in front of their own scribes, for a scribe would rather not finish a text than to knowingly introduce inaccuracies. Argue as they might, the scribe always had the final say. And, of course, women were not allowed to be scribes.

In the morning, the two women sat across the table from Luccia, steam from their teacups rising in front of their faces. Giovanna was dressed for presentation, with her optimism and her credentials. Fiona was hidden in the folds of her cloak. Time to find a scribe. At evening's end, Giovanna sat again in front of tea looking surprised and troubled, Fiona in front of wine trying to suppress her rage. They had been rebuffed in office after office.

"We'll try again tomorrow," Giovanna said resolutely, but Fiona turned away. The next day, they were refused again. A transcription of an established work demanded a patron, and they had none. No bookbinder would take a volume that wasn't from a monk or a certified scribe. And they had merely to open the book to a diagram of the female anatomy before the scribe slammed the pages and pointed Giovanna to the door. On Giovanna's last stop, they threw the book into the doorframe and heckled her into the street. The Inquisition would take notice of a book like that, the scribes shouted. You'd endanger us all.

When Luccia welcomed her mother home, Giovanna blew past her, stormed into the kitchen, her skirts slapping against chair legs and doorframes. She pulled two wine glasses from the shelf.

"Even the apprentice laughed!" she fumed to Fiona. "I am a professor, being laughed at by a sniveling boy."

Fiona stood and tapped her stick on the floor, her face downcast. Then an idea made her flinch and she turned her palm upward to Luccia.

"An apprentice, that's what we need."

The women stood shoulder to shoulder, regarding Luccia and Giovanna made mental note of how tall she had become, how her shoulders were pressing on the seams of her dress. At least with their own apprentice, they wouldn't have to pay a patron, just the bookbinder. Luccia had a good hand, and read Latin of course.

The next morning, the three were rebuffed again. An apprentice needed a mentor, the scribes complained, and none of them would take her on. We'll instruct her ourselves, Giovanna argued but they were shown the door. By the end of the day, they were reduced to approaching a single scribe in a low stone building so far on the edge of Salerno that they had to cross the paddocks of the swineherd to get to it. When Giovanna stooped into the doorway, the scribe was just ushering out a man with a torn coat and a wild hat whose papers spilled out of his dirty fist and whose language was almost unintelligible. There were no other customers, no chatter, no din of exchange. But the reaction from the scribe was the same. No girls, no Trotula, no childbirth.

Giovanna sent in a stream of colleagues and friends to apply gentle persuasion. A group of women came in to ruminate on future business. Friends brought in fruit and candles to hold a celebration though they knew the decision hadn't been made, boisterously making reference to Giovanna's standing at the university, followed the next day by an apothecary who stopped in to hint at a sudden lack of ink, lack of herbs, lack of quills for any but the best customers. The scribe sighed, with one of Giovanna's hot buns in his hand.

"You could sharpen quills on that child's nose," he muttered, but motioned her to a tall, narrow desk in the back of the room.

He tolerated her scratching quill across paper, while he waited for her to share her dinner of bread and eggs. She was there more than a week before he finally strode over and put his hands on her papers.

"No, no," he grumbled, "the binding requires three inches from the edge. Start with your border. Look at this, useless, ruined. And the slant of your hand must remain consistent, to the end. Not just of the page, but of the book. Look at this! Like four old women at a country fair scribbled it. And don't give me that flinty stare, child."

Begrudgingly, he trained her, at first hovering nearby, then darting in after hours of silence to snatch the page and crumple it. She growled between clenched teeth, re-tied the scarf around her head, but her next attempt produced better results. She was tense all day, her shoulder muscles and hands cramping and every so often she would look up and check his whereabouts, as if she were working in the paddock of a bull.

To Luccia, being a scribe's apprentice was second best to the life she had had before. It didn't have the fragrance of herbs, didn't lull her with the aroma of plants, and walking home in the evening with her mother she would inhale as if she had been under water. She touched the bushes and the branches, neglected friends. After a few months of working with the scribe, though, she could conjure the smells and leaf-patterns just by the sound of the plants' names.

"Who is your illustrator?" the scribe barked at her one afternoon as he sat by the window. She completed the word she was working on, then looked up and re-focused her eyes, quill poised in the air.

"Good, you didn't stop mid-word. Now who is your illustrator?"

Luccia stretched her cramped and blackened fingers. He unfolded himself from the window seat and put his hands on his knees. "What sort of rag-taggle group are you, you have no illustrator?" They stared at each other, and the scribe shook his head, knowing what sort of group they were. He gathered his brushes and set up a station beside her. Luccia looked over at her pages, where instantly the leaves in question, just the right color, exactly the vein network shown in the original, bloomed on her page. She breathed deep, inhaling it, relaxing into it.

"How many languages do you speak?" he said as he brushed quickly across the page, rendering a sprig of rosemary.

"Two. Latin and Italian."

"Insufficient. You must learn at least two more. Every culture has its secret," he said softly. "Only language gives you a path to the secret. We'll start you on French in the morning."

"You don't need language to talk to the plants," she said, expecting Fiona's skepticism or worse.

"Of course you don't, but you need it to talk *about* plants," he said, his eyes sparkling.

She smiled slightly and nervously touched the scarf on her head. Geography for Fiona, herbology with her mother, and now languages for the scribe. "But the manuscript!" Luccia protested weakly and he waved away her objections.

"Brain enough for both," he said. "Run along now, it's getting late. I'll have caught up with the illustrations by the morning, and then we'll really get the work done. There's an extra charge for this, of course. Tell your mother."

Laid over the litany of Trotula's knowledge was the challenge of new French vocabulary words that the scribe barked at her from across the room. Learn about the herb, smell it though it wasn't there, write about it in perfect hand, speak its magic in French, watch the old man make it blossom on the page. Soon transcribing became as thrilling as any chase through the streets.

"A noble task, my dear," one of the midwives said, holding Luccia's chin in her hand and staring at her eyes. "You are blessed

with a noble task. Trotula … you keep us alive by keeping her alive."
Luccia clutched her quill and felt tall.

Every time Luccia offered up a manuscript to the
bookbinder, she nervously awaited its return, wondering if they
would refuse to bind it, if they would deface it or lose it. But every
new manuscript bound and delivered was celebrated.

Eventually, however, their arrangement aroused suspicion. A
little man with a bulbous nose and a tattered jacket that nearly
reached to his calves arrived from another scribe's office,
interrupting them as they sat with their desks next to each other. He
stood in front of Luccia's desk with his hands on his hips and his toe
against the chair as if he would kick her into the street. He
disdainfully examined the page on her desk, with his mouth curling
and twitching.

He turned to the scribe. "What kind of scribe lets a woman
into the profession?" he sneered.

The scribe rubbed his brushes on a rag. "One who knows a
good piece of business."

The men switched from Italian to a language Luccia didn't
understand, and the visitor made disdainful reference to the books,
and then he turned to her. He pulled the shawl off her head, jerked
her off her stool and pontificated on the fact that she was merely a
girl.

Just then, Luccia's mother entered the room to collect her
and Giovanna saw her daughter standing protectively in front of her
pages, the man shaking Luccia like a rag doll. Giovanna crossed the
scribe's office, pressing her daughter with her hand into the flesh of
her thigh, and she grew into a ferocious griffin towering above the
little man. She screeched about her position at the University, her
connections with the authorities, the indecency of frightening a child.
The little man slithered away from Giovanna, still lethal but
temporarily vanquished. Straightening her daughter's clothing and
buttoning her collars, Giovanna took a last look around the scribes'
den and marshaled her daughter out the door.

After that incident, the scribe was sullen and began grilling
her mercilessly on her French, then decreed that she would begin to
study German. One week into her studies, he announced that he

would teach her to illustrate as well. Not the usual course of a scribe's apprenticeship.

"But clearly," the old scribe said quietly, the two of them regarding each other sadly, "you're destined for many burdens alone."

Giovanna accompanied her daughter to work in the morning, Luccia slowing their journey by touching the plants along the way, twisting off a leaf and rolling it between her fingers. Her mother ceremoniously installed her on the tall stool and took another brutal look around the room, but softened when she caught the scribe's melancholy eyes. Luccia kept her head covered and her face to her work. The manuscripts went to the binder and didn't return, which frightened Luccia but she bent over her task.

The night after her 12th birthday Luccia heard a lone woman arrive late at night, when everyone should be in bed. Luccia saw her tattered and wet and watched Fiona disappear, then return with a group of students. Previously, a late-night arrival had meant that school books were more closely hidden under the women's wraps; special potions were secreted behind bricks instead of baskets and a few women buckled under the pressure and left. This time, however, it produced a frenzy among the women, including her mother, who packed up Luccia's clothing, and organized a rendezvous in a darkened courtyard of the university.

"You have 100 manuscripts of Trotula hidden under the boards of this wagon," she whispered, putting the reigns of a donkey cart into Luccia's hands. Luccia peered into the empty wagon. Her manuscripts. All the books that went to the binder and disappeared. "Here is a list of their destinations. Don't stop until you have delivered them all."

Luccia looked at the paper, then back at her mother. "But these are in… France, and...Denmark!"

"You know your map well, I don't doubt you'll find the locations, but you have to be smart, Luccia. Don't ever let anyone find them on you," Giovanna whispered ferociously as she pretended to make the wagon ready. Suddenly, she put her forehead against the girl's cheek and cried. "It's gotten so much worse, dear. Worse than I ever thought it would."

"Come with me," Luccia said frantically. "Mother, you have to come with me!" This was not part of the plan. No one had told her that she was going to be sent away. She had studied hard, become a scribe, done everything they asked but no one told her this would lead to separation. Sent out of Salerno? Impossible. "Especially if you're in danger!"

"I hadn't thought it would come to this," her mother wailed, stuffing a sack of food and a boda of water under the wagon seat, "in our Salerno!" She pulled her hood closer around her face. "Too suspicious to be together. You wouldn't be safe. You can do this, my sweet. Don't tell anyone who I am or where I live. For your sake."

"But when should I come back?" Luccia whined.

"I'll join you... when this is over."

Just as Luccia was going to protest — when would that be, where should they meet — she saw the glint of Fiona's Celtic knot in the darkened archway. "A hundred manuscripts?" Luccia said incredulously. Perhaps this was a plan, not a dismissal.

"I've been hiding them in my rooms at the university. It's Trotula, sweetheart," she pleaded. "Luccia, sweet dear," she whispered, putting a boy's cap on Luccia's head. Giovanna hung around Luccia's neck a small glass vial entwined with pewter roots. Giovanna's eyes darted to the side as she saw Fiona enter the courtyard then duck quickly through a doorway. "Take a few drops of this when the sadness is too great."

She marshaled the protesting Luccia onto the wagon seat and smacked the donkey's ass. "Always with you..." Giovanna called and as Luccia turned to cry out to her, she saw two men take her mother by the arms. Giovanna pulled away from them and straightened her shoulders like a duchess but didn't turned back to her daughter or answer her cries. Luccia grabbed the reigns, struggling against her desire to jump off the wagon seat and run to her mother. She saw Fiona at the side of the building flagging her on. Fiona ran parallel to the cart for a few yards, and Luccia turned face-front, doing her part in the charade.

Trained in subterfuge and herbs, Luccia began her new task, feeling the vial bouncing against her chest as she lurched over the cobblestones, then over the rutted roads, twisting in her seat for some sign of Fiona, some miraculous sighting of her mother.

Her first stop was marked as Rome. She knew the map in her head but had never been out of Salerno. It had been just an academic exercise, something to do while her hair was being brushed. She didn't know how to travel, she didn't know how to cross the terrain of Italy.

Luccia trembled on the wagon seat at midday and stopped every time she caught a glimpse of blue jays, iris or peonies, thinking it was Fiona's cape. She spent nights rocking back and forth, clutching her blanket around her like Fiona's cape, rubbing her hand across her hair, calling to her mother and Fiona, begging the spirits to send someone to guide her, someone to reinstate her feeling of safety. She sat at crossroads unable to decide what to do, woke in the night without anyone, waiting, listening, trying to be strong when she was paralyzed into inaction. She held handfuls of leaves to her nose to breath in their calming coolness. It was one thing to feel old enough to become a scribe who was ushered around by her mother, but quite another to be sent away. Still, she had a duty. She had been trained in her task, surrounded her entire life by people who had given up their homelands for the honor of medicine and so she headed north, to Rome.

Luccia bemoaned the fact that there were only two genders and three ages to be — young and vulnerable; adult and dangerous; old and expendable. At night, at least she could curl up as a sheep, or burrow like a wood rat in the hay. To earn a meal, she hauled straw, loathing the hot, dead smell of it. She liveried chickens but growled over feather mites and chicken shit, and she lay night after night wishing her mother would hold her cheeks in her long, thin hands. She traced the clutching roots across the glass vial as if they were tracks to home. By the time she had reached the outskirts of Rome, she had cut off her hair, donned the clothes of a boy, snared a few birds and cooked them.

As she neared the city, the people seemed more suspicious so she decided to pass through the remaining villages as a spindly old man with a bandaged face and shaded eyes.

The night she was close enough to Rome to see the light on the horizon, Luccia made a fire by the side of the road and stood facing the city, cupping her mortar and the vial like talismans. She had never seen a town so large and its light looked like it was devouring the horizon. Her insides were hollow at the prospect of arriving but she remembered her mother's strength in the scribe's office and because of her fear, she stood in front of her fire and made her presence huge as Giovanna had done. She cast a shadow across the meadow in front of her and Luccia filled herself with the strength of her own mirage.

Suddenly, her mouth was covered from behind and she was thrown down into the grasses. She scrambled away, panting.

"Fiona!" She jumped into her arms and Fiona cupped her head and held her chest, rocked her for a moment. Then Fiona pushed Luccia backwards.

"You're not ready," Fiona growled accusingly, pacing in front of Luccia, then pushing her cape back over what were now trousers. She flung back her hood to reveal a shaven head. "You know what to do but you don't seem to know when to do it. Have you not noticed where you are, little shadow?"

Luccia looked around her but said nothing.

"Have you seen any cats in the last few days?" Fiona demanded.

"Cats?"

Fiona walked behind Luccia, folded her cape around them and pulled the girl to squatting, turned her to the side. She pointed at a tree just thirty feet away. Luccia raised her face to regard the branches, gasped, then tried to scramble backward. The flames of her fire glinted off the luminescent eyes of dead cats, more than a hundred of them, strung up by their necks and dangling in the tree. The firelight glistened on their hanging tongues and danced across their pelts.

"You're upwind, so you didn't notice, did you?" Fiona said, pulling Luccia closer and looking around.

"The donkey reeks so bad I can't smell a thing," Luccia whined.

Fiona stood and kicked dirt into the fire pit. "Ack, you can smell oregano in a hurricane but you don't know the smell of death unless you're downwind. You're not ready, little one. Pack up your things quickly. This is clearly no place to stay."

"Who would do that?" Luccia's mouth filled with bile as she turned back to look at the carnage again, afraid to inhale.

Chapter Four

Fiona shook her head at Luccia's ignorance. "Of course you know the Latin name for catnip, but nobody bothered to tell you what a dead cat meant." She picked up the provisions that Luccia had lain by the fire and made her way toward the donkey. "Well, now you have to learn quickly, little shadow. And you have to use your head, not just your nose! They kill the cats because they think cats are the consort of the witch."

"The witch?" Luccia sneered, stumbling after her and holding the donkey's head while Fiona put the bit in its mouth. "Everyone has a cat or they're infested with rats."

"Exactly," Fiona said, "But it seems that if you're smart enough to take care of yourself you're being branded as a witch these days. And that's what you have to know. I told your mother — for the love of God, we argued about it incessantly. I told her she couldn't just fill your head with tales of medicine. You're a good little spy, shadow, but you don't know who you're running from and that's damn dangerous. Ack, get over here, you stupid donkey. God, how I hate donkeys. Luccia, dead cats mean the burning courts have been through here. You should have veered off this path a long time ago, little one."

"You've been nearby?" Luccia said, her eyes filling with tears.

"I have. I had a set-back or two, or I would have been here earlier. It's been breaking my heart to not ease your pain but I had to know if you were ready, Luccia. At least you figured you should cut your hair. I had to keep my distance until I got rid of my own hair and... well, you'd be damn conspicuous with a six foot, red-haired

31

banshee by your side, wouldn't you? Ach, up we go now," she said, climbing into the wagon and taking the reigns. "Come here little one." She opened her cape and pulled Luccia close again.

Fiona held Luccia while tears rolled down her cheeks. They rode until they were exhausted and then hid themselves in a knoll. Just before daybreak, Luccia rolled over and nudged Fiona.

"When's mother going to join us?"

Fiona pawed around, pulling up her blanket and patting herself for her pouch. "I don't know, Luccia. She made it out of Salerno, and I sent her on ahead to Ireland, where she'd be safe."

"Ireland!" Luccia wailed, pulling away from her. She could hardly imagine her mother leaving Salerno.

"Ah, the hardest thing in the world is for a mother to decide that she's more a harm to her child than a help." Fiona slipped a pinch of her revolting herbs into her cheek.

"You should put some mint into that mixture," Luccia grumbled. "And occasionally rinse your mouth with sage water."

Fiona gave Luccia a challenging look. "She's a professor, little one. She has a gift, and it made them want her more than they wanted an old cow like myself. Some of us they sweep up in their net, some of us they hunt down," she said, struggling to untangle her blanket. "Your mother was hunted, little shadow. She had no choice. You weren't safe as long as you were with her."

"And how is it that she's safe without us?" Luccia demanded. Fiona sighed, and pulled Luccia into her arms. Even the smell of Fiona's breath couldn't keep Luccia from nestling into her.

In the morning, they began another part of Luccia's apprenticeship. Fiona set about to teach her to read the countryside, to hunt for wild herbs, track allies and notice the evidence of death, pending and past. Too many women had been taken off the road as they walked bold-faced toward a town. The roadways were especially dangerous for women carrying Trotula, herbs, or any evidence of a medical practice.

The tree of dead cats was just the first lesson. Fiona taught her to scan distant hillsides for random poles— burning posts where women were brought from the countryside, tied up and burned alive. They practiced their disguises for riding the roadway, they invented corrals and hiding places for the wagon and the donkey, they ducked into the forests with nothing but a single bag of water, a flint and a bird snare. They agreed to use the call of the mourning dove to signal each other and Fiona made Luccia follow her through the forest with the sound. Fiona taught her to track the secret gardens of the herbalists — hidden in the forests to divert suspicion, tucked into groves of trees, never too overt. A patch of tansy grew forty paces from the path to the house, here a strip of mandrake along a creek bed, a cluster of mushrooms surrounding a tree. Fiona taught her to notice the little cups of cloth that were hung under the heads of fenugreek to catch the seeds. They crept through the woods, following the trail of herbs, then doubling back, slowly making their way in the direction of Rome. At night Fiona grilled her on the clues she had seen.

Two weeks into the lessons, Fiona caught her arm and pulled her to a crouching position.

"What do you notice about this patch of herbs, Luccia?" Fiona whispered. Luccia thought it looked very lush. "It's a very long way from the last one, and the rosemary has gone to flower." Luccia looked slowly around the grove of trees. "The herbalist hasn't been through here in a while, and that should make you question why." She turned to the girl to be sure she was listening. "Untended gardens, an herbalist carried off, do you understand?"

Fiona and Luccia hitched up the wagon and decided to dress as men.

The herbalist barred their entrance with a broom handle. Fiona unveiled a copy of *Trotula Minor* and opened it to a page that outlined the herbs needed to expel an afterbirth. The herbalist hurried them inside, bolted the door and shuttered the windows.

A thin woman with darting eyes and trembling hands, she told them that she had left her gardens untended because the clergy had rumbled through there two weeks ago and she was too frightened to venture out again. Whenever a burning court went through an area, she explained breathlessly, there were stragglers who lay in wait for frightened women to flee. They kidnapped the women, delivered them to the burning court, collected a fee and sometimes returned to squat the women's land. Instead, she had chosen to be a near prisoner in her own house, and Luccia could tell from her eyes and Fiona's reaction that it had been a close call, that the herbalist had been forced to weave a story to save her life, and the veil of it still hung over her eyes.

Fiona, the herbalist and Luccia hid all but a half a dozen manuscripts deep in the woman's root cellar, in the darkest corner behind a false wall of mud bricks where the herbalist had put her mortar and pestle, her trowel and tinctures. She regarded the books as apparitions, both admiring and fearing her guests, pushing cautiously past them to busy herself with a meal.

The midwife stood at the window. "Someone's coming," she said, grabbing the bowls of half-eaten soup, throwing things around the room in a panic. "Clergy and two others. Into the root cellar, all the way to the back."

Fiona and Luccia dove into the cellar and scrambled to the back corner just as the last board was laid to block out the sun. Fiona lay in the dark on the floor and Luccia curled next to her, overcome with the darkness and the smell of loam. Fiona lurched beside her and Luccia, startled, turned to her just as she began to shake and expel breaths in harsh little bursts. "Count," Fiona whispered, as she lost control of her arms and legs and her back bucked off the hard dirt floor. "Count!" One burdock two burdock three burdock, Luccia whispered in Fiona's ear, but the shaking continued and Fiona's little sounds became more garbled. Luccia covered Fiona's mouth. She lay down and buried her head in Fiona's shoulder to keep her steady. They pitched on the floor for six thousand burdocks and then Fiona lay utterly motionless, trying to regain use of her mouth.

Finally, the herbalist opened the cellar and Luccia called her for help but when she saw Fiona, the herbalist wrung her hands and wouldn't enter nor extend a hand. "You have to leave!" she shouted, backing away with frightened eyes.

"She can't move," Luccia called from the pit.

"You have to leave here. What is it?" the herbalist challenged.

"It's not catching," Luccia assured her, though she didn't know what it was.

"Take her and get out!" the herbalist shrieked.

"I can't do that. She can't move!"

"Then leave her here but you have to go. I have no idea when they'll return. If they find you... Now go!"

Luccia pivoted on her heel, trying to find an answer, desperate to stay by Fiona's side.

"Take care of her!" Luccia demanded, but the herbalist muttered incomprehensible protests, grabbing at Luccia's clothing to pull her up from the cellar but then running away to the other side of her cottage, tottering back and seizing a bit of Luccia's sleeve. Luccia thought of her mother's promise to join her when she had finished. That promise drove Luccia to collect the half-dozen manuscripts and put them in a gunnysack, then clamber out of the cellar. She could deliver the packages and return for Fiona, she reasoned, unable to think clearly. As she had done nearly every day since she was nine years old, she would deliver the packages, return home for hot buns and cider.

Rome was a jumble, and Luccia disguised herself in a raggedy old cape, crouching in corners to gain the time to make her way through so many people, down so many strange streets. Her games of cat and mouse through her mother's town had made her keen to the whereabouts of midwives, until she could stand at a second story alcove, look across the town square and see them moving through the city as if threaded to one another. Sometimes she had climbed to the belfry of the university and saw their movements as a tapestry, knowing that she was the shuttle that could run undetected through their waft. Fiona had now taught her to track the movements of priests. But in Rome, there were so many priests that she felt smothered, unable to find their pattern. And the signs of danger that she had been taught to see had transformed the task: it wasn't a game anymore.

All over Rome Luccia saw evidence of the campaigns that had been nervous discussions in her mother's house and pointed lessons from Fiona. Rooms hung empty that should have housed a midwife who was to receive a package, perhaps give her a roof and a meal. Doors were slammed in her face. Women at addresses that she was certain were correct let their eyes glaze over and their voices rise as they denied knowing the woman she sought, or even knowledge of medicine. Luccia slept on the pews of a church dressed as an old man, received a piece of bread in the morning, and began again. Return to Fiona, she thought. Deliver the books and return to Fiona.

After she was jostled down a flight of stairs and thrown into the street, she learned to follow women, to make silent contact across a marketplace, slip the manuscript into their basket. She confronted them on the street, jumping out of a dark corner to beg for money. Safer to accost them as a crazy old man than have a learned discussion with them as women, she grumbled as she hunted through trash for her dinner. At this rate, it would take her another week just to deliver the manuscripts that were destined for Rome.

Luccia turned a corner, four manuscripts left, four doctors to contact, when she felt an enormous rumbling. She looked up at the buildings that surrounded her, expecting them to break loose. All the other sounds of the city seemed to be still for a moment, paused in surprise. Dogs slunk into alleys, the street were strangely bare. Luccia's chest clenched and she looked up the lane to the square. People ran down five narrow streets that converged on the *piazza*, tossing aside baskets and buckets as if expecting lava to burst through the stones. Up the streets, forcing the few stragglers into alcoves and doorways, came horse-drawn wagons, the wooden wheels as high as a tall man's head, the sides made of freshly stripped logs. The horses strained against their load, stamping the ground and dislodging stones. Men rushed in with bundles of branches, then unloaded enormous mounds of wood, built a pyre that snaked across the piazza in a labyrinth. The sound of women crying echoed off the narrow stone walls and Luccia turned, wide-eyed, not knowing where to run, feeling naked in front of an unknown threat as people ran by her, ignoring her.

The next set of wagons held an enormous number of women, some crumpled naked on the bottom, some tied to the slats with their arms straining above their heads. Young women incredulous and enraged, old women resigned and half-dead, even little girls who sat in their own blood, lost in the nightmare. Luccia thought she couldn't be seeing this, not women bloodied and broken, with bones showing and knives still in their flesh. Dead bodies were piled on one another in the carts like a slaughterhouse parade, and behind the carts, the shackled and crying women being marched forward in a great horde. Up the other street came a similar procession, some women with necks still encased in collars with spikes that dug into their flesh, with stains from the rapists on their clothing, blood dripping onto the pavement.

Luccia folded herself and her gunnysack of books into a corner behind a rain barrel and lost track of time as the screaming was joined by the sound of piling wood, by the sudden influx of Romans who came to jeer and throw food. Luccia thrashed, turned, trying to prevent both witness and discovery. The women were corralled and the fires lit, the city went mad with vengeance, with imploring prayers and screaming, with the stench of burning flesh.

Luccia ran through the night sensing hands about to seize her, though none did. She ducked through the countryside, the sack bouncing on her back, running bush to cave to ditch, weeping and retching, clutching her hooded cape to her as if it made her not just a boy, but invisible. Who wanted a body in a world like this? A body was just a target. It brought the fires, so she would have no body at all if she had had her way at that moment. Despite the effectiveness of her disguise, she hid from view, pulling the leaves of the bush in front of her up to her nose. She recited plant names and families as prayers, recited their properties, the names of their cousins that could be used for medicine, the tinctures and potions they made. Think of the plants, she counseled herself, and put one foot in front of the next.

When she returned to the herbalist's cottage, she found it in ashes on the ground, one burnt corpse tied to a post and she crumpled to the ground, covered her face over the accusation of the blackened face. Fiona, she cried, and cut down the corpse, laid it gently on the ground. Too short to be Fiona, she thought, the tears flowing down her face, and she turned to the charred logs that were the herbalist's cottage. The cellar. She pulled the rubble aside and wormed her way through any space big enough to accommodate her, digging and calling to Fiona. She dug with sticks and her bare hands, soon unable to distinguish between the dirt of the cellar and of the earth around her.

Though she spent two days digging, she couldn't find a second body anywhere. Had Fiona escaped, or been carried away? And there was no sign of the books, though in a fire they would have been ash mixed with the dirt. She cried, folded herself like a pill bug in her exhaustion, rose from the dirt covered outside with black soot and inside with a charcoal smell that invaded her pores, coated her nostrils and lungs. A distraught, soot-covered woman keening at the site of a burning was guilty by association. If she couldn't find Fiona here, she should leave.

The flames of Rome flashed in front of her. It had been subterfuge that had saved her. It had been disguise, in having a body that wasn't her body and she flinched at every creaking branch and hooting bird, thinking of who she could be, how she could hide.

Luccia had nothing — no donkey, cart, nor Fiona. No mother. Not even a hometown, because Salerno had turned on her mother, turned its back on them. Rome had taught her the extent of horror. Fiona had taken ill with a strange affliction and couldn't be found. The only thing Luccia had was the list, four manuscripts left over from Rome and the hope that perhaps Fiona were still alive, possessing the same list and well enough to track her as before. Luccia trudged into the woods stuffing leaves into her pockets, and headed north with the goal of Marseilles, traveling only at night, hiding during the day, a delirious young boy who occasionally sipped from a vial kept inside his filthy shirt.

Two weeks into her journey, she heard the mourning dove in the early evening and she stopped by the side of the road, turned in all directions, afraid to be unafraid. Behind her, a donkey cart lumbered up the road, then pulled alongside her and she covered her face with her sleeve at the stench of the manure that was piled in the back. A raggedy man with a hooded face barked at her to climb in beside him.

"Couldn't smell your own stead for the stench of the shit, could you?" Fiona said to her, grinning from ear to ear and holding out her hand to Luccia.

Luccia clutched the side of the wagon to keep from crumpling, her chin fell to her chest in relief. She sprang forward onto the wagon seat, grabbed Fiona and shook her, clung to her, slapped her on the back and spat into the dust to keep the tears from her eyes.

Luccia settled beside her. "So you're what I've been smelling for an hour. Marseilles?" she asked Fiona.

Fiona smiled. The plan was understood: come hell or high water, follow the list. It gave both of them solace. Fiona slapped the donkey with the reigns but it stopped in the middle of the road. "God, how I hate the donkeys."

Luccia kicked its rump and it started to plod down the roadway. Luccia looked back at the cart, turned to Fiona and inquired silently about the books.

"They're all there but the ones you took," Fiona said. She saw a nervous flutter in Luccia's eyes and turned back to the road, measuring her words carefully.

"I was very frightened for your being in Rome," she whispered but Luccia threw her shoulders back, gritted her teeth.

"They killed the herbalist and burned her house," Luccia whispered back. Fiona bowed her head and turned away. Luccia didn't tell her how she had frantically dug for Fiona, or how Rome had shown her the horror from which her mother had tried to shield her. "Are you alright?" she asked instead.

"I'm not much protection for you, little one, and I'm damn sorry," she said, her voice breaking. "My body just buckles under the pressure." She pulled her hood back and Luccia saw that Fiona's mouth was as misshapen as it had been during the seizure. She wiped the spit from the corner of her lip onto the sleeve of her tunic. "Afterward it doesn't seem to put itself back properly anymore. Your mother was the only one who could concoct something to keep me right."

Luccia ran her hands along the lining of Fiona's cape.

"Woad," Fiona said quietly.

"With privet fruit in the dye," Luccia whispered, and clung to the edge of the cape. Fiona, the books, back again, more precious now. Come hell or high water, the list. And hell was clearly here, so it would be the list, Luccia thought, trying to re-order her life. The days of quiet copying, the purposeful scratch of her quill across paper, gracious study time seemed like life in another world. She had listened to the women's plaintiff cry for the manuscript without understanding. In Salerno, every book was honored, but outside Salerno... she thought, trembling. Fiona wrapped her blue cloak around Luccia's shoulders.

At night, Fiona cooked while Luccia huddled with her back to the fire, shaking, accepting her meal with shame. It took Luccia another two weeks after Rome to be able to light a fire without breaking down. In the night she screamed about enormous wheels and spikes. Most mornings, she woke up with Fiona spooned into her, her cupped palm just a twig's width from Luccia's mouth.

Fiona didn't ask Luccia about Rome again: the story of her own mother and the ravenous river fought against the inside of her teeth, and both Luccia and Fiona recognized how fragile a barrier that could be. Instead, they traveled north to Livorno, to Genoa, and on to San Remo, becoming women again when they were to meet women, men when they traveled the roadways, splitting up when necessary. They took on a feral look, living in hollowed-out logs, in the forest, for a while in a cave by the side of a river, sleeping on the beach, gathering edible plants, fishing, snaring small birds and rabbits.

She and Fiona presented books in Marseilles, in Toulouse, rode north to Lyon and started south again. Whenever she was alone, Luccia tipped the elixir from the vial onto the end of her tongue. It was her only solace, two drops of a liquid that she couldn't yet decipher, tasting of licorice.

It became a less than orderly journey. So many of the women were dead, what were they to do with the manuscripts? Giovanna had had a clear plan for the books: first priority was the women remaining in universities so that Trotula could be taught to the next generation. Then came the women in the hospitals, and those few who openly practiced medicine. Some of the women had moved on, though, and they followed their trail across entire countries, only to discover that there was someone practicing medicine in hiding in the towns along the way who could have used the book.

They had to travel south in the winter and then back north again as the weather permitted, all the time dodging the outbreaks of the witch trials. Fiona struggled with her illness, insisting on separating herself from Luccia whenever it overtook her, so that they spent as much time doubling-back to find each other as they did moving ahead. They tried to gather the names of midwives and doctors who might want the book, even though they weren't names her mother had given them. And sometimes they just scattered like frightened rabbits: when a priest questioned them on the road or something made Fiona shiver in the middle of the day.

Chapter Five

*I*n addition to their book delivery, Fiona and Luccia pursued Giovanna. They heard about an herbalist who was hidden in the caves in Southern France, and through a series of midwives and herb merchants, set up a rendezvous. They waited in the woods at a checkpoint, but another woman arrived instead and when she let her hood fall to her shoulders, both Luccia and the woman started to cry. Luccia and Fiona continued their journey, then heard of another plan, waited on the outskirts of another city, without finding Giovanna. After half a dozen failed rendezvous that cut Luccia to the quick and left her weeping for days, Fiona began heading out without her.

Finally, Fiona returned wrung out and exhausted. She sat beside Luccia and a dying fire.

"There was a boat she was supposed to be on but it sank. And a town she was supposed to be in but it burned. Either way, I'm afraid she didn't make it, little one."

Lying in Fiona's arms, Luccia cried all night. Her tears poured out, the night marked by the bitter smell of Fiona's breath and her resigned weeping that had turned to calm, steady breathing.

"In the end, little one," Fiona whispered to her, "grief is a selfish emotion. The dead are off to a better place, and we're left here to feel sorry for ourselves in our loneliness. Sleep now, little one. Sleep."

In the summer of 1471, Fiona gathered a few provisions, and promised to meet Luccia south of the tiny village of Tasse, France. She had taken two books, gone off into the woods and Luccia was convinced that she saw Fiona's right arm start to flail as soon as she left. It was a scalding hot season, and after two days, Luccia stumbled along the banks of a creek clutching her stomach because she had either eaten some bad berries or a bird that had eaten some bad berries. Either way, she had to hide the wagon and its books in a thicket, dress as a girl, and get at least to the outskirts of a village before she collapsed. It wouldn't do to be in the forest and it was too dangerous to pass out beside the contraband.

Luccia and Fiona had been sent by a midwife from Toulouse to find Simone Tasse, not a medic but a supporter, and as their life had evolved into a series of clandestine jumps from the shadows of one woman's life to another, Tasse's village was a welcome sight. Especially since Luccia crouched in pain by the side of Tasse's stables.

Clutching a gunnysack with a single book and a small piece of bread, Luccia watched Simone Tasse stride from her stables toward a warehouse. The woman's gait was so large that village children running behind her couldn't jump from footprint to footprint — she was short and twice as wide as a man with body parts that seemed to defy containment — breasts heaving and swaying inside her corset, rising against her gauze modesty panel. Her legs gobbled up the ground, nearly shredding the skirt that covered them. Simone picked up heavy tack as if it were a handkerchief, though it made her muscles strain the seams of her dress. She shoved the saddle into a stable-hand's arms, spewing language at him that would land a man in a brawl. Her yards of caramel brown hair were so thick that Simone had woven it with cowhide thongs and lanced it to her head as if it were an unruly piece of luggage strapped to one of her wagons. The sun was blistering and the air smelled of horse sweat and hot dung as Simone turned to the rain barrel, flung off the heavy lid with one hand, and dowsed the front of her chest.

A thin, dusty driver walked up beside Simone and muttered under his breath. Simone looked startled, then grabbed the reins of his horse and drew the animal in front of them for cover. The driver continued to speak beneath his breath and Simone forced open the lips of the gelding.

"Don't look so frightened," she growled, half at the horse, half at the driver.

"It's different this time," the driver said. "They're the big guys."

"A couple of broken down priests," Simone dismissed. "Pay them, feed them, tell them there's no midwife here: it's always the same."

"It's the Bishop, ma'am. And I'm tellin' you, they're heading right this way."

"The Bishop!" she said with uncharacteristic excitement. "Then there's nothing to worry about." Simone inspected the horse's ears, then tenderly stroked its muzzle. "He's a man of God. Certainly not one of those profiteering clerics. Now take this animal up to the top pasture."

The Bishop, Simone thought, smoothing the front of her dress out of instinct. She had told her drivers to be alert for the itinerant priests who roamed the countryside creating trouble, the stray burning courts that barreled through the village but never bothered to stop. She always liked to know what was going on near her corner of the world. But the Bishop. A Godsend. A great honor to have him here. She hurried toward the inn. She must be certain the dining room was clean, that he was welcomed with the best linens and port. It was doubtful he would stop except to water his horses, but perhaps he would bless them. Did she dare hope for a chance to pray together? She had to change and get her rosary for him to bless.

As Simone turned toward her little house at the end of the lane, Luccia stumbled from the side of the stable holding her sack to her chest, and vomited into the pathway.

"Mother of God!" Simone charged over to her and took Luccia's arm, righted her, then looked around for horse or companion that might have arrived with Luccia.

"Where did you come from?" Simone asked.

Luccia tried to straighten herself and smooth the front of her dress. "The forest from the south."

"Where are your people?" Simone asked as she paced around Luccia, the ground trembling under them with every footfall.

"The plants are my people," Luccia said, out of breath.

Another herbalist fleeing north: it didn't really matter what they were fleeing from. Husbands or judges, Simone knew flight and was willing to shelter a runaway for a time. But the Bishop was *en route*, and she wanted to put her best foot forward.

"This is no time to be sickly," she muttered to Luccia. "The Bishop is coming." She summoned a stableman with a single wave of her arm. "Hide this girl in the inn. And fill her with water."

The stableman guided Luccia to the inn across from the barn, muttering about how she smelled like a wild dog, that she had bugs in her hair and black filth caked on the back of her neck. He warned her not to steal anything or make a sound and that if she vomited inside the inn he'd personally kick her into the stables. Luccia was in no state to argue. Feverfew for nausea, she thought. Agrimony and five-finger grass. Sage to clean my blood, but she was too weak to say anything at all. He tightened his grip on her arm, put her sack on the table, laid her in a child's bed set into the wall beside the fireplace and removed her boots, covered her.

"I better not have to burn these blankets when you leave," he grumbled, and pulled the curtains around her. As it was the first indoor bed she had lain in for quite a while, she fell asleep.

What seemed like minutes later, she was jolted awake when the door was thrown open and a man folded himself up to fit through the door, then untangled himself on the threshold. She peeked out from the bed curtains, careful not to be seen. He was a tall, gaunt man whose head nearly scraped the ceiling of the room— he swatted at it resentfully — then stepped forward on legs bent high like a bug climbing a stalk toward prey. He wore the broad-brimmed hat of a German professor and it was coated with road dust, jammed down on stringy black hair. The flesh of his face hung so loosely on his bones that it seemed to be melting off his scull. He had heavy drooping eyes, a bumpy forehead, a short nose that came to a sloping end, and a mouth so down-turned that he appeared to have been frozen in the middle of a nightmare, morose and only half-awake.

He stomped his boots on the threshold and swept sleepy eyes once around the room. A clean little well-scrubbed stone house with gleaming beams, low ceilings, a big hearth whose mantle displayed mismatched china plates like prizes, a pewter mug, a sooty candle snuff, a brasserie that would be handy in the winter. Lace on the windows had been many-times mended and fervently washed. It reminded him of his mother's house before her demise, and of her precious care of anything that remotely looked like gentility. If his mother had only known how far away genteel had actually been. The room made him feel uneasy and yet he felt himself settle in. He sighed sadly, as he opened a book in his hands.

A Bishop followed on his heels, stepping around him, hiding his hands inside his cape and sneering at his surroundings.

"Pestilential stench," the Bishop muttered, kicking a chair out of his way.

The professor shrugged indifferently. "Bishop, when do we reach Toulouse?"

"Several more days, Professor Bremer," the Bishop said in a bored, indulgent tone and turned away.

The Bishop held his sleeve over his nose. "What died in here?" He reached back through the door and pulled a child into the building. "Is it you who stinks, little ward of mine?" he bellowed, throwing the child into the room ahead of him where the boy crashed into the legs of a chair and cut his cheek. "Find me a seat. I should send you back to the orphanage in Basel for all the good you do."

The professor snapped his book shut and grumbled. "Indeed you should, Bishop, at least to stop the tedium of shouting at this boy."

The little boy who had been thrown on the floor, no more than eight years old, dressed in a novice's habit but dirty, with matted hair and oozing eyes, gathered himself as if already dodging the next blow, and scurried across the room to gesture to a chair.

The Bishop crossed the room with a huff and plopped himself into the large chair in front of the fire, propped up his muddy boots and pulled off his gloves. "And they say peasants work hard. Where is the staff?"

A small man scurried into the boarding house, sheepishly introduced himself as the blacksmith who also served as the alderman, and rubbed the mud off his old boots onto the back of his pant legs. Bowing and scraping, he begged pardon again.

The Bishop smiled slightly, offered his ring to be kissed.

"You understand that we are on a mission from God," the Bishop intoned, and the alderman bowed again. "This land must be rid of evil, rid of those who ply the Devil's trade. Have you a midwife here?"

"No Bishop. We have no doctor of any sort," the alderman said apologetically. "Someday we hope to attract one but we are simple people who have to muddle along until then."

The professor transferred his book under his other arm and rubbed his forehead in exasperation. "No doctor, Bishop. There is nothing here. When the heat of the day dissipates let's be on our way. There is nothing to be gained."

Nothing for him, anyway. It was the midwives he wanted, or more to the point, their records, their recipes and tinctures. It wasn't his fault they were heretics. While they were being arrested he went into their homes and took their books, their vials, studied them at night. He owed it to medicine. It wasn't his fault that he was the son of a poor widow and couldn't afford university. He wasn't even a professor but they called him that because he wore the cap of a man he had beaten at cards. It could have been his. It should be his. Admittedly, he couldn't read Latin — just German and bar maid French. But that's why he needed the midwives and the witches — they wrote in their native tongue, not Latin. He could read it, he could study. Latin was something you needed university for, and there was no education in his future except for the one he made for himself. Sometimes he could question the women...beforehand. Before the Bishop got to them. If their knowledge became his, at least he'd have something.

He didn't practice medicine but he would, someday, when all this was over, this chasing the Bishop around. They'd accept him. They'd have to. He'd prove his knowledge and they'd let him into the profession once and for all. Maybe to a teaching post, even. Rightly so. His saddlebags bulged with the journals of these wicked women. Macon was the big herb market in France and he wanted to study more before he reached there, to be ready. There was no time to waste in a little back-woods livery stop like this.

"Bring me the tax records," the Bishop ordered, and the alderman scurried out.

When he returned, the alderman offered up a ledger of tax records that was seized and studied by the Bishop while the alderman stood as if at attention and the professor wandered on aimless spider legs through the room.

"Tasse," the Bishop pronounced, after a moment. "Simone Tasse. She is the wealthiest woman in the village?"

The alderman cleared his throat.

"Oh yes, by far. In fact this is her inn," he said, sweeping his hand grandly around the room. "She will be very disappointed that she wasn't here to greet you. I think she's...dressing for your Grace."

"I need no woman to dress for me," the Bishop sneered.

The alderman shuffled his feet nervously. He owned the blacksmith shop and Tasse was both grit in his wound and his partner in building the village. His business depended on her, but there was no way for him to expand his business from shoeing horses to owning horses because she was always launching another caravan of wagons into Paris before he had even thought up the plan. Her enterprise had mushroomed around him until he was barely more than a stable hand for her. She was haughty. A shrew. And yet there was something magnificent about her, something shining and indefatigable, he thought, glancing at the Bishop to see if he could read his thoughts. Solid as her stone house and sometimes he just wanted to crawl in and close the door behind him.

"She takes part in the May Pole celebration?" the Bishop asked.

"Well the whole town does," the alderman said dismissively. "It's just a spring celebration..."

"The entire town?" the Bishop stood sharply, slapping the book down, and leaning across the table toward the alderman. "The whole town?

"Of course not the entire town, just...most of the women," the alderman blustered, spittle jumping onto his lips. What was going on here? Was the Bishop going to say Mass or burn the place to the ground? Why the focus on Simone? What would it be like to see Simone Tasse go up in flames? A cold sweat gathered on the alderman's forehead. He thought about her money filling the village coffers after she died. The Bishop turned his back on the alderman who nervously bit his lip and tried to still one trembling leg.

Fritz Bremer heard the conversation as a tedious drone, and then noticed the gunnysack on the edge of the table. Attuned to the hiding places of books, the professor noted the shape that defined the sack and without interrupting the Bishop, he moved to the edge of the table. Stealthily, he picked the sack up by the neck, and heartened by its weight, settled himself in a chair.

Bremer's breathing slowed as he turned the pages of *Trotula*, stunned by the illuminated diagrams of plants. It was written in Latin, cursed language, but his eyes gobbled up what he assumed were the descriptions of ailments and their cures, the treatises on disease. He gripped the sides of the book as if it were a plate of the week's only meal. Where had this book come from, in a town that had no midwife? And no ordinary midwife would possess such a book. It contained more knowledge than all of his saddlebags, tenfold. It was the education he had been denied. It was the sum of this long, ugly journey. And it was a secret to keep from the Bishop. The books and remedies of witches, the Devil's work, he would say, and throw this volume and all the professor's books on the pyre with the women.

"And Tasse is without a man?" the Bishop asked the alderman, folding his hands into his sleeves.

The professor quietly moved to the alderman's side. Did Tasse own the book? And if so, where had she found it? Tasse couldn't be eliminated before the source of the book was discovered.

"A husband?" the alderman laughed. "She'll have none of that. No indeed."

"You're an idiot," the university professor growled in the alderman's ear, looking sideways out of his half-lidded eyes, the words barely moving his flaccid, scowling lips.

"I beg your pardon, sir?" the alderman whispered.

"If they kill her the Church takes her money. If you marry her, you take it. Given the choice..."

"And have you ever heard her speak of the Devil?" the Bishop said without turning back to the alderman.

"Certainly not, your Grace," the alderman said, confused. "She's a devout Catholic, and as I mentioned, she is no midwife."

"Heretics have many disguises," the Bishop said quickly. "These are evil lives, these witches," he muttered as he looked around the room for his ward. Having found him on a little stool by the fire, the Bishop grabbed him by his matted hair and marched him across the room. "A social pest and parasite," the Bishop said, bending over his charge, "a devotee of a powerful and loathsome...."

The little boy laughed with the sound of chickens being killed. The Bishop pressed the little boy into a crouch on the floor.

The cackle of the child's laugh and the sharp sound of his knees hitting the floor made Luccia freeze in her bed. Looking down, the shoes of the Bishop were so close to Luccia's face as she hid in the bed that she could see mud clinging to the soles.

"You should pray, little boy. Pray the Devil never finds you." The boy pressed his hands on the floor. The Bishop turned away from the child but Luccia's heart stopped as the Bishop's boot crushed the boy's hand and the child took an intake of breath but didn't let it out. The boy prayed through gritted teeth as the Bishop ground his heel into him. "A loathsome, obscene creed, witches are."

The professor continued to mumble in the alderman's ear. "But if you implicate her, and then marry her, you're as likely to go on the pyre as she. They're very thorough like that. You'd become the faggot, the kindling to set the blaze."

"Remember the Book of Revelations," the Bishop intoned, "the great whore that sitteth upon many waters with whom the Kings of the earth have committed fornication...'"

"Oh, not Tasse," the alderman quickly added. "Contributes heavily to the Church. Nothing of the witch in her, no indeed," he said nervously.

The Bishop whirled around to the alderman, twisting the boy's hand with his shoe and then walking away. "You can make such a pronouncement? You know better than the Holy Inquisition? Bring her to me and I shall be the judge of that."

The child, Peter, stayed on his knees in the same spot, but now held his bruised hands in prayer. Luccia could smell him and her hands hurt in sympathy.

Then she saw the book open across the seat of the chair, and her breath caught in her throat. The bed felt cold underneath her. Her head swirled from her own ailment, from the plight of poor Peter, the proximity of the Bishop, the discovery of the book. The boy was praying with his eyes closed, and both the professor and the Bishop had their eyes locked on a little man's sweating face. Luccia scurried to the end of the bed, pulled the book toward her and secreted it under the mattress.

When Simone passed the alderman as he left the inn, she noticed his frightened eyes and disoriented nature but she was accustomed to his being unable to handle the twists and turns of an ordinary life. He was a sniveling, gutless man and when he stopped in mid-step at the sight of her, she sailed past him with her chin up, annoyed that he had met with the Bishop before her. She smoothed the front of her best dress, and slowed her stride to appear less of a farm hand and more of a lady. Perhaps the Bishop was here to discuss plans for improvement to their little church at the end of the village, or to ask her opinion on the conduct of the local monk Brother Brian who could certainly do more to fill the pews on Sunday.

"Your Grace," Simone said breathlessly as she swept into the inn and curtsied deeply. The Bishop reluctantly offered his ring, which she kissed passionately, and as she gathered her skirts to stand, he wiped the ring on his vestments. "It's a tremendous honor to have you in our tiny part of the world, your Grace."

He raised his eyebrows and waved away a fly. Bremer was staring into the fire, reveling over his discovery of the book.

"Madame Tasse," the Bishop said slowly, "or is it Mademoiselle?"

"Mademoiselle," she said, throwing back her shoulders with pride. She had built the livery business on her own after her father had drunk up the profits from all but one wagon. She had acquired the inn after ten years of hard work and was responsible for the employment of half the village. It would be a joy to have it recognized by the Bishop.

"We are a devout Catholic village, your Grace," Simone said, settling into a seat in front of the Bishop. "I, personally, tithe heavily, and I insist that every one of my stable hands attends Mass every Sunday. Is there any possibility of your saying Mass for us?"

"Certainly not."

"Of course not," she said blushing, squirming slightly in her seat.

"Do you consider yourself the watch-keeper of your people's devotion?" the Bishop asked, looking toward the windows.

"I do," she said proudly.

The Bishop whirled around, the lace on his vestments dancing through the air as he leaned into her face and shouted. "How is it that you take on this task over the man of the cloth?" He raised his voice to a thunder. "Do you consider yourself above the Church?"

Simone sat back, aghast, her hands suddenly flat against the table, her breath lodged in her throat.

"Hell is filled with women with no masters — the succubae, the incubi, the witch, the whore," he snarled. "Remember the Book of Revelations. 'I saw the woman drunken with the blood of the saints and with the blood of the martyrs... And I,' the Bishop pronounced with a sharp finger in the air, 'shall make her desolate and naked and shall eat her flesh...'" he said, his face just inches from Simone's. "And burn her with fire. And in her," he said, "'I found the blood of prophets and of saints and of all that were slain upon the earth.'"

"Good Bishop," she said, standing though her knees were shaking and her breath was labored in her chest. "You will find no one like that in this village. Perhaps in the cities but here we love and fear God, and do His bidding."

"You have no man, Mademoiselle, why is that?" the Bishop snarled. "You don't care for the... member?"

"Your Grace..." she stammered. "I am... a virgin. I know nothing of... members, save those of the animals in the field."

"A goat, perhaps?" he said. "Is it cold, Mademoiselle? The Devil's member is cold. Is your partner a goat?"

Simone was aghast, blushing to her hair roots. Here he was, in her inn, accusing her, of all people. She had been fooled by her own devotion, ensnared by a flaw in her system that was supposed to alert her to danger "I am... a devout... and virginal Catholic."

Professor Bremer turned back to the room and, discovering the book gone, slammed his hand on the hearth. Who had taken it? He strode through the room on his spider legs, peering into chair seats, the top of the table, the windowsills. His pathway out had just disappeared, he thought frantically, his eyes as wide as his drooping lids would allow.

The Bishop glared at him momentarily and Bremer stopped mid-step, crossing his arms over his chest and pretending to peer out the window. Alerting the Bishop would just worsen the situation, with an outcome that would not benefit him. No one should be carted away until the book had been found.

"Bishop," the professor moved toward the table so suddenly that the Bishop flinched. He lowered his voice to a whisper. "You have no need of a tiny piece of property here in the middle of nowhere. Save your strength for Toulouse where... receiving an entire city block from a... coven of witches, would do you well, indeed. Toulouse, Bishop." The professor stepped back and raised his voice. "We have traveled far today. Perhaps the fine lady would ... offer us a bite to eat, and we can consider this matter another day. Peter here, is in need of... attention."

Chapter Six

The little bell in the church sounded, and Simone breathed a sigh of relief. "My staff will show you quarters and fulfill your requirements, your Grace. I have instructed them to lay out our very best. For myself," she said shakily, "I don't like to be late for vespers and as I retire shortly thereafter... I beg leave to see you after morning prayers."

The Bishop turned furiously to the professor and Bremer knew it would go hard on him in the ensuing days, until they came across a midwife or a band of women the old fool could send up in flames. But he stood his ground, and the Bishop finally waved Simone away and turned again toward Peter.

That night, the wind tore down the dark lanes of the village, howling against the stone walls. Luccia was still sick, but had learned through her travels that it's best to know first-hand what events are about to transpire: after Rome she lived in fear of being swept into events. She needed to see how large the entourage was, whether there were soldiers of the Bishop encamped outside, take an assessment of where things were. She breathed in the reassuring bouquet of the surrounding trees. Poplar, pine. Mostly, she needed to separate herself from the book, adopt a new disguise as a stable hand perhaps. She hid the book in a haystack on the far reaches of the property.

Simone lived at the end of the lane. The alderman had to rap several times on the door before her maid answered and he squirmed inside, forcing the maid to close the door behind him. Simone was sitting at a desk, staring on her daily reports but not working, her hands deep into unbound hair that poured like caramel from the crown of her head, down her shoulders, into a puddle on the table. She was shaking, perplexed over her error — her belief that devotion would keep her safe, that this witch thing had been the work of renegade priests. Now here was the Bishop, spitting in her face. Simone Tasse, pillar of the church, dutiful, generous. She shuddered over what the Bishop had said, and what she knew they did to others but assumed they would never do to her.

She had been abandoned by her faith, judged unworthy, as she had as a poor, fat little girl with her mother dead and her father slumped drunk by the rain barrel. They had tried to send her to live with old man Vrie when her father had died and she knew what horrid fate she would meet in his bed so she had clambered onto her father's wagon seat — Mother Mary her feet didn't even touch the floor boards — and had lashed at the villagers with the whip to keep them away. She had ridden off to another town. A month later, she had returned, triumphant, shuttling flour from the mill to the baker. Oh, that day she had come back, their jaws had dropped. And now they weren't going to usher her out this way, as a witch, marched naked through the square with all her hair shaven off, walking backwards to finally be turned to meet her Inquisitor. Not Simone Tasse. Sitting there, with her hair unbound and a bleak future before her, she was unwilling to call on the Blessed Virgin to protect her. She needed to save herself.

She looked up from her papers and saw the alderman.

"Henri," she said with disgust and surprise. She was in no mood to contend with her witless adversary.

"They've come for you," he said breathlessly, breaking his hat in his twisting palms.

The maid gasped, stepped back a few paces from Simone, then pulled her cloak off a peg. "I'm sorry ma'am" she muttered, then flung open the door and ran out of the house.

Simone, startled from her chair, began to protest the maid's departure, but thought better of it. When they come for you, they string up your servants as well.

"As usual, Henri," she said sarcastically, "you're four steps ahead of the rest of us."

"They'll have you for witchcraft." The alderman leaned on the table. "For consorting with the Devil."

"I consort with no one," she growled, then twisted her hair in her hands. "Now get out of my house."

"As much evidence as they need, Simone. A woman without a man? And a wealthy woman? Surely a witch."

Simone glowered at him. It was true that things had gotten worse recently. The stories coming in from her drivers raised the hair on her neck. Previously, they had been only occasional tales, told when they thought she couldn't hear, but now the men arrived pale and frightened, sometimes sitting in the hay loft with their faces in their hands before they could address her.

"There's only one way out," the alderman continued.

"I've paid my way out of this kind of mess before, alderman, and you know it, so don't tell me there's only one way." Simone feigned confidence.

"Marry me," he blurted.

"What?"

"You could…marry me."

Incensed, Simone stood up and came around to the front of her desk, grabbed the alderman's arm and flung him away. She outweighed him by nearly two hundred pounds and with fury in her eyes, he didn't dare to collect himself from the floor.

"Marry me," he said again, timidly, curling into a ball. "They have only one charge against you and that's that you're not married."

"You've been scheming for my money for years, you sniveling squirrel's ass!"

"Better to have half of your estate than no estate …no… life," the alderman pleaded.

She turned away at the thought of such a man. But he was right, Simone knew. She couldn't stall any longer. The Bishop had made it clear that he wouldn't leave empty-handed.

"Marry you?" she growled. She strode toward the alderman so violently that the floor shook. She grabbed him by the collar and pulled him to standing. A filthy, witless, disgusting little man. And he was her ticket to life.

56

"You want to *marry* me?" she sneered and hauled him with one hand onto her desk. She held him down with one massive hand on his throat and pulled apart his threadbare pants with the other.

"I'll show you marriage," she said. Members, she thought. She'll show them… members. He whimpered as she pulled his cock out and roughly made him hard as if milking a cow. Hauling her girth onto the desk, she mounted him, with a scowl on her face and tears in her eyes that this should be the way she gave up her virginity. That this act could save her life. She scooped him up like a rag doll and clumsily pounded him into her, thinking about goats, crying over the end of the solace and illusion. When he came she snarled and fell forward onto her fists, which hit the table beside his head like hammers on a nail.

"You're mine now, little man, and if you betray me," she said, tearing a swatch from his pants and shaking it in his face as evidence, "I'll see that you burn beneath my skirts!"

Early the next morning, Simone, in a simple white shift with the alderman sweating on her forearm, presented herself to Brother Brian for marriage. The stable hands were there, so fresh from daybreak chores that the straw still clung to their pants.

With the alderman to profit from Simone's fortune there was no easy access to the tax records that had disappeared as quietly as the copy of *Trotula*. And there was no other woman in the village with enough wealth to make a trial profitable, so the Bishop, who had slept through the daybreak nuptials, now furiously ordered the entourage to leave. No one in the group mentioned that in the middle of the night, Peter had been tightly tied by the neck to the handle of the well.

Bremer strode back into Simone's inn as the Bishop's servants prepared the carriage. "Where is it?" the professor snarled, the corners of his mouth quivering in his pasty cheeks.

"Sir?" the alderman asked timidly.

"The book! I want the book." He leaned his spider body forward across the table.

Simone rushed to the hearth and brought forward her Bible. The professor flung it to the floor.

"I keep the tax records in my home," the alderman's voice shook. "I can fetch them…"

"Not those," the professor growled, then straightened as he regarded the faces of the newly-weds from under his drooping lips. Unlike the Bishop, who could become lost in his own fury, the professor prided himself on his ability to see a lie tightening a liar's lips, to know an innocent by their steady shoulders.

"Professor, the carriage is ready," a servant called from the doorway.

The book had been here. But the book was not theirs.

"The Bishop commands you to... join him at once, sir."

There was no use in continuing with these two, and desertion of the Bishop would land *him* on the pyre. But the book was the key to his future. His possession of it — and his alone — would allow him to march into the university, a scholarly and honored man. He would disdainfully throw bread to the peasants as had been done to him. He would have silver candlesticks on his mantle and a headstone for his mother. He would have this book.

The Bishop, with pokers for eyes, burst open the door and the professor straightened.

"Don't keep me waiting...Fritz," the Bishop growled.

With a long, thin arm, the professor reached out and slapped Simone across the face and swept out of the building behind the Bishop.

The entourage set out toward Macon while Luccia watched from the hayloft, struggling for a glimpse of the little battered boy, hoping Fiona didn't stumble into their path.

Luccia slept indoors, her blankets stayed dry, nothing dropped from webs above her, nothing hung from the trees in front of her, though she cried in her sleep over nightmares of a boot crushing hands and a nagging feeling that she should follow the little boy Peter and rescue him.

At sundown a week after Luccia had moved into the house, Fiona appeared in the crossroads dressed as a woman, dragging one of her feet a bit. Luccia, threw a pitch fork to the ground, flung herself on Fiona and knocked her down in the dirt, holding her so tightly that Fiona finally pulled away, gripped Luccia's chin and looked into her eyes for evidence of a Rome-sized catastrophe.

"I'm fine," Luccia said quietly, running her finger over the Celtic broach. She didn't want to make Fiona feel worse for being sick and staying away. "Really, I'm fine. A Bishop came through here and... I was afraid they'd run into you." A Bishop with a child, she wanted to say. She nestled into Fiona, then pulled away and helped Fiona to her feet.

Luccia took Fiona in to meet Simone and after a moment, the two adults shooed Luccia outside and closed the door behind them. Several hours later, Luccia crept to the inn windows to see what they were doing, and Fiona had one of her gangly legs propped on the edge of the table, a mug of beer in her hand, her head back and laughing. Simone had her head on her forearm, her breasts resting in an enormous mound on the table as she laughed.

Luccia slept spooned into Fiona that night, the joy of her arms around Luccia banishing the dreams of the boot, the bones, and the sores on the little boy's hands.

In the morning, Fiona sent Luccia to gather the donkey cart from the woods, and she retrieved the volume from the haystack as well. Simone met them in secret at the side of the barn and insisted they take the cart to the very back of her stables, lift the baseboards and show her the books. Fiona had let her in on their plan.

Late that night, as the alderman snored in the back bedroom, Simone lit a lamp and poured over the manuscript, letting her tea chill beside her. So this was the book the professor had been looking for.

"Any one paragraph of this book would have you two burning in the square," Simone said. "We have to hide these, immediately. The Bishop was just through here, there's no telling who has circled back."

"Will you help us?" Fiona said. "We could carry them one at a time but it's slow going and we could do it so much better under the cover of a livery business such as yours."

Simone regarded them cautiously. "There's no one else with these books?"

"The monks won't copy them because of the anesthetics and the scribes won't produce them because they're about women," Fiona said.

Simone leaned back in her chair and rubbed her face with her big hands. She had spent the last five years harboring midwives who were fleeing the courts, women who had gotten skittish in Macon and were on their way to boats out of Marseilles. There had even been a close call last spring — two young things who had moaned like swamp reeds. Simone had burned the sheets after they left, not really believing that they had been touched by the Devil but by horror. Even that had been nothing like the Bishop's last visit, and now nothing like this shipment. This wasn't a hot meal and a ride out of town, this was a request to plant both feet into the thick of it.

But Simone knew that she was a woman of extremes: when confronted with the world's insistence that she be banished after her parents' deaths, she became the pillar of the community. Startled by the Church's unwillingness to see her virtue, Simone now decided to embrace vice.

Fiona and Luccia had grown used to relying on women who were passive supporters, who slipped them a piece of bread or a hiding place for a day. But within a month, Simone was not only transporting manuscripts, but the illegal herbs they mentioned as well. Not just motherwort and Lady's Mantle to regulate menstruation and provide a sedative for post-partum anxiety, not just lavender for stings and headaches or raspberry leaf for the uterus and chaste tree that drove out all thoughts of baby-making, but those herbs that the Church was always looking for, the abortive agents tansy, pennyroyal, wormwood and betonica. Luccia was impressed by Simone's ingenuity — she invented a way to shape-shift an entire wagon, creating leather sleeves filled with contraband herbs that she fitted to the wagon's axles. She stuffed herbs into hand-made worm holes in the planks, tied little tufts of sheep's wool onto the mandrake branches so they could be sorted from a simple load of kindling. She created thin boxes nailed to the bottom of the seat that were just the right size for the manuscripts. Simone's favorite tactic was a bold one that she trusted only her best drivers to use: throwing bunches of pennyroyal and tansy in with great mounds of bog myrtle and pyrethrum and passing the entire shipment off as insect repellent.

Luccia set up a small laboratory in the back barn, determined to make as many medicines as she could with the herbs that presented themselves. She tended the animals, shoveled, cleaned, and spent her evenings by candlelight mixing and brewing, hungry to create, using whatever tools Simone had handy, comforted by the steady feel of a mortar in her hand. She made tinctures of Pasque flowers for the stable-hands' cuts that they accepted first with suspicion and then with appreciation. It was the only medicine they had encountered in quite a while. And while it seemed odd to take medicine made by one so young, the tinctures worked. Luccia brewed hop and valerian tea for Simone's melancholy, an infusion of licorice, golden seal, marigold, and chamomile with comfrey and marshmallow leaf for Henri's gastritis, and mixed wormwood and balmony into the animal's food to fight worms.

The shipments were orderly and regular, and Simone kept her eye out for the spidery professor and any word of the Bishop. Folding her arms across her broad chest, Simone described the professor to both Luccia and Fiona, trying to impart a sense of urgency, a sense of fear.

"A face like clay. You must keep your eye out for that one," Simone warned, but the two regarded her calmly.

"We've got a eye out for them all," Fiona said, digging a seed from her teeth and spitting into the dust.

"No," Simone said. "This one asked specifically about the book."

Luccia stiffened. She thought of her mother who had been hunted, and her assumption that she and Fiona were just trying to avoid the net.

"A face of clay?" Fiona repeated.

"And a German professor's hat," Simone replied.

Fritz Bremer felt every bump and pothole on the journey north as a personal affront. He had been at the behest of the Bishop for three years, as he had no other means of support — no real education, no trade of any kind. He needed that book but there was no convincing the Bishop to return to the site of his defeat, and defection was a dangerous business. He would have to bide his time. It had always been a reasonable arrangement for the professor, after he abandoned his conscience over the burnings, which had required a single week of excessive drinking and a hangover that had lasted two.

He occasionally suffered from boredom, from stiffness in his joints from riding, from indigestion over the relentlessly changing food, from irritation over the daily savagery to the boy and the smell the child emanated. But since encountering the book, and being forced to leave without it, he was consumed with rage. His stomach burned night and day, until he had to sleep sitting up. He incessantly dragged his fingernails over the back of his neck as if trying to dislodge insects that weren't there. His blood had changed its constitution as his mother's had during the winter when she boiled ink pots on the fire. Then her hands were covered with lamp-black to the forearms, she had streaks on her face that wouldn't come off, and the air in their little room was so thick with the fumes of linseed oil and charcoal that their clothes and the bedding became gray. In those months she would wheeze like wind being pulled from a mine, then mutter incomprehensibly to herself and tear at her hem. Little Fritz prayed for spring, for sunshine, and for a night without muttering and his mother's black and bloody phlegm, for laundry to replace the ink so that his mother could spend a week inhaling deep in front of the window and coughing into a cloth, scrubbing the room, the curtains, the candlesticks, coming to her senses. "You'll be a gentleman like this," she would say in the summers, holding up the foolish lace collars and the improbably delicate shirts that she cleaned.

What book was it, he muttered, bouncing over the ruts and reaching his spindly arm down his back to scratch. After he had seen it, he had torn up all the other books in frustration, knowing them to be a paltry imitation of the one he had held at the inn. He hadn't thought to look at the title of the book, so instead, he asked the witches. Before the Bishop got to them as before, but now after the Bishop had nearly finished with them and they were weeping, or worse. Bremer stood in the dungeons, unflinching, and asked. He asked during trials, before dunkings, before the pyre, and the cow-eyed stupidity that stared back at him made him think that he had ink in his lungs.

Chapter Seven

Fiona and Luccia stayed with Simone for eight years, donning different disguises for secret exchanges that were sometimes successful, sometimes sad. In every new area where they traveled, Luccia would pull the mule up short and jump down from the wagon, trod into a field and touch the grasses, the flowers, as if announcing her arrival to them, asking them what they knew.

Luccia collected herbs on every journey, and the secret compartments were as full when she returned as they had been when she left. Luccia worked with *Trotula* then started improvising. Her chemistry grew more sophisticated.

The books made their way secretly across Europe, and Fiona told Luccia of, but would never show her, a convent where the education-hungry daughters of the rich had been sequestered and copied *Trotula* to replenish the supply. Fiona's hair turned gray at the temples, but her limbs seemed to cooperate.

Luccia, however, had arrived at age 20, and despite the eight years at Simone's, appeared to be no more than 14. She menstruated only occasionally. After a long trip, Fiona unfolded her clothing on her bed, and looked over at Luccia.

"You don't seem to be aging, little one," she said, going back to her unfolding. "Why don't you age, Luccia? Your breasts are tiny and you're nearly 20. It was good for the disguises on the last journey we took together, but it's making me wonder. You've got the skin of a baby."

Luccia ran her hand across the smooth surface of her chest. "Aren't you taking my mother's potion, too?" she asked Fiona.

"The potion? You think it's the potion?"

Fiona looked around to see if there was anyone near. Even living in Simone's village, there were secrets that only Fiona and Luccia shared. "I'd be much worse off without it," she said. "Stiffened up and crippled. I should have been dead long ago."

"Don't say that."

Fiona shrugged. "You, though, little shadow, you should put it away."

"I can't put it away. It's from my mother, Fiona. She wanted me to have it."

"Yes, but not to stop aging altogether," she said, inspecting Luccia's eyes and prying open her teeth for perusal. "Maybe it's because you were so young when you started taking it. This worries me. Do you not know what's in it?"

"Me?" Luccia protested. "You're the one with the degree."

"You're the one with the gift. Both your mother and I knew that. I've no clue. I can smell the licorice root, of course."

"It overpowers all the other ingredients."

"Which is probably why she put it in there: to throw anyone off the track. Your mother was so amazingly good at this. Have you no idea at all? You know every herb ever grown. Does your nose and that leaf-crowded brain of yours not tell you anything?"

"No. Mother bought things that came in on the boats. There's nothing growing around here that smells like this liquid." Not that she had tried to decipher it, she didn't admit to Fiona. Why hadn't she? Did she need to believe her mother had magical powers?

"Well, you have to stop taking it. My God, little one, give it to me."

Luccia recoiled from her outstretched hand. "No."

"What do you mean, no? Give it to me! You can't live forever, Luccia. Why in the name of God would you want to?"

"She wanted me to have it."

"You can't be serious, little one. Have you no desire to be… a woman?" Fiona challenged.

"When the pain was too great, mother said. Well, it's almost always too great, Fiona."

Fiona took Luccia in her arms to comfort her, but slipped her hands under the leather thong of the vial and started to remove it from Luccia's neck.

"No!" Luccia shouted, pulling away from her and going outside to pace around the compound in the dark.

She walked around the village inhaling the smell of peat and horses. If she stayed young she could always wait for her mother, couldn't she, and refuse to acknowledge that Giovanna had died, that they had found her and burned her like the rest? If she remained a child wouldn't she always be the one Giovanna had left behind and Luccia would never have to acknowledge that at some point she had decided to live her own life, abandoning her mother? Who wanted a body to grow old in a world like this? If time was boundless, would tragedies seem smaller?

But Luccia knew that if the contents of the vials were keeping her young and Fiona healthy, then deciphering the tincture was essential. Were they the same medicine? What would happen when they ran out? Luccia resolved to begin her enquiry in the morning.

"Why would she give us something that is bound to run out?" Luccia asked furiously when she returned to Fiona's side. "Why would she give us something that can't be duplicated?"

Fiona smiled indulgently but said nothing.

In the years that Luccia and Fiona stayed with her, Simone gave birth to seven children. The first time, Simone was striding across her stable yard like any other day until she gave out a yell, slammed her fist on the wooden top of the rain barrel and shattered it, waddled to a pile of clean hay and spewed out her daughter.

Simone named her Helene and she was a handful. Despite her sudden yet equanimous birth, Helene grew to be a furious baby, squalling and fitful, as if she embodied the rage Simone had felt at being forced to marry the alderman. Kicking and screaming, flailing her little arms inconsolably, Helene was carried by first one servant than another, until the staff finally just chased Simone down and pushed the raging bundle back into her arms. She grew to be a hailstorm of a girl, at two years old frequently seen in the pathways shaking her pudgy little finger at the sky, babbling over some unseen injustice.

Her sister, Isabelle, was born the following year in a birth as passionate and ecstatic as her sister's had been easy and haphazard, and Isabelle grew to be a dreamer, not railing against reality but weaving a world of her own that no one could enter and none could dislodge. Virginie, born fast on the heels of her sister, was devoted, but craved the written word, the visions of others, the concrete. As if Simone's rage dissipated with the birth of each child, one grew up gentler than the previous. Marie Clare, who would turn out to be the middle child, was middling in all things, calm in a storm of sibling furor, moderate in her habits, able to sit in the crossroads of her mother's enterprise entranced with the ebb and flow of other people and their tasks, calmly certain that the horses would step around her. Simone, after rescuing her from her dangerous, dusty spot beside hoof prints, strapped her to a little chair that she then nailed three feet in the air on the side of the barn and Marie Clare, her pudgy little legs dangling and bouncing in her seat, would clap and coo as the engagements of others danced around her.

After each birth, Simone's breasts filled up until she waddled over to the barn to shove a tit in the baby's mouth. When little Marie Clare was
dangling on the side of the wall, Simone would stand, turn her head, and continue to bark orders at the men. Or she would sit for a moment, cross-legged in the dust, with the children climbing into her lap and grabbing at her nipples, sucking the sweet milk that came in torrents or spewed out in a spray when the baby was pulled away by an older sister, until the milk ran across Simone's breasts, the children's clothing, and puddled in the dirt for the dogs to lick. Simone lived with butterfat stains on her clothes for a decade.

A boy slipped out of Simone like an after-thought, born frail and tiny like his father, and died before he was moved from the cradle. When Henrietta was born she was barely able to lift the deathly cloud that had visited the family and Teresa, born the following year, had an oddly shaped face. These two daughters who brought on the end of Simone's childbearing years clung to her like broaches.

One spring, Fiona suggested that they head south into Italy. While Luccia at first longed to return to Italy, if for nothing more than the food and the sun, she couldn't bear to return without her mother, to return to the land of the original betrayal. The university was still open, Fiona said. They still accepted women students but Luccia was steadfast in her refusal to join Fiona. Salerno had had its chance, and it had shown her its true colors. Fiona weakly mentioned women who needed books there and that she would go without her. Luccia agreed to meet Fiona in Marseilles in four months.

It was a surprising time of peace. Bishops were focused on building churches rather than the trials and so women opened their doors to Luccia with only slight hesitation. Midwives sometimes even had celebrations at her arrival. Luccia was able to dispense with much of her subterfuge, grow her hair long and dress like a woman but she maintained a stony grip on her suspicion. She paced through every house, carefully peering out windows and ordering that shutters were pulled, curtains drawn. She never used her name or revealed her previous destination, and she considered the women's jubilation an indulgence.

Luccia followed at the heels of the midwives, taking notes, writing down remedies, and checking them at night against *Trotula,* then adding them to her own collection. Her mother may have hoped she would become a doctor, but Luccia considered herself simply a gatherer of facts, a recipe holder, a chemist. These women could look up the recipes, but they had an essential skill she didn't have: they heard the messages of the body. Luccia chided herself for learning it backwards, for letting Rome burn knowledge out of her, but in some ways was grateful for it. The women doctors in the hospitals, the midwives in the villages, saw the needy and could sense their illnesses. If Luccia had been any more compassionate, she reasoned, any more intuitive of people's suffering, she didn't think she would survive. As it was, she led a life of collecting, inventing, archiving and preserving, which was dangerous enough in a world hell-bent on dissipating and forgetting.

Luccia set out for Marseilles in 1478, excited to see Fiona.

As Luccia and her mule made their way south, him with an old hat to shade his eyes, her humming a little tune under her breath, she dodged a band of monks on the roadside beating themselves with whips and stuffing their faces with fruit as they passed her in the opposite direction. She had grown accustomed to the oddities of men in the Church but was surprised that they were carrying on by the roadside instead of hidden behind their walls.

She couldn't yet smell the sea, but the landscape had changed somehow and crows were clustering in the trees. She asked the plants for a clue, but heard nothing and let it comfort her. Perhaps she was further away than she thought, because she had expected to be joined by farmers heading into town to sell crops, to be jostled by tinkers and wayfarers, to weave her way between herds of sheep. But the roads were empty except for dogs that gathered in the forest knolls.

As Luccia drew closer to town, the dogs were clustered in packs and they began to stalk her and she drew closer to the mule. But before she could mount him, she heard a woman crouched in the weeds, across the lane, keening over the corpse of a man at her feet.

Luccia dropped the reins of the mule and rushed forward, then stopped when she saw that the man's face was half black.

"Do you need help?" she called fearfully, just as the woman spewed a green vomit and fell like a log at his side. A huge flock of crows descended upon the two and Luccia backed away, flailing her arms at the birds and chasing after the mule that was bolting.

Struggling to keep the frightened mule in tow, Luccia called for someone to help, stumbled further down the road toward cottages, but the doors were flung open and left to bang in the wind. When the dogs started darting in the doors, Luccia mounted her mule and covered her nose over the smell from the cottages, spurred him on toward the city, frightened.

On the outskirts of Marseilles, a small band of people clinging to parcels and the sealed coffin of a child saw Luccia on her mule and started running down the road. Luccia pivoted in her seat to see what was behind her that made them charge and when she turned back, they were on her, pulling her from the mule.

"Get off me!" she shouted. "Thieves!" There was no one on the roadway to help her. Luccia broke a twig from a tree and beat at their hands but they threw her down and three of them mounted. The look in their eyes reminded her of the midwife with the cellar.

Shouting at them, she gathered her saddlebags of manuscripts, lunged for a few of the bags of herbs she had hidden before they dug their heels in to the mule's side and trotted away, the ones still on the ground clutching the saddle and running alongside.

Luccia turned in the lane, looking for an answer as a shiver ran down her spine at the thought of mobs in fear. She backed away, then stood her ground, shaking. Fiona was in Marseilles, and if women were going up in flames she might be in the middle of it. Luccia covered her mouth to keep herself from moaning. She wanted to run back to Simone. But Fiona. Luccia bit her lip and pressed on toward the city.

By the time Luccia reached the interior streets of Marseilles she was frantic, off course in a terrain she had previously known backwards and forwards. She lost her way several times, blocked by barricades and cordoned-off streets, stumbling through deserted boulevards. The city had shrunk to a third of its size, eerie and hollow, the low-lying smoke drifting through the city, a single church bell ringing in defeat. Luccia walked as if weights were tied to her ankles. A horse cart tromped by, laden with bodies, arms and legs hanging out of the back, leaving a trail of lime behind it.

When she finally reached the square where she and Fiona had always met, it was deserted, half of the buildings nailed shut with boards and a whitewash sign of the cross, half of them with doors flung open as if someone had just that moment fled, their best possessions still on a little table by the door. Luccia called to Fiona. The silence pushed her back down the street.

Clutching her volume, holding her little cloth bags to her nose, she walked among the sick and the dead. The Plague, she thought, here, as it had been one hundred years ago. She had heard of it, but never seen it, never witnessed the pustules and blackened limbs of whole families dead on their doorsteps, the foaming mouths of a few twitching by the well, and as she stumbled through the city, terrified, she stopped at a pile of clothing stripped off the dead that was taller the height of two men. She was bewildered by parts of town that had been gardens turned into graveyards with no one to erect a tombstone, the dead laid out naked and foul, dusted against the flies. Bodies, wretched bodies, she thought. The survivors she encountered were dulled with the task in front of them or half mad with grief and fear of the water, the air, the touch or the sight of the sick.

All services seemed to have ended, all shops were closed. There were no food stalls or produce carts. She watched men beating each other at the water spigots, and covered her nose over the stench of the funeral pyres (at least this time burning the dead), more foul from the sickness of the flesh.

Surely Fiona had left all this? But she would have returned for me if she were leaving the south of France, Luccia reasoned. And with her ailment, wouldn't she be more susceptible than others? Luccia's desire to run away was building to a panic in her chest, and it fought with her need to find Fiona. If Fiona were ill, at least she could tend to her, so Luccia headed toward the hospital.

She had never made deliveries of herbs to the hospital before because it was controlled by the new doctors — surgeons who would cut off a hand that could have been healed, whose knowledge wasn't based on the teachings of the past.

This day, doctors were nowhere to be seen and bodies were piled in the alcoves and the walkways. Luccia moved among them as if in a trance, her elbows close her to sides, her little bags and manuscripts against her chest like armor. There must have been 700 of the sick in the room, Luccia estimated, and just two nurses staggering between the beds with little more than a beaker of water, numbed to the praying and the crying.

"Fiona," she asked them tentatively, but they recoiled at her touch. "A nurse named Fiona O'Connor?" They shoved her aside and continued. Luccia forced herself to search the faces of the sick for Fiona, stepping back as the patients reached for her.

"I'm sorry," she said, her voice breaking, her eyes huge in her head. "I don't have anything for you. I don't...I don't..." Luccia was reduced to muttering, to guttural sounds as she moved through the room, horrified at what the body could endure, praying that she wouldn't have to search the faces of the dead. It was worse than a burning, to see what could happen to a body from the inside out. No villain, no perpetrator, just decay. Luccia stood frozen in the middle of the aisle, clutching her sack to her chest like a child's blanket. Afraid to breathe in, afraid to be heard, Luccia trembled while little sounds escaped from her throat.

Through this dying throng walked a creature in a brown leather cape, leather head to toe, with a beaked headdress, like an enormous bird of prey. But the patients raised their hands up to him, grabbed his gloves, pleading. The bird looked in Luccia's direction, then suddenly dropped the cup in his hand. Extracting himself from one of the patients, he strode over to her, he grabbed her hair and dragged her across the room.

"Leave off," she screamed, "I'm not sick!" She struggled against him, but he was too strong and he pushed her through a labyrinth of hallways. He pulled her into a tiled room, grabbed the manuscript and bags of herbs from her hands and tossed them aside, dowsed her with water, tore her clothes off and doused her again. She tried to fight but he pushed her to her knees and picked through her hair. When he flattened her on the cold tile floor and started pawing at her labia she was sure she was going to be raped, so she kicked his beak as hard as she could. When he tumbled sideways she scrambled backwards like a crab. He pulled off his headdress.

"God dammit, Luccia, will you not hold still!"

"Fiona!"

"Get up!"

Luccia struggled to her feet. "This blasted habit of yours of appearing out of nowhere!"

Fiona yanked her to a door at the far end of the room. She pushed Luccia inside and slammed the door behind her. After a few minutes, Fiona entered again, dripping and naked herself. She tossed a blanket that Luccia wrapped around herself and then curled into a chair. Her fear mingled with her relief at finding Fiona.

"You scared me to death!" Luccia shouted.

"Well this is the place for it: fear and death. What are you doing here, child?" Fiona said, slamming her hand on the table. "Has the word not gotten out?"

"We had no idea."

"I suppose that means they're all... dead before they get even that far north, eh?"

"It's the Black Death again?"

"Oh, yes. But you're still not ready!" she shouted. "Marching right into the jaws of death! You've no sense at all. What are you doing?"

71

"Meeting you. Delivering herbs. It's what I do," Luccia said fiercely, drawing her blanket around her.

"And a course nothin'd beat you back — not even the dead by the road!"

"And leave you in the middle of it? I should think not." Luccia didn't say that she had been unable to think of what to do except to keep going, keep searching for Fiona.

Fiona sighed with disgust, pulled her blue cape over her shoulders but didn't cover her nakedness. The vial from Luccia's mother hung between her breasts. "What am I to do with a girl who's got splendid brains and absolutely no sense of survival. We're defenseless against this, Luccia. No one's ever devised a medicine.

And they just keep coming. Lines of the sick. I spent my whole life tryin' to protect you, and you just walk right into it. You shouldn't have come," she wailed, her voice breaking. "If I thought you could get back to Simone without contracting the thing I'd send you home right this minute."

"I'm not leaving without you," Luccia said, setting her sharp jaw.

"Then we're dying here, little one." Fiona dropped her head and started to cry but covered her mouth with both hands. "I've seen more death than the Devil over these last months, Luccia. You can't stay here. I've seen things that would tear your heart out." She crumpled into a chair at the head of the table and wept. Luccia went to her side, stroked her shoulders and her red hair, until Fiona reached out and pulled her into her lap, cradled her head in her big hand. "My sweet Luccia," she cried, burying her face in the girl's shoulder. "My only consolation was that you were far away and safe. Nothing has made my heart fall like the sight of you in the archway of the hospital. If you had had a single boil... well," she shook her head and closed her eyes, "saints and ministers of grace, defend us." She crossed herself.

"Fiona you're so thin," Luccia said softly.

"There's nothing to eat," Fiona said, straightening. "The baker's dead," she recited dully. "The butcher's dead. Everyone shies from the food that's left for fear of the contagion that's on it, and I don't blame them. But there is something to drink," she said, brightening slightly. "Here's a little liquid I can introduce you to."

She stretched her long bare legs out and put her feet on the table, wrapped her cape over her lap. "Bury me in this cape when I'm dead, will ya, child?"

"You're not dying, Fiona," Luccia said, though with less conviction than usual.

"*You're* not dying, little one, still not even getting old. In a place like this you look even more improbably young. The rest of us are taking our chances." She pulled over a jar and two cups, poured a small amount in each. Luccia raised it to her lips and tossed it back, then gasped and coughed. Fiona laughed.

"It's for sipping, little one."

"How should I know?" she said defiantly. "What is it?"

"Brandy. Invented by the monks in Modena, Italy a bit ago. Of course it'd be the Italians."

"And of course it would be the monks. Brandy?"

"The French have taken it on these days. It'll put a wild head on you soon enough. Have another."

Fiona's sour breath was tinged with the smell of the brandy. She lit candles and the two of them sat with Luccia's blanket and Fiona's cape gaping, downing beakers of brandy. They mournfully shook their heads over the state of the world, and quietly tried to recount the whereabouts of any of the women they had known as healers.

"So you're a doctor now," Luccia said.

"They've no idea I'm a woman," Fiona said. "Better a man with a beak than a woman. It's filled with herbs, this beak. The others thought it would protect them from the sickness but it's really just to keep the stench at bay. There seems to be no escaping this one, my dear."

Fiona poured herself another glass, set the jar down with a thud and laid her face on her forearm. "As long as you're here, I could use the help, Luccia."

Luccia pulled her blanket closer around her. If she stayed in the room she would be spared more of the hideousness outside the door. She tried to summon the griffin-like strength of her mother. Duty called, but she trembled and averted her eyes. "I...can't, Fiona."

Fiona stood and rummaged in a box in the corner of the room. "We need another suit for you."

"Fiona...I can't... go back out there."

"True enough," Fiona said sadly, "there's no cherubim and seraphim about the deaths out there but..."

"They're too...sick," Luccia wailed.

Fiona righted and turned to Luccia, startled by the fear in her voice and the terrified look of her eyes. "What sort of a doctor will you be if you can't stand the sick?"

"I'm not...a doctor," Luccia said fiercely, starting to cry.

Fiona dropped the blanket she was pulling from the box and wrapped her cape around her. "Your mother worked tooth and nail to teach you..."

"To be an herbalist!" Luccia roared. "Plants, Fiona."

"You were to be a great doctor, Luccia. Your mother..."

"Then my mother should have stayed and taught me!" Luccia growled.

Fiona slammed the lid of the box and charged across the room. Luccia stood her ground.

"Plants! Break a limb off they grow another. Chop it to its trunk and the shoots sprout up two feet away, Fiona." The two women faced each other with rage in their eyes.

"There are tissues in the body as interesting as twigs," Fiona roared.

"Plants don't scream," Luccia said ferociously. "They don't know grief or pain. You pinch off the flowers, buds grow on either side."

Fiona turned away but Luccia strode to the other side of the table to follow her.

"Even if you tear it out by its roots, Fiona, the seeds spray to the ground and it begins again."

Fiona raised her hand and Luccia flinched as if she was going to be struck, but Fiona laid her palm against the sharp angle of Luccia's cheekbone. "Your mother thought you'd drop off a few books, then settle onto the path of a doctor, maybe become a professor."

"I've strayed off the path, Fiona," Luccia said, ashamed.

"It's not you who have strayed," Fiona said quietly, "it's the path."

Chapter Eight

"Come on, little one," Fiona said, stumbling into a nightgown and pulling back the curtains separating her big bed from the rest of the room. "Curl up with me like the old days."

"Not if you have any of that disgusting chewing mixture in your cheeks," Luccia said.

"Oh fine, first you frighten me, then you lay down the law and now you're insulting me. Come to bed."

In the morning, Fiona slammed into her gloves and jammed her beaked hat on her head. The conflict raging inside her at least gave her more energy to face the day. She wanted to protect Luccia from the horror, from exposure to the Plague, but she felt she should demand that Luccia rise to her mother's challenge and become a doctor. Perhaps Fiona had steered Luccia too far off the path with her talk of senseless candle making and animal husbandry. She hadn't helped her learn and had allowed Luccia to silently suffer the effects of that first burning in Rome. Hell, she had sent her to Rome. And now a great doctor had veered off the path.

When she woke, Luccia was ashamed and relieved at the same time. Then she noticed that medical books lined a high shelf around the room. At least this was something she could do: avoid the sick but hunt for a remedy to make them well.

That night she stayed awake as long as she could, and fell asleep with her head on her arm amid the open books, and a sheaf of papers, a quill still gripped in her stained hands. When Fiona returned from her rounds, wanting to cry over a healthy child she had plucked from the side of her char-black father, she found Luccia slumped over the books as she had found her and her mother so many nights. At least Luccia worked hard.

In the morning, Fiona had come and gone, leaving only an emptied chamber pot, a dent in the brandy, and a piece of bread for Luccia.

That night, Luccia curled herself on the floor in the front of the door, knowing that Fiona would have to push past her to get in. The door slammed her in the back and Fiona stepped into the room naked and wet.

"Juniper," Luccia said in her half-sleep, struggling to her feet.

"Sleepin' on the floor? Pneumonia won't get you as fast but it'll get you nonetheless. Go to bed." Fiona stepped over the piles of books that Luccia had gone through and discarded.

Luccia scrambled to the base of her table. "Burn juniper, Fiona."

"I believe we're way past a little juniper. Where did you come up with that?"

"Look, John of Burgundy, a physician of Liege. There's reference here. I need to find what else he's written. 'The Black Death comes in three forms,'" Luccia read. "Bubonic from the bite of the fleas, pneumonic from the spittle of the infected, and septicemic from the oozing boils."

Fiona threw her cape over her shoulders, and hurried around to Luccia's end of the table, her nakedness glowing in the candlelight.

"They told me I was crazy but I knew this was from the rats," she said. "The rats and their fleas. What good is it to explore the world if all you do is spread disease, I ask you? Where did you find this?"

Luccia pointed to the page. "Burn juniper on the hearth. Blood should be let once a month."

"Well, there'll be no blood lettin' here."

"I agree. But if he's mentioned here, he'll be mentioned elsewhere. Perhaps a whole volume," Luccia said.

"And where do you think you're gonna find a whole volume? The doctors have all fled and the university's closed."

"I just need the libraries, Fiona, I don't need the damn librarian or the doctor."

Luccia stood resolutely tracing the pattern in Fiona's broach while Fiona paced through the room considering what to do next. "Juniper eh?" she asked sadly. "Alright then, little scholar, in the morning we'll go on a hunt together. It's not going to be pretty, Luccia but you've got to help me." She sat down to write a list of the addresses of doctors in Marseilles.

In the morning, Fiona had risen, suited up and returned with a beaker.

"Rosemary oil," she pronounced, "from the kitchen of the hospital." She rummaged in the old chest where she found another pair of brown leather pants and a hood.

"Against the fleas," Luccia said and Fiona nodded.

"Piss now and not again all day," Fiona said. She pushed Luccia toward the chamber pot, then rubbed rosemary oil on her legs, her wrists and neck. "Luccia, never, ever, under any condition, show your skin anywhere but in this room. Better that you didn't talk, either, because we wouldn't want them knowing about the woman thing. We have to keep on our rounds finding the sick, and in between, we can look for the books. It's only humane that way. And we better find an axe. The doctors may have fled but they most certainly locked their doors."

The two women held hands with fear and resolution in their eyes. They each sipped from Giovanna's vials, donned their beaks, and strode into the city. At the first doorframe, Fiona pushed Luccia aside, and entered first. Luccia followed at Fiona's elbow, then crumpled against her at the sight of a woman and her children dead in the corner, ashen and stiff, covered with boils. Fiona sent her outside, then returned after a moment, closed the door and gripped Luccia's arm as they stumbled through the streets. Each house they went into was more crowded with death than the last.

On the first day, Luccia was sorry she had come but felt remorseful and weak over her regret. The horrific memories stuck in her mind in isolation. She didn't remember the number of dead to step over as they were felled on a staircase, or later that day of ever seeing the bodies of children thrown onto a fire, though Fiona said that at one time they knew all of these surrounding facts. She remembered standing at the base of a bed, a pair of legs convulsing under the blanket, wishing they would stop their twitching, and when they did, wishing they hadn't. She remembered the grip of Fiona's hand on her arm as she pulled her into kitchens, their clumsy gloves sorting through bottles to find oil, their boots tromping through gardens to find juniper, the tug on her clothing by people in pain, the wicked bite of the cold water that Fiona poured over her.

And in the weeks that followed, she remembered suiting up as if numb, as if she had shape-shifted into the leather doctor's apprentice but had forgotten to take her brain. She remembered great billowing clouds of incense from the church and in the hospital, the moment of fear when her gloved hand gripped a doorframe, before stepping through thresholds. And the mounting pile of books they collected from the homes of doctors, smaller than the mounting pile of bodies. She considered the suit a blessing: the beak kept people at a distance and the net face-plate in front of her eyes dulled the sights in front of her. It was a far-flung Hell outside the beak. If she held her head just so, she wouldn't even see the children below her.

They came in droves, dying or afraid of dying, afraid of living in a shrinking city, hungry in a city with no food, thirsty in a city where the water was suspect. Those without boils were passed off as the frightened and Fiona lived to regret that decision: she stood at the base of a man's hospital bed and realized that he had died, untended, of measles. In Marseilles, Fiona silently battled smallpox, measles, leprosy, Saint Vitus' dance, and the Plague.

Luccia had the nurses enlist anyone who was walking to collect juniper. She carted juniper back in great armloads, strapped it to her back until she was bent over, a brown leather bird carrying her own nest. They burned the juniper in a circle around the hospital entrance.

Luccia set up a small laboratory in an alcove of the hospital, deep behind the central floor. Only there did she feel safe and sequestered enough to remove her beak. She brewed juniper oil and rosemary water while the nurses and the surviving families gathered the healthy and dowsed them, swabbed them, sent them off to gather more juniper. She never left her laboratory without her beak and suit, she rarely spoke to anyone, but went back out for more plants.

Luccia added bog myrtle, elder leaves, and lavender to the list, even brewed strong infusions of chamomile.

At night, Fiona and Luccia poured over the books.

"Oh for the love of God," Fiona muttered one evening, "'Wear a broad-brimmed hat to shield from the moonlight that brings the Plague,'" she slammed the book closed. "With doctors like these it's a wonder any one of us is standing. We're going backwards, Luccia. We used to know so much. Occular surgery for cataracts — we've known that in Salerno for a hundred years, and now they're saying the Plague is from the moonlight!"

"And that toadstools gathered from a dead tree will put life back in a corpse," Luccia read tiredly.

"It's always the children that get to me," Fiona said. "The look in their eyes."

Luccia crumpled in front of a new stack of medical books, unable to turn the pages.

"It's because of the witch thing, you know," Fiona said tiredly. "Witches consort, they say, so they killed all the cats and in come the rats with the Plague. Burn us alive, burn us covered with pustules, Luccia, sometimes I wonder what sort of world the Church wants."

Several times, Luccia woke up with Fiona in a seizure beside her and spent the night holding her down, but both of them would get up at dawn to begin their work again.

They were exhausted beyond reason, surrounded by those frightened beyond sanity. Her mother would have known what to do, Luccia thought, as Fiona slept with her head on the table and her hand on the brandy jug. Her own inventions had been minor compared to the task at hand. Luccia flung open the heavy cover of another book, expecting nothing. At first she thought she was so deliriously tired that she just saw what she wanted to see. John of Burgundy. Violets, roses.

"Fiona!"

"Go to sleep, girl. Got the far side of town to go through in the mornin'."

"John of Burgundy. The Plague... here it is! 'The Plague should be treated with teas of dictamnus, scabious, roses and violets,'" she read, pounding her finger on the book.

Fiona roused herself. "Scabious? Devil's Bit? It's growing in profusion on the west side of town."

"Dictamnus, scabious, roses and violets," Luccia said. "And the boils should be lanced."

"Lanced?" Fiona whispered, her head two inches off the table. "Of course. A septic boil that's lanced will stop the spread of infection."

"Hands should be kept clean but avoid baths because they open the pores," Luccia read.

Fiona stood, grumbling her regret over their nightly bathing, then looked around her room, picked up a bottle of spirits of alcohol and called Luccia over. Dousing both of them up to their wrists, she lit their hands on fire and as they shook their fingers to put out the blaze, they regarded each other with new determination. Fiona was pleased by the new glimmer in Luccia's eyes.

"The sick are hard to look at, Luccia," Fiona said. "And these have been some of the worst. But healing, now that's a miracle worth watching."

They suited up at dawn, discarding the hoods, relying on just the rosemary oil and the leather pants, a pair of gloves, a cotton mask over their noses and mouths.

"Who's around to arrest us for being women now?" Fiona quipped, and they set out.

Luccia re-directed the cadre of the well to collecting rose and violet petals, which they stripped from the gardens of the rich. The survivors brightened over Luccia's new enthusiasm, and they brought in the dictamnus roots and Devil's Bit by the bushel.

Luccia, renewed by the smell of the plants and a course of action directed by herbs, set up a great pharmacy in the middle of the hospital courtyard. She had doors torn off houses to serve as tables, commandeered ale casks and enormous copper bowls from the baker. She had huge mortars cut into logs. As if to make up for her initial revulsion over the patients, Luccia worked as if possessed, chopping until late at night, not resting to eat. She mixed and poured until the medicine slopped out of bottles and she had to look frantically for new vials.

Little children fetched wood while widows stirred the pots. Fiona lanced boils while volunteers cooked bandages to cover them.

They burned juniper night and day, its oil soothing the lungs of the patients and they ladled out medicine to the throngs. Because Fiona lit her hands on fire after every lancing, and Luccia did it several times a day, they became known as the Fire-Hand Doctors, asked for by name.

Luccia pressed bottles of the remedy into the hands of anyone who planned to venture outside the city limits. She carried a caldron of it to the livery office, stood outside the church and then she and Fiona hit upon a plan. They rolled a huge cask out of a restaurant and poured the wine onto the cobblestones.

"Now we musn't waste it all," Fiona said sheepishly as she filled her tankard and drained it a second time.

They filled it with Luccia's medicine, set it on a pony cart and walked through Marseilles calling like fishmongers.

"Medicine...for the sick. Medicine...for the well," Luccia called up to the windows, her voice quavering as she wondered what sickness might emerge. "Bring a cup, get a cure," she called. Devil's Bit, violet and roses, she recited under her breath, as if it would quell her fear.

Fiona stepped in front of her and inspected those who emerged. "Let's check those arms now," she said, running her hands down the armpits and chests of a young woman. Those with boils were put in cart and taken back to the hospital.

"Do you have a flask?" Luccia asked. "A little bit every day. Don't guzzle it, it won't help. Just a little bit every day."

The next day they brought a bell and Fiona insisted they give it a chipper ring to distinguish it from the bell of the body cart. "Med-cine," Luccia called. "Rose med-cine," she sang.

After days of walking the city, they returned to neighborhoods they had visited before. Fewer of the sick emerged, more fresh faces, though frightened and sad, stared through open shutters above. After two weeks, women emerged with laundry baskets on their hips and their children clinging, but walking, down the steps in front of them.

"Your color's good," Fiona said, surprised. "Anyone in there sick? No?" Fiona turned to Luccia. "Anyone in this block? Well get yourself another beaker of it. Luccia," she said, her mouth open incredulously, "Luccia darlin', ya did it!"

Fiona pulled her up where Luccia was bent over the cask, filling a cup for a child. Fiona hugged her, turned her. "Look at that," Fiona said, striding over and opening the blouse of the young woman. "The boils have receded! Look at her out here standin' in the sunshine. You did this, Luccia."

"No. No I didn't. John of Liege did it."
"You, Luccia. You fought hard to find somethin' that others had buried. You're going to be a great...apothecary."

Fritz Bremer enjoyed the feeling of his new horse between his legs, the look of his trousers and his fine polished boots — a gentleman's boots. The Bishop had died an ignominious death, coughing up blood as he thundered about hell-fire, lying in bed crying out for wine while Peter, now a misshapen young priest, sat at the bedside hiding his glee behind praying hands, remorseless in his inattention. His cackling laughter was heard more than once during the Bishop's internment. The Bishop's death had released both Fritz and Peter from their duties and they immediately sold off the Bishop's vestments and pilfered his gold. The book, Fritz whispered, and Peter signed on with the self-proclaimed professor through a well-worn habit of following. They rode south, back towards Simone.

Book Two

Chapter Nine

*D*espite the years, Simone recognized the professor the minute his horse pulled into her crossroads. His fine clothing couldn't make up for the way his face sagged around his mournful mouth. She gathered her daughters and hid them in the cellar, except for Helene, who wouldn't budge from her father's side as he lay dying in the bedroom.

Helene, a defiant child and mature beyond her 9 years, had never seen the professor but had been involved in several clandestine herb deliveries and understood deep in her bones the risks her mother described. But her love for her father — and her habitual refusal to do what her mother asked — kept her by the bedside, holding the old man's hand. Simone trembled as she looked out the window, then crumpled into a chair next to the bed, and cried, surprising her daughter with her fragility.

"Helene," the old man muttered deliriously, his backbone disintegrating and his mind going, "a basket by the door…Two spoons now. Two."

Simone thought it was no coincidence that the Bishop's henchmen were tethering their horses in her crossroads the very day her husband lay dying. They must have set out for her the minute her husband had fallen ill, Simone thought, confirming again that he was her protector. Her daughters loved him, she thought, averting her eyes from him and weeping harder, and so, in a way, did she. This time they would take them all, her and her beloved daughters as well. As if he could sense her distress, the old man moaned and called out about chickens in the rain.

Simone heard the clerics throwing open the door downstairs and shuddered as Father Peter limped into the room, followed by the professor, who strode to Helene's side before Simone could draw her near.

"Leave us," Father Peter hissed, and Simone pushed her startled daughter out the door and quickly down the stairs.

The professor leaned over the dying alderman. "Such a lovely place you have," he muttered, and the old man spoke the name of his wife. "A blessed family," Bremer continued, and the alderman muttered about a son who had died, tears rolling down his cheeks, then listed his daughters' names as a litany. "And... the books," the professor snarled with his lips puckering.

"Ah, Luccia," the dying man uttered deliriously, "such a smart one. Hair, so dark. Blackberries come late. If the branch is broken, then you can't...Father, bless me," he called to Father Peter.

But the priest didn't hear him. He watched the professor stride out of the room, and with a sneering glance back at the old man, he followed.

Bremer startled a young stable boy by appearing as if he had dropped from the tree. "Pity Luccia won't be here for the old man's funeral," he hissed.

"But she's due back from Marseilles any day now," the boy said, still holding the water bucket above the trough. "Has he much time, the master?"

Bremer closed his veiled eyes even further and stripped his horse from the post, mounted without a word and rode off. Father Peter clambered awkwardly onto his own horse and struggled to catch up.

When Bremer found her in the Marseilles hospital, he knew instantly it was Luccia. Not because of her coal black hair, or because people in the streets had enthusiastically told him the whereabouts of the Fire-Hand doctor and the Italian apothecary, but because as he stood in an alcove watching her at her table, he fumed. The oils and elixirs coalesced in front of her, the herbs quivered as her hands passed them by. She moved as if the potion would put out a fire that was burning toward her.

Bremer gripped the edge of the wall and then pulled his hat off because there it was — the book. Propped up on a bag of herbs was the same book he had had in his hands, its fine illustrations visible from across the courtyard.

Despite Bremer's tendency to surprise people by moving with insect-like stealth, Luccia saw him before he touched the open page of *Trotula* beside her. Luccia kept pouring the medicine into the jug in front of her but it had been so many years since Simone's warning that she didn't recognize him. Luccia didn't see the hat in his hand and after the putrid, misshapen faces she had encountered fighting the Plague here, his sagging cheeks didn't alarm her. Besides, there was a group in the town square who were trying to leave the city. If she could just get a full jug to them before they left, they could carry it into the countryside.

"Hold this," she said to him without introduction or courtesy, handing him a sieve to place over the top of another jug. "Are you sick, or here to help?"

"Not sick," he hissed but Luccia didn't flinch at the sound of his menacing voice, simply pointed to another jug for him to place in front of them. Taken aback, Bremer complied.

"If you're traveling, would you take a jug of this medicine with you? Give it to anyone. A doctor or nurse if you can find them, but otherwise just ... give some to everyone you meet. Sick or well. Pour it into their cups or... into their hands, it doesn't matter but don't let them put their mouths to the jug. Can you do that?"

Bremer dropped the sieve, nearly knocking over the jug. Luccia caught it before it spilled more than a small puddle and gripped the neck. "It's not a miracle," Luccia continued. "Just a medicine. Against the Plague," she said, brightening. "Can you imagine? Finally a medicine against the Plague."

Insolent bitch. Bremer wanted to hit Luccia's chiseled face so hard that she would break through the table and hit the floor as dust. Hardly a woman yet and spouting that she'd found a cure for the Plague! He stepped backwards and gathered *Trotula* to him.

"That's not for taking," Luccia said and stepped forward to retrieve it but Bremer held it to him and glowered at her.

"Where did you get this book?" he snarled.

He had none of the markings of a dangerous man, Luccia thought, other than the look in his eyes that could be the madness of the Plague: he wore no Bishop's vestments, not even a priest's frock. Luccia thought that he was calling into question the effectiveness of her medicine so she squared her shoulders. "I am the daughter of a medical professor from the University of Salerno, Italy. I have copied the volume myself. The medicine, however…"

Before she could finish, Bremer's lips started twitching and his eyelids slid lower. Wretched whore! This little witch with her education, her Latin, her smug assurance. How dare she speak to him directly? The Church cut out their tongues for such an offense. This was the witch he wanted. This was the midwife he had been driving himself across Europe to find, tolerating their sniveling and shrieking and their sickening tears. This book, and this … excuse for a woman. Now he had them, and his blood felt like iron, his nose was filled with the smell of ink, and a dark acid from his stomach invaded his pores. He knew every shackle, every pincher and technique and now that he was so close to what he wanted, what he deserved, he couldn't stop gritting his teeth to speak. He reached out and grabbed the girl's neck and slammed her on the table where she knocked over several beakers and crumpled to the floor. Behind him, in the alcove, Father Peter cackled.

Luccia scrambled backwards when she heard the laughter and, when she saw that the boy was now a priest, she blanched at her mistake. She had taken this other man for the sick, and then she saw the hat he had in his hand and her book that he held against his body like a prize. Bremer reached down and pulled her to standing, choking her with his grip. She heard several of the patients behind her call out for help.

Bremer had to control himself to not kill her on the spot, but he needed her to read him the book. She would be his teacher — by torture, by imprisonment, by whatever means necessary, this whore of the Devil. He dragged her across the hospital floor, gagging her and cursing at her with guttural noises that came from deep inside his throat. He was too blinded by his rage to see Fiona running toward them, her red hair like a fire trail behind her, and he was too absorbed in his near victory to let go of her, or to free his hand to defend himself when Fiona slammed him in the head with a jug. He stumbled backward and the book slipped from his hand, as did Luccia, who twisted, scooped up the book and ran through the hospital. Fiona picked up a poker from the brassiere beside the table and drove it into his shoulder.

"Bless my child, father," a woman's feeble voice called as she carried the corpse of an orphan girl toward Father Peter and Bremer, showing them the child's black boils that were weeping and eyes red-ringed with contagion. "Bless my child with your Holy kiss," she said. Father Peter covered his nose and grabbed Bremer who had crumpled onto the table. The two backed out of the hospital toward their horses.

"Don't just sit there trembling! Pack your things," Fiona grumbled, flying through the little room they shared. Luccia sat in a chair, angry and immobile. "Now!" Fiona shouted, throwing a nightshirt at her and rolling up two blankets.

"We can't go now," Luccia said, letting her hands fall onto the table in front of her.

"There's not a moment to lose! Those two, the ones Simone warned us about all those years ago, they'll be back with an army in a heartbeat."

"We have the medicine, Fiona," Luccia said, confused. "We should make the medicine, now that we've found it."

"Luccia, love," Fiona said pointedly, "we've done great work here, and admittedly there's more to do." She strapped the blanket rolls together with shaking hands. "But if they return for us, they'll burn us to cinders and all the sick with us. Better for everyone if we're gone. Now put the recipe on the table, and leave it to someone else."

"The medicine is more important than our lives." Luccia stood and faced her across the table.

Fiona stared at her, then continued to stuff clothing and papers into a satchel. Her life and Luccia's were two entirely different matters. She would have let the entire city die if she had to exchange it for Luccia's life. Maybe not, but right at this moment she was breathless and frantic over the sight of a man's hands around Luccia's throat. Mary mother of God. She would rather her own mother had been a sheepherder than have saved the church president's wife. If truth be known, she would have preferred that Giovanna had been a glove-maker's assistant than a gifted medic. At least she'd be here, and Luccia wouldn't be in danger. The same old danger that had been stalking her since Fiona had been a girl.

"Here," Fiona said, her voice shaking, dragging a dark wooden box decorated with studs from under her bed. "Put a vial of it, and the recipe, into the box and we'll make more, heal everyone we can everywhere we go."

Luccia was shocked that Fiona was willing to run. She had never seen her so frightened. On the other hand, Luccia had never been so frightened. The feel of Bremer's hands on her throat. He had been able to drag her across the floor like she was a rag-doll. Luccia knit her fingers together and rubbed her forehead. Luccia hadn't seen Fiona running across the floor, just heard her from a distance and then saw the point of the poker pierce his skin. She looked down at her dress and flinched at Bremer's blood that had spurted onto her bodice.

On the other hand, why had they spent all these years risking themselves during the delivery of books and herbs, if their lives were now more important than the medicine? Everyone she had been raised around had sacrificed their lives for medicine. Her own mother had sent her off with dangerous books rather than shipping her directly to Ireland.

Fiona's lip was trembling and her eyes were wild.

"You're being hunted, do you understand that?" Fiona's voice shook. "He could have taken the book and fled, but he didn't. He could have taken the medicine and fled, but he didn't. He wanted you and the book. Hunted, like your mother. The net, Luccia, is something you just live with, feeling it behind you. But the hunt, little shadow, is something you've got to act upon. You've got to avoid."

When Luccia didn't budge, Fiona put the materials into the box for her, shoved it into Luccia's hands, then picked up a shovel beside the fire. "So help me Mother Mary, you walk through that door with me, or I'll knock you senseless and carry you."

Luccia cast her an angry look, but walked through the door. Run or stay, she had her opinion, but she wouldn't live without Fiona.

"'Course with cheekbones like those you'd probably split the shovel before it would split you," Fiona muttered under her breath, and pushed the girl forward.

They skirted the sides of buildings, scurried through deserted streets so they wouldn't be followed, and when they reached the outskirts of Marseilles, they ran. Fiona overtook her and Luccia ran behind her the rest of the day, astounded at Fiona's energy, wondering if she really would have hit her with the shovel. She watched the steady gallop of Fiona's legs and the undulation of her spine, feeling the fresh air of the countryside pour into her own nostrils and drive the stink from her lungs. They stopped to light their hands on fire, though they hadn't touched anything contagious all day.

Luccia was surprised at the relief she felt over running. She ran away from death, lime, boils, vomit and the pyres, from a book thief and the thought of being hunted. She fled from discovery, from guilt, from confrontation, from being seen, from the grip of a man's fingers on her throat. They threw themselves into streams and scrubbed their skin raw, then fled from what had felt like the inevitability of a hideous demise, and at the end of the day, they descended together into the sleep of escapees.

Bremer woke up in a dank abbey with an infection in his shoulder and a trickle of blood pooling in his cranium. He checked under his armpits for boils, ran his bony hands down the inside of his thighs. His flaccid lips puckered around words that he couldn't form, but he made a mental note: a tall redhead as well as a granite-faced girl.

In the following days, Fiona and Luccia walked in near silence, picking up a piece of cloth, fashioning a walking stick, digging up a bite to eat, until they found the countryside populated by the living, the blossoming, with crops in the field. Luccia gave doses of the medicine to anyone who would take one. They laid on the riverbank to fish for dinner and their own sense of safety. Now with Bremer looking for them, they couldn't go back to Simone's and endanger her and her family. They had to go somewhere new, somewhere no one knew them. They netted birds from the trees as if capturing their future.

One afternoon, Fiona spotted the low-hanging smoke of the first village they had seen and she stopped in the middle of the lane as if hitting a wall.

"We shouldn't go there," Fiona said, her voice breaking.

"Fiona, there's food there. Maybe they need a midwife." Or the medicine, she thought.

"We can't go," she said, crouching down and beginning to shake. "He could be there..." she pulled at her hair, rubbed the corner of her eyes. She pivoted on her heel away from the village.

Just as Luccia put her hand on Fiona's shoulder, Fiona threw their meager bedroll over her shoulder and darted into the bushes. Luccia followed, trying to grab her forearm. "Fiona! It's fine, Fiona. We don't have to go there," she called.

Luccia tried to keep up with her as Fiona fled through the brush.

"We'll live out here. Fiona, stop! No reason we shouldn't. We've been doing fine, don't you think? Fiona!"

Fiona stopped and held the bedroll to her chest. Luccia looked up her length, into her frightened eyes.

"Right here," Luccia panted, pulling Fiona to the forest floor. "Right here." Luccia rolled Fiona into the bedding where she shook so hard that her arms flung about like branches in a storm. Luccia cried quietly at her side. All those exhausting nights, all the death had caught up with Fiona. She had seen so much, done so much. Fiona slept and then woke to cry so long that she had to slap her own face to shock her forehead into relaxing.

Luccia wracked her brain trying to think of a remedy for her, to diagnose, to make a connection between the body and the brew. It didn't come easily but for Fiona's sake, she would try. She tried to make tea from the weeds around them that would either feed her, calm her or heal her. Skullcap, wild oat, vervain: nothing could counter all those silent days in the beak and the hunted feeling that must be returning from her childhood. Nothing Luccia did made a difference, and she thought sadly of the times Fiona had gone off by herself, to suffer through the seizures alone.

Luccia sat beside her for four days while Fiona cried, flailed and slept. Luccia had to get Fiona out of this thicket: she had exhausted all the berries and the tubers in a radius that was as large as she dared venture away from Fiona. They needed to keep moving.

In the morning, Fiona's seizure was better and Luccia crouched beside her as she stooped over lady slipper tea.

"We should keep moving if we can," Luccia said softly. They had to get word to Simone, to warn her. And to say goodbye, she thought sadly.

Fiona straightened her shoulders and set down her wooden cup. "Where?"

"Through the forest," Luccia said, "no villages or towns, don't worry. But we should try to continue if we can." Fiona shook her head in agreement, then let her head fall onto her chest, inconsolable.

Fiona and Luccia set off on a little deer-trail that took them further into the woods, Fiona stumbling beside Luccia, lost in her own world with one drooping leg catching her on roots and vines. Luccia kept her eyes open for mushrooms, berries, wild fennel, and a good place to snare rabbits. What she found, as she pulled a couple of eggs from a nest and then shimmied down the tree, were increasingly dense patches of pennyroyal. They had stumbled into the land of a crossroad's apothecary. Of course she was deep in the woods where only a tracker could find her, and Luccia crouched in humble appreciation of her, and to scan for potential danger from either Bremer or others.

"Let's camp here," Luccia said.

Luccia made a small fire, cooked the eggs, and the two of them ate it with tubers she had gathered *en route*. She sat expectantly, glancing into the shrubs behind them while Fiona struggled with another seizure. Hopefully, Luccia thought, they were far enough off the road that they wouldn't attract highwaymen or Bremer, discrete enough that they didn't bring danger to the herbalist, but she hoped their dinner's enticing aroma would bring her to them.

She stoked the fire while Fiona slept, then fell asleep sitting up.

In the middle of the night, Luccia heard the mewing of cats, and when she woke up, groggy and disoriented, she had eight cats sitting on top of her. Luccia tensed over the sight: while she was comforted that they were alive, cats still held a special fear for her. There were more than 40 cats at their campsite.

At the edge of the firelight, Luccia was startled by a figure crouching in the darkness whose eyes didn't shine the same as others. It was a tiny woman with cats climbing over her. When she saw Luccia flinch, the woman chuckled, brushing the cats off her shoulders.

She was so small that the cats seemed to overpower her. She pushed her hair from one side of her head and her teeth gleamed in the moonlight. Her skin radiated softness and she made little half-gestures with a right hand that was framed by woven bracelets half way to her elbow. Her left hand remained hidden within her cape until she slowly withdrew it and put the point of a dagger into the ground.

She looked at Luccia, ran her tongue over her teeth as if genuinely amused, then stood and walked forward, grasped Luccia's elbow and stood her up. The faces of Luccia and the stranger were quite close while the cats wove in and out of their legs, entwining them.

Luccia, suddenly aware that she must look like a forest rat, smoothed her hair to check for twigs and bugs and the things that had taken to living there since she and Fiona had begun their journey. The stranger's breath got shallow in a way that Luccia didn't know and each time Luccia inhaled she was filled with the smell of lavender, the woods around them, the moss under their feet, the cats. Luccia swayed, thinking it was the night, the disorientation of being awakened. She couldn't look in the woman's enormous walnut eyes. It didn't seem necessary for Luccia to question the stranger suspiciously, though she wasn't sure why.

"Luccia..." she faltered, "Alimenti, and this is Fiona O'Connor, both of us from the medical university in Salerno, Italy."

"Oh my," the herbalist gasped and stepped backward. "A Salernita...a true physician. You are known to the four corners. It is an honor to have you in my forest. Jacqueline," she said, and Luccia put her hand in Jacqueline's as if gifting her the bones inside.

"No...not a doctor. Just a...chemist. Could I ...put on tea for you?" Luccia said, nearly tripping over the fire to get to the pot and the cups.

"Come to my cottage, Salernita," she said, and Luccia turned instantly to wake Fiona so they could follow this cat-woman. Luccia shook Fiona, too urgently for her condition, then kept her hands pressed on Fiona's arm in case she jolted awake and it started a seizure. Fiona moaned and Jacqueline and Luccia helped her roll to sitting. Fiona, with Luccia silently measuring with her, took inventory of her limbs, her facial muscles, all the things that usually deserted her during this time.

"The leg's abandoned me a bit, shadow," she said quietly with her lips distorted and numb. Luccia helped her to her feet. Fiona towered over Jacqueline as Luccia introduced them. "Good even' fine woman," she said, struggling to bow. "Out so late?"

"I gather herbs at night. To avoid detection," she said with a smile and a resigned tilt of her head. "It would be better just after the morning dew is gone, of course, but I can't be in the fields during the day. It's just too dangerous. Besides," she said, smiling at Luccia, "I would miss my moonlight, and the cats think it's just grand that I'm out on their schedule." She regarded her cats, and then laughter came pealing out of her mouth so bright and shiny, a laugh so untainted by bitterness that Luccia was surprised.

"Has the Plague been through here?" Luccia asked, looking for signs of dementia in the laugh.

"No. We have been spared," Jacqueline said.

"And the burning courts?"

"I'm told they rumble through but they never find us. The forest is kind," she said with a deep, warm voice.

And what does that say? Luccia thought to herself, looking at Jacqueline's full lips: unabashed laughter is more foreign to me than weeping? She checked the woman's face for pockmarks, her shoulders for sign of deformity but she was straight and plump and ...luscious. Luccia had never thought of a person as luscious. That was for fruit, or... herbs that carried a high water content. The pods of tamarind or legumes with furry shells?

"Come, little Salernita," Jacqueline said, sliding her hands up Luccia's forearms, "you seem to have lost your way."

Jacqueline's house was a labyrinth of rooms cut into the side of a long, narrow hill. Luccia was pleased to see stands of boughs at the ready to cover the windows and doors in case the Church's entourage happened by. They were far enough off the beaten path that Bremer wouldn't find them, she surmised.

Jacqueline took her hand to lead her into the house, and Luccia felt her lungs contract in anticipation. Fiona backed away from the doorway entirely, unwilling to enter, still too tied to the horror that she had seen in dark corners of unknown houses. She limped backwards, muttering her apologies. Jacqueline guided Fiona to a log near the door, and bent to make a fire for them in front of her house.

Jacqueline crouched, making a sweet tea in a small copper pot. The fire's reflection danced across the folds of the many skirts she wore. Jacqueline wore a bright red skirt under a blue one, a flowered skirt under that, and several colors of slips. Every move she made had a different sound, a different color, and Luccia struggled to keep her guard up while relaxing into the solace of it.

Jacqueline threw back a tangle of wiry chestnut hair that lifted off her shoulders to ride a thermal driven by the fire. An army of cats curled on her shoulders, above and underneath her shawl, and stretched out on her forearms when she was still for a moment by the fire. Their fur was as much a part of how she looked as her own hair, and even though Luccia had only known the woman an hour, she resented the way the cats walked across her body, lounged on parts of her as if she were inanimate. Luccia could have sworn that there was a gray tom who paced across Jacqueline's lap as a gatekeeper, his wicked, glowing, slit eyes on Luccia.

Jacqueline moved around the fire on her haunches, sinuously weaving among the split wood, the branches and the fire, with her skirts rustling.

"Fond of the cats, are you?" Fiona asked. Her face muscles were back to normal but she tried to pull an uncooperative leg underneath her.

"I am a simple farmer," Jacqueline said with deference, "and these a few contributions of my secret farm. Cats for all of Europe. To re-populate. We have lost so many. Yes," she said, stroking the head of a cat and welcoming those that jumped on her in response to her words. "And we need you so much."

The fire flared up, the pot boiled, and Jacqueline filled a hammered copper cup with tea. She stood, and with a wide grin, ceremoniously offered it to the darkness above Luccia's head. Neither Fiona nor Luccia were able to turn before a hand reached in over their shoulders and seized the cup. Fiona leapt unsteadily to her feet and Luccia grabbed her arm, then whirled around at the ready. Into the circle of light thrown by the fire stepped two women, their bare arms gleaming with sweat and marked by forest dirt.

Fiona stepped out of the light of the circle. The women moved into the space she had cut. The first to reach the cup was in deerskin pants with a sling-shot and a leather bag hung over her belt, a large dagger in a sheath with a handle that was cut from a bone, now brown with blood and use. Her blonde hair, twisted like a rope, hung down to her waist, as if it were another tool of her trade.

"Ah, home at last," Jacqueline squealed, dancing around Luccia to reach the women. She flung her arms around the dagger-armed woman who encircled her waist and pulled her in.

"Marcelle," Jacqueline muttered, and buried her face in the woman's neck. Jacqueline touched the cheek of the second woman, a pale, insubstantial being whose clothing was undecorated and hung from her shoulders.

Marcelle, however, kept her eyes on Luccia and Fiona, and after a minute, twisted Jacqueline around to face them.

Marcelle passed the cup to her companion, who quickly sipped the hot brew, handed back the cup, then stepped into the shadows again. Jacqueline quietly called after the skittish woman.

"*Poulain*! We call her Poulain," Jacqueline said to them, "the colt."

"More stray cats?" Marcelle pointedly asked Jacqueline, nodding her head in the direction of Luccia and Fiona.

"Marcelle," Jacqueline admonished.

"Marcelle nothing," she said, tossing the last of the tea into the fire. "We cannot have these people here. Pardon, no offense," she said to Fiona and Luccia, "but these are not days for hospitality."

"Why aren't they?" Jacqueline said, pulling away from the circle of Marcelle's arm. "I can't live here alone like a nun all the time when you go hunting. At least Poulain used to stay with me. Now I work all night in the fields and I sit alone all day waiting for you. That's no life, Marcelle. Besides, you don't even know if they want to stay. They are here for tea."

"Oh, tea," she scoffed. "Were they followed?"

"Of course not," Luccia insisted.

"Oh, no?" Marcelle sneered and Luccia bristled.

"She knows," Fiona said. "We're your compatriots. We've just come from fighting the Plague in Marseilles and I doubt there's anyone alive who's seen more, and in the case of Luccia here, eluded worse, than us. So you can rest easy. We were not followed, and we'll bring you no harm."

"Your presence brings me harm," Marcelle spat and she moved away.

"Marcelle!" Jacqueline growled.

"We'd love to stay," Luccia said, jumping up again and taking a step toward Marcelle. Fiona raised an eyebrow.

"Marvelous," Jacqueline said, standing and walking the darkness where Marcelle had disappeared. "Companions, Marcelle."

Marcelle muttered a gutteral reply.

Chapter Ten

In the morning, Marcelle was up first, hard at work cutting up the deer the two had felled, before Fiona and Luccia had even rolled out of their blankets by the cold fire. Marcelle piled great bloody chunks of venison on the surrounding logs and when Jacqueline emerged, sleepy and content, she stoked the fire and brewed morning tea, while cats wound among them all.

"How can you stand the screeching of these damn cats in heat?" Marcelle growled to Jacqueline, gesturing at them with her bloody knife. "All night, like the sound of murder. I can't stand these cats."

"You have your job, I have mine," Jacqueline said, offering a cup that Marcelle waved away before returning to her work.

"You're an herbalist," Marcelle scoffed. "Herbs don't camp out on your body."

By noon Marcelle had butchered the boar and was stretching the hides of the rabbits while Fiona and Jacqueline had set to salting and putting up the meat. They stopped for a meal but Marcelle continued until the entire bounty was cut and she covered with blood and flies.

Jacqueline set down her empty plate and took Marcelle's hand, the rest of the women following her into the woods to a hot springs where Jacqueline guided Marcelle into the water. Marcelle, pushing Jacqueline's hands away from the top of her pants, splashed water on herself and scrubbed the meat pieces off her hands, then pealed off her shirt and threw it on the bank, trying to hit one of the cats. Jacqueline, still dressed, in the water to her thighs, approached Marcelle again. Luccia watched. She was accustomed to women tending out of a sense of duty, scrubbing their husband's back while their minds are thinking of their children or being anxiously attentive to avoid a fist. She had even grown accustomed to Simone's tepid attendance of the alderman that occasionally bordered on tender. Luccia, however, was not accustomed to what she saw here.

Jacqueline laid Marcelle back as if praying, pushing water with a tender hand up Marcelle's belly, between her breasts and around her neck, cradling Marcelle's head with the other hand. Marcelle's breasts were full and firm, rocks in the stream and the river tumbled around them, as did Jacqueline's hands. Jacqueline started to untie her own blouse but Marcelle stood up, slipped her big hands inside and lifted Jacqueline's blouse over her head, then roughly pulled Jacqueline to her, Jacqueline's little breasts fitting into the space on either side of hers. Finally, with Jacqueline still tight within the circle of her arm, Marcelle stripped off her pants and threw them soaking onto the riverbank.

Jacqueline and Marcelle had moved down to a bend in the stream and Jacqueline's tangled skirts were floating, untended, in the current toward them. Marcelle lifted Jacqueline onto the moss-covered roots of a tree that held her like a chair. Luccia could only see her long chestnut hair, and even the cats, who surrounded Jacqueline day and night, had a hard time climbing to reach her, most of them hanging back and crying on the sheer sides of the bank.

Maybe it was the light. Maybe it was because Luccia had disliked Marcelle when she had first met her and so her nakedness seemed more startling. Maybe it really was because Marcelle's breasts were exceptional, but Luccia watched Marcelle touch Jacqueline, watched a streak of light play across Marcelle's breasts, then her shoulders as she leaned into Jacqueline. A body. A luscious body. Luccia wanted to have breasts like Marcelle's, she wanted to know how to touch Jacqueline with that much power, that much tenderness, to be that commanding woman who took her pants off last.

"Luccia."

She readjusted her gaze. Fiona ordered her. "Wash the road off you, Luccia."

Luccia stripped off her clothes and threw the vial on the riverbank beside them.

For two weeks, Marcelle was hardly seen outside the hut. Fiona had relented and come into the hut and she and Luccia sat alone at the table on the other side of a curtain that divided Jacqueline's bed from the rest of the hut, while Luccia was transfixed by the moaning, crying, laughing sounds from the other side. Jacqueline had gotten giddy, there were no unkind words between her and Marcelle, and Marcelle walked around with her rope of a braid undone. She even occasionally tripped over a cat without swearing.

One morning, Marcelle literally kicked Jacqueline through the curtain that divided the rooms. Jacqueline, clutching her blouse to her, tripped into the room, her top skirt on backwards.

"Ask her," Marcelle called from bed. "You can't let them go any longer."

"Luccia, sweet girl, would you help me tend the herbs today?" Jacqueline asked.

"Every day," Marcelle called.

"I thought you did that at night?"

"Harvest at night. It's the harvest that is dangerous. Come with me today, and see where they are. I'll teach you. You can tend my herbs. It would mean so much to me."

So Jacqueline and Luccia set out through the forest, dropping balls of animal fat and meal for the cats as they walked. The cats dropped from trees, emerged from burrows, each new litter greeted with joyful congratulations from Jacqueline, until there was a vast herd of fur trailing behind them.

They paced through the forest, from Crampbark, St. John's Wort, motherwort, to the raspberry. From a patch of monk's pepper, and finally, to the pennyroyal and tansy, each crop more secreted than the next as they made their way into the woods. She had planted the crops behind trees, under a fungus outcropping on the trunk of the old pines.

The only crop that waved bravely in the sun was Jacqueline's field of lavender, which she dashed into, arms outstretched and her knees bouncing high. Luccia followed behind her, alarmed at her display, incredulous at her joy.

"Ah, the sun," Jacqueline said, falling spread-eagle on her back into the lavender. Luccia lay down beside her. "If I didn't have this lavender in the sun, I would go completely mad living in hiding in the forest all the time. Bad enough," she said, rolling onto her elbow and looking into Luccia's eyes, "that I am stuck here in one place, but that it has to be a little hole in the dirt, in the shade, in hiding."

"Why do you stay?" Luccia asked. "You could raise cats anywhere."

Jacqueline looked at Luccia, sat up, her hair wild and glinting, her blouse open. She picked up a handful of dirt, rich and black, brought it to her nose and Luccia could smell its peat. Jacqueline let it fall through her fingers, then pushed back her hair, smudging her cheek with the dirt. "You have never been in love?" she asked quietly. "Hum? Where is your heart?"

She drew close and cupped Luccia's sharp face in her hands. "You have never been touched by someone, hands like bark that cut your skin but you think that if they took their hands away you would die?"

No, Luccia wanted to exclaim. The body is pain.

"Come," Jacqueline said, dropping her hands from Luccia's cheeks so that Luccia felt the air scald her skin. "We have work to do."

They wove their way through the forest while cats slithered between their feet, Jacqueline describing the layout of her crops, the markings on the trees that Luccia should notice so she would know where they were located, the instructions for the weeding and care.

At night, Luccia sat by the fire and made up the meal balls for the cats and listened more closely to Jacqueline giggle, then suddenly grow silent. Luccia's own breath caught in her throat at the sound of Jacqueline's labored breathing, her sense of distress.

"I've made a fire outside," Fiona said, stepping into the house and seizing the bowl off Luccia's lap. "You can finish your chores there."

Luccia wandered through the forest haphazardly, trying to find the spot in the lavender where Jacqueline had fallen in abandon. Coming back to the camp, she crouched in the bushes by the creek to watch Marcelle draw Jacqueline onto her lap again.

"Back to your post, little shadow," Fiona said, grabbing her by the elbow and pulling her out of the bushes.

"I am not little," Luccia growled back at her. Fiona raised her eyebrows, then used a single finger to pull out the collar of Luccia's shirt and peer into her clothing at her erect nipples.

"Finally that's true," she said, letting go of Luccia's blouse and walking away. Watching Jacqueline and Marcelle, Luccia smoothed the front of her blouse and wondered where she had put the vial.

Accustomed now to sleeping outside the house, Fiona and Luccia were awakened by Jacqueline shrieking as she stumbled outside. Marcelle was several paces in front of her, hair braided, dagger strapped to her side again, a leather sack packed and strapped to her back. Jacqueline clutched her blanket around her, tripping over its hem, nearly stepping on cats that were disoriented by the commotion.

"There is plenty," Jacqueline wailed. "Stay a few more days!"

"If I tell you three days before I leave, we fight for three days," Marcelle grumbled, kicking a cat out of the way. "If I tell you two days, we fight for two days. At least this way, we fight for one hour."

"I hate you. I hate you when you go," Jacqueline said but Marcelle gathered her in her arm and kissed her as if she might breakfast on her mouth. Jacqueline's blanket started to fall but Marcelle gathered her tighter and dug one hand into her hair. When she finally let Jacqueline go, she turned, nodded to Fiona and Luccia, and walked off toward the forest. Poulain — startling all of them except Marcelle — stepped out of a clump of nearby trees, laden with her own pack, and took her position at Marcelle's side.

"I am the one who should be on the road," Jacqueline shouted after them. "But no, it is always you. I think maybe you don't even hunt. You just go." Luccia stepped up beside Jacqueline, inhaling her smell of blanket and warm bed.

"We won't go," Luccia said with as much firmness as she could muster, and clumsily put her arm around Jacqueline's waist.

"That's right," she said, surprised at Luccia's closeness. "At least I have you, Luccia. I have you, don't I?"

At Jacqueline's side, Luccia became a farmer — taller, stronger, with a sickle in one hand and the memory of Jacqueline's waist in the other. Her skin darkened in the sun, her hands grew callused and rough. She cut and bound lavender, beat enormous batches of stalks for the heads. She slashed fungus from the trees, dug for tubers, chopped the raspberry bush and harvested the fennugreek.

As her sickle sliced rhythmically through the stalks, Luccia thought about Jacqueline, not just her beauty or the new skills she had taught her, or the way Luccia's life here was demanding that she be strong, not just smart. Jacqueline had a joy that pealed out of her without suspicion or defense. Every dinner was a feast, every morning was greeted with ebullience, every cat, bud, or clump of dirt was honored. Luccia couldn't remember knowing someone who didn't constantly look over her shoulder. Even Fiona, who had worked hard to emerge from her trauma into a cheerful acceptance of life, seemed draped in sadness compared to Jacqueline. Every moment the air poured into her lungs, Jacqueline was fully immersed in life. When she fought with Marcelle, she did it with all of her claws. She held nothing back, ever. Not when she laughed, not when she argued, not when she took Marcelle to the stream.

Jacqueline's two-fisted grip on joy induced a hunger in Luccia. She cut the fields quickly so she could return to process the herbs with Jacqueline. She over-ate at dinners so she could linger with Jacqueline by the fire. She never went into the fields without sharing tea with Jacqueline first, even if it made her late. Luscious, she thought, unlike anything she had encountered.

One noon, Jacqueline brought a beaker of water for Luccia and as Luccia raised it to her lips, Jacqueline reached out and touched Luccia's sweat-soaked shirt, touched her breast. With the water still clinging to Luccia's lips, Jacqueline pulled Luccia to her and kissed her, then she lay down in the lavender field, descending as if the falling had taken hours, her blouse open, her skirt rumpled, hair mingling with the lavender, and Luccia followed her, filled with the smell of her own sweat and the pounding sound of the blood in her ears. Luccia's hands tentatively slid over Jacqueline's breasts but Jacqueline took Luccia's hand by the wrist and slid it into the waistband of her skirt. She taught Luccia to play her, and when she rolled Luccia over and spread herself on her, Luccia humbly took a lesson. Not the body as battleground, nor the body as target. The body as music.

Jacqueline taught Luccia to command her with her hand and lose herself in Jacqueline's reaction, taught Luccia to send herself into her fingers and let the brain and heart of her float around them, and in the days that followed — the time of her naked in the moss, the time of her on Luccia's lap in the peat, the morning of her pressed against a tree — Luccia learned to stalk Jacqueline's climax, needing it more than Jacqueline, needing it far more than her own, sweet though that new feeling was. Luccia needed to hold Jacqueline's face in her hands and feel her grow utterly still, this vibrant, moving woman who gobbled her life, who grabbed it tight-fisted, flailing about in it, her Jacqueline with fire in her cat-eyes. Luccia would tentatively take Jacqueline's chin in her hand and Jacqueline would grow utterly still, parted lips impatient for Luccia's tongue. She needed the right to make Jacqueline wait, to pin her arms back and drag her teeth across the musky softness of her ribcage, to make Jacqueline descend from her full-of-life position to a state of whimpering impatience, moving with the journey of Luccia's fingers. The body as power, gently used, for good, for joy, for love.

Afterward, Jacqueline would be up again, chirping, this time cheeks flushed, eyes glazed over, nipples shining with Luccia's spit, dancing around in some silly little combination of skirts or a tangle of necklaces each with an odd story and she would be ravenously hungry, as if she'd hiked the forest for a week, desperate over cheese and bits of meat that would fall out of her mouth when she laughed at her own hunger. At the fire in the evening, Luccia noted smugly that Jacqueline cooked not for Marcelle, but for her, hovering over her shoulders, attentive and tender, serving Luccia enormous plates of venison, pork and fennel.

One afternoon, lying in the lavender field in each other's arms, Luccia dug her hands into Jacqueline's hair. "Why do you love me?" she asked timidly, fearing the answer. Jacqueline chuckled, and ran her hand down Luccia's chest.

"Because you are strong."

It was the last answer that Luccia had expected. "I'm not!" Luccia protested. She had hidden behind a rain barrel in Rome, within a beak in Marseilles. She had assumed any disguise just to shield herself. Jacqueline had no idea how many times she had skulked and shrunk from discovery. Now she was even shrinking from her duty. She should be fighting the Plague. She should take her remedy to the other port cities that were being decimated. Instead she had run into the woods after Fiona and now was lolling about with Jacqueline as if the woman were a plate of sweets. "I'm a coward, really," she said quietly. There was so much more she could have done.

"Luccia, someone who loves you doesn't see who you are, they see the glow inside you," Jacqueline said, stroking her face, "and it is your honor to live up to the shine."

The following morning, Marcelle stepped into the clearing with a string of rabbits on her left and fish on her right. She called to Jacqueline who was sleeping soundly beside Luccia. Luccia covered Jacqueline's ear with a pillow and stepped outside, her hair crumpled from the bed, topless, cinching her pants.

Marcelle looked at Luccia from under her eyebrows.

"Welcome back, Marcelle," Luccia said, crossing her arms over her naked chest and planting her feet firmly, her eyes directly on Marcelle's, but keeping tabs on her dagger.

Marcelle dropped her catch into the dust and slowly walked around Luccia, bumping into her shoulder. She stepped wordlessly into Jacqueline's room and was greeted by a shriek. Despite what Luccia wanted to hear as she stood with her back to the cottage — the sound of protest, of refusal, then the emergence of Jacqueline — she had to admit it had been a joyful shriek and that it was now silent inside. The morning air was acid on her skin again.

Fiona came out of their hut and tossed Luccia a shirt. "Care to tend herbs?"

Luccia couldn't stay to hear any more, now that she knew what the sounds meant, so she grabbed a boda of water, and glancing back at the cottage, set off with Fiona.

When she stormed back to the encampment after several torturous hours, Jacqueline and Marcelle were fighting by a cold fire. Marcelle had been trying to make her give Luccia up and Jacqueline, hands on hips, eyes ferocious, refused to choose between them.

Fiona made dinner, trying to break up the tension by slamming the pans around. While the pots boiled over the fire, she threw her shoulders back and announced in her most imperious tone that Jacqueline should meet Simone and that a joint venture should be forged. There had been no sign of the professor for quite a while and perhaps it was time to connect them. "Look what we could do with the cats and the herbs if we joined forces with Simone again!" she proclaimed. Luccia thought about taking the Plague remedy through France, thought about her neglected manuscripts back at Simone's and was glad of any plan that would knit her deeper into Jacqueline's life, especially one that gave her a way to avoid watching Marcelle and Jacqueline together. Jacqueline danced around the cold fire. Her cats, Jacqueline said laughing, on the road as she should be. Luccia put her hand on Fiona's shoulder, happy that she was straight-backed and strong enough to present herself in public.

The close call with Bremer in the hospital prompted Fiona to insist that they cut their hair and pass as men. She shaved hers off entirely since he had seen its distinctive color and Marcelle crossed her arms over her chest and chuckled at the sight of them. Fiona seemed unnaturally tall and thin with her shining, bald head and close-cut men's clothing, and Luccia's angularity was much more pronounced without hair.

"You'll be fine unless they arrest fence posts and the chisel that cut them," Marcelle laughed, and Luccia knew Marcelle was just glad they were going.

They stayed off the main road, never went into public houses, chose another route mid-journey if they heard about a court. The burnings continued, so despite Luccia's protests, Fiona ruled out any stops at universities, for fear of Bremer, and they both agreed to stay clear of hospitals, deciding that they were overrun with doctors of the new order. Midwives and women doctors only, an ever-shrinking group, but they did their part.

Luccia traveled when Marcelle returned, and Marcelle left to hunt when the time was right. When there was overlap, there was trouble. Marcelle was surly and confrontational and Luccia lost all her confidence, which allowed Marcelle to be even more aggressive. Marcelle refused to share her meat with Luccia and Luccia made a point of displaying how much money and goods the herbs had made them, how important the Plague remedy was. Rabbit entrails wound up under Luccia's pillow, and Marcelle developed a mysterious rash that had a very unpleasant odor. They didn't speak. Jacqueline, unable to pamper either one of them without incurring the wrath of the other, stormed off to gather her hooded cape and threatened to leave for good. Since both of them knew that she meant it, and understood that their ability to make her come was more important to them than her coming was to her, they made a pact. Unspoken, but made nonetheless.

Fiona ordered her camp life around visits to the hot springs and setting in a store of fermented spirits. Pears when they were in season became pear beer, pear wine, pear brandy then on to apples and berries. Fiona stumbled around the camp so drunk that she slept in the dirt under a tree. One evening, tottering around the encampment while Luccia and Jacqueline sat holding hands by the fire, Fiona strode forward, slurring her words. She pointed at Luccia and the absence of the vial.

"Now you're alive," she growled. "Now you're riskin' it. You had to claim a life, Luccia, not postpone it."

"I was alive," Luccia protested.

"You were alive but you had no life. Life is risk, little one."

"And what was the Plague, and the professor...and Rome?" Luccia demanded.

"Well you did a damn good job in Marseilles, I will say that. Tenacious. And the world's a better place for it. But that was danger. This is risk. There's no risk like love."

"You're drunk, Fiona."

"I am, indeed," she said, but shook her head over Luccia's lack of knowledge of the world. Didn't she know that the loss of Giovanna hurt Fiona more than any Plague, horrible though it had been? That the thought of losing Luccia was far more frightening than death? She turned as Luccia stormed off. "Welcome to the messy, glorious, risky world, girl. Your mother'd be proud: not over the fun and games, but that you had the courage to put down the vial and live. You can't begin if you won't admit to an end."

Luccia grumbled under her breath because it hadn't been a conscious decision. She had misplaced the vial from her mother. Had no idea where it was. But it was true that she hadn't been looking for it. It had gone from sacred talisman to misplaced object.

Fiona slowed her drinking and increased her spirit making, bottling enough to sell. They built another hut that was half filled with herbs and beer and half with sleeping cots for Fiona and Luccia when she wasn't otherwise preoccupied. Luccia collected any medicine she could find or buy, brought it back to analyze it, document it, reproduce it in a little laboratory she set up in their sleeping hut.

They plied a quiet trade, building a new route through Europe, with bags of herbs, the Plague remedy, a manuscript, a few casks of beer. The Plague had dissipated, leaving as fast as it had arrived, and while Luccia was relieved, she packed a few bottles of remedy just in case.

They brought Simone back to the encampment, and she sat by the fire and got drunk with Fiona as if she'd never tasted spirits in her life. The herbs were taken to the cities, their requests for more brought back, the herb farm expanded, and they wove the intricate threads of a life, entwining scores of women.

Chapter Eleven

O ne spring, Fiona and Luccia had set out to make deliveries, leaving just as the bushes parted and Marcelle stepped into the clearing. Fiona bade her welcome but Luccia turned her back and headed out, unwilling to see the look on Jacqueline's face.

They were only a few hours ride away from the encampment when Fiona started twitching, which made her horse skittish. Luccia pulled her horse up, hauled Fiona behind her onto Luccia's horse, bound her wrists around Luccia's waist so Fiona wouldn't fall off and break her neck when the shaking grew worse, and, tying the other horse's reigns to her saddle, turned them toward home.

Marcelle and Jacqueline, dining in front of a small fire, had not even had time to duck into the house yet when the pair rode up. Luccia jumped down, and the three of them helped Fiona into bed, where Marcelle held Fiona's hands at her side. The routine for Fiona was pre-established: they had a tea that wasn't terribly effective, and a system for keeping her cool and comfortable. The potion created by Giovanna could elongate the periods between episodes but was nearly useless once they began.

Luccia fell to her knees beside her godmother's bed and wished she hadn't lost her own vial. She uncorked Fiona's and brought it to her nose. It smelled the same. An elixir that kept Luccia young and Fiona strong. What could that possibly be? And how could she have so glibly lost the last thing her mother had given her? When the pain was too great, and it just wasn't now. She must decipher it, she must create more of it, to spare Fiona from this. But for now, time was the only thing that quelled the shaking. Defeated, confused, Luccia strode outside.

Looking at Jacqueline, so recently in her bed and now poised to enter Marcelle's embrace, Luccia surprised herself by mounting her horse again and bringing the second horse to Jacqueline. What surprised her more, however, was that Jacqueline mounted the animal and left the encampment with Luccia.

Jacqueline rode as if fleeing a fire, oblivious to the bottles of wine and the bags of herbs that were tied to the saddle and hidden within the blanket roll. And Luccia sailed after her, laughing at Jacqueline's delight in her freedom, in her choice to join Luccia, in her success in keeping Jacqueline from Marcelle. It was one of the first times Luccia had seen Jacqueline without cats surrounding her, without the shade falling across her face and she thought Jacqueline was splendid, her hair wild and her cheeks flushed and when she dismounted at a cross-roads Jacqueline laughed so deep that she doubled over.

So when Jacqueline mounted the horse again and took the left fork of the road, rather than the right fork that Luccia had planned to take, Luccia followed without hesitation. They wound across the hills, then ducked into a section of the forest that Luccia hadn't seen before. She assumed that Jacqueline was just moving with abandon.

Instead, she took Luccia deep into the forest and tied their horses up at branches behind a rock outcropping. Luccia tried to take Jacqueline in her arms, hoping they had stopped for an interlude, but Jacqueline pushed her away with a chuckle and stuffed the bags of herbs into the front of her blouse.

"We're first, so we're responsible for the fires," she said, motioning Luccia into a clearing.

Luccia looked around for others.

"Fiona will recover, Luccia," Jacqueline said, touching her face. "Maybe someone here will have a suggestion." Luccia turned again. "Firewood," Jacqueline dismissively ordered and Luccia obediently gathered wood as instructed until they had an enormous pile of kindling and logs.

"No no, not all in one spot," Jacqueline admonished and she dropped another pile into the clearing. "We'll have a dozen fires, in a ring."

"I thought you never left the compound," Luccia challenged, wiping her sleeve across her sweating forehead.

Jacqueline smiled. "Perhaps I exaggerate a bit," she said coyly.

Luccia stepped forward with alarm as several cloaked figures walked up behind Jacqueline, but Jacqueline pivoted, and took their hands in greeting. They started the first fire, and Jacqueline sent Luccia off to find more kindling. When Luccia returned, a pot tended by the new arrivals was boiling and Jacqueline offered Luccia a cup of tea, which in her thirst and her fatigue Luccia took without question.

The evening took a strange turn after the tea. Luccia had drained the cup before she realized it was thorn apple, a painkiller that brings waking dreams. She looked into the bottom of the cup but then saw Jacqueline striding toward her, smiling broadly and she smoothed her hair, relaxing into the disembodied feeling of the brew.

Women stepped into the clearing, tossed back the hoods of their black cloaks, and laid out beakers of healing salves. Little fires and caldrons made a ring in the clearing and while Jacqueline helped put a goat onto a spit and laid her fennugreek and tansy out, Luccia wandered the crowd peeking into cloth bags, asking questions that might help Fiona. Several times when she encountered a cautious face, Jacqueline would call across the fire circle to introduce her and Luccia would then be privy to recipes that she hadn't learned in Salerno, hadn't heard from doctors. She had been delivering her wares to the hospitals, to the midwives and women doctors in cities with established practices. She had always thought that her people were women doctors. True, she knew how to track the herb farmers in the forest, but had never been invited into the community of women who were gathering to compare and trade the homespun medicine, the folk remedies. She hadn't realized they were different, but all around her were remedies she'd never seen.

They wore black to avoid detection in the night, met at crossroads far from the villages and its authority, and they were spies who impressed Luccia with their ability. They tucked herbs into the hems of their skirts, stuffed medicines into the tall points of their broad-brimmed hats. She had to meet them all, hear them all, and so she peered over the shoulders of old women as they showed younger ones how to extract the bile glands of lizards, the sinew of rabbits while the air was filled with elaborate smells that challenged Luccia's nose. She had to know it all.

By the time the moon was directly overhead, there were three-dozen women in the clearing drinking hot wine, exchanging wares, eating goat, and the complexity of their remedies impressed Luccia, while their secretiveness saddened her. She wondered what the world would look like if these women had been free to hang a shingle. Why should they be reduced to working in the woods instead of presiding over a laboratory like the ones in Salerno? If they had had any one of them in the hospital in Marseilles, could they have fought the Plague any better? They were healers and criminals, she thought sadly, as fire was both cooking circle and pyre.

A cloth laden with four kinds of mushrooms was thrust in front of her face. Luccia lifted them, turned them over, inspected the gills and the stems, until she heard chuckling and finally looked into the face of the woman holding them.

"Isabelle!" It was Simone's second daughter, the dreamy one.

"Luccia, have you been drinking the tea of Mme. Boudlain?" she laughed. "What are you doing here?"

"More to the point why are you? Is your mother here?"

"No, no. Helene brings us." She pulled Luccia down into the duff, crouched over her cloth and cut her a tiny piece of mushroom. "Here, a present. Chew it well."

"No."

"Yes, it will go well with the tea," Isabelle said and Luccia's love for her and her sense of discovery made her chew the leathery, bitter mushroom.

"The crop of fools," Helene growled, crouching beside her sister and scowling at Luccia, who clumsily threw her arms around them both, so glad to see them again, even if Helene admonished Luccia as if she were 15 and Helene were the 25 year old.

"Henbane on you!" Isabelle intoned with mock seriousness at Helene as her sister ducked back into the darkness on the edge of the fire circle. Isabelle cut a small piece of mushroom for herself as Luccia slumped to the ground with a grin. Isabelle laid her head on

Luccia, who sheltered her in her arms and listened to her catch up on the news while the women seemed to be floating above the ground and dancing above the trees.

When Isabelle moved off to trade her mushrooms, Luccia let her clouded eyes sweep over the gathering, passing over a group of old women making brooms. At any gathering, in any village, there was always an old broom maker — the trade of the very poor, of the destitute widow, since branches were there for the taking, and brooms needed to be replaced every month. But Luccia tried to focus her eyes because there was a small crowd in front of the broom-makers, and it seemed odd to Luccia that brooms would be needed here when they could be made or bought anywhere. She struggled to her feet and walked over to the group.

A wizened old woman in a patched skirt gestured to the women in front of her, her wrinkled hands festooned with rings and bracelets, while two dozen little leather bags and suede-wrapped bones hung from her neck. Her piercing blue eyes were framed by long silver hair. Behind her were a large pile of twigs and half a dozen smaller piles of plants. The women in front of her were pointing at the piles of herbs and the old woman bent over to grab a handful, combining them with others, then passing them to an old woman behind her. That woman selected a handle, or took a staff from the woman ordering the broom, gathered the plants that had been selected, and wove a skirt of willow twigs around it. When she had finished, the woman who had requested the broom pulled other plants from inside her cape and secreted them within the bristles of the broom. Luccia stood, peered closer. Willow twigs, a mild painkiller for the exterior. Inside the bristles now were cohosh, and digitalis.

Luccia regarded the piles again. Dried stalks of borage against sorrow, comfrey root to not only knit bones and flesh but to stimulate the ovaries and testes, shepherd's purse for menstruation and other kinds of bleeding, boneset and on the end, a pile of mandrake, blessed secret between Fiona and her mother since Luccia was a child, Satan's Apple, thought to bring madness — powerful, mysterious mandrake, enough on the pile in front of her to put an entire village to sleep for a very long time. Ready to be smuggled within an innocuous skirt of willow, the trappings of women's work, a powerful force passed off as the effort it takes to sweep dust.

It seemed a very long ago that Luccia had felt at home in her mother's study, had felt herself surrounded by her people. Now she looked around the fire circle and felt part of a different clan, this band of smugglers and healers, the Wicca. Someone was brewing a tincture of borage, she could smell it. And the broom, the mandrake broom, welcoming her home.

She dropped, unsteady, to her haunches. Fiona had been trying to teach her this for years: that few things contain the same essence all the way through. Trees had gnarly bark but were sap-soaked in the middle. Women were weak yet harbored an internal strength. The disguise protected a messenger who was strong. Fiona herself had reserves that her body belied and Luccia had walked out of Rome without a scar but her mind had not fared as well. And maybe, just maybe, in this era when so many were crushed in its spin, there was a way to skirt the maelstrom.

When the summer ended, Poulain disappeared for several months and then returned, pregnant and hungry. Jacqueline, as was her way with all things, laughed and joyously welcomed her home, feeding her for hours, washing her in the stream, then just sitting naked in the water with the girl on her lap, holding the girl's belly in her hands while the cats lined up on the streambed. Fiona and Luccia stood on the riverbank with their arms crossed over their chests, scowling, while Marcelle raged at it all. She was afraid a man would come looking for Poulain, leading their enemies to the idyll in the woods. Fiona was just flat out disapproving.

When the time came, Poulain howled and thrashed like a dying dog but birthed a baby boy she named Jean into Fiona's arms without serious incident.

As a baby, Jean tottered around the sandy clearing in front of Jacqueline's home. The women spent their time with Jean scrubbing dust out of the fat creases in his neck, sponging off his tiny, soft butt, making him howl as they pulled twigs and vermin from his hair. The little boy grew up wild, clothed in a leather thong, with a wooden sword and a twig knife, disappearing into the forest with his mother without a word, taller and more gangly each time he reappeared.

At every reunion, Jacqueline was more disgusted by his appearance, calling for buckets of water to be heated and a stiff brush brought to scrub him. At the same time, they feasted at his every arrival. Marcelle, who took him on whenever his mother got frightened and fled into the woods without him, taught him to hunt when he was 6, and when they sat down to the pheasant dinner of his first kill, he had eyes that were voracious for the hunt.

Luccia tried to teach him stealth but he had a recklessness that she couldn't break; he was too cavalier in his willingness to pop out of his cover and pick up a stick to fight. He thought part of the game was to drop down on top of her from tree branches. There was none of the rabbit in him, only the bobcat. He could not be the hunter and the hunted and despite her best efforts to teach him to evaporate and shape-shift, he had too much of Marcelle's fury in him, too much of her fight, and that kinship gave Luccia another reason to resent Marcelle.

His hair grew long, dark and matted. His brown eyes were bright and he was an attentive little boy, bringing Jacqueline, Marcelle, and Fiona cups of tea at the end of the day, then quietly coaxing Poulain in from the bushes so he could crouch in front of the fire and rub her feet.

Luccia built another small shed beside Jacqueline's house, planed a board for a desk, collected the quills of wild geese and turkeys, and spent warm summer afternoons hidden from the sun, the sound of her quill on the thick paper she bought with every extra *sou*s from every remedy sent to the village market or through the Wicca.

She copied *Trotula*, her thread through life. The concoctions and potions of Trotula's world captured her in tunnel vision in her little shed, the afternoon sun struggling through the creaks in her roof, the sound of the hot afternoon bugs and the birds heralding the time of day. The papers littered her table, one pile for Trotula, one pile for a volume of the Wicca wisdom, combined with her own remedies. The recipes crowded her head, took over her sense of time and space, until she lived most of her hours picturing herbal lore like a schematic in her mind, the stem of an herb family with branches of cures, each gathered from another time and place. They raced through her, and she had to hold herself very still to allow them to order themselves in some semblance of a line so that she could record their composition. Poulain brought her lunch, and sometimes Jean would pound on her flimsy door insisting that she come and play. But she persisted, scribbling for hours, sometimes after the sun had gone down and the moonlight was up.

The unique contents of Luccia's remedies, their purity and efficacy made the Wicca crowd around her to ask her what more they could do with their own tinctures. What could strengthen the effects of cleansing sage? What could one combine with comfrey to knit a bone faster? Crouched together discussing combinations of plants, Luccia was inventive and forthcoming, spinning recipes with them in an excited exchange that made her stand up, bright-eyed, gesturing and chattering. Jacqueline sat proudly at her elbow.

Word had gotten out about the apothecary, and the sick arrived at their hidden encampment. Each time she saw them coming through the woods, Luccia shut herself away in her laboratory and refused to open the door. If they came on the arm of a Wicca, Jacqueline asked for the witches' diagnosis or brought them to Fiona, then turned them away gently and crept into Luccia's lab, quietly asking Luccia for a remedy for a particular organ or ailment. Jacqueline carried it to the circle that night. Those who came alone, guided by legends, suggestions or desperation, were taken to Fiona, given broth by Jacqueline who then crept to Luccia with her question.

Rustling into Luccia's laboratory after a visitation, Jacqueline plopped on a stool, folded her blue skirt over her red, and jammed her bracelets up higher. She glared at Luccia, her teeth clenched.

"How can you know so much, and see so little?" Jacqueline fumed.

Luccia stood behind her table, gripping her mortar, leaves stuck to her wrists and branches to her blouse. She hung her head, and pushed her hand deep into a pile of white sage leaves.

"I prefer plants to the body," she said weakly.

"Well you don't prefer them to my body," Jacqueline said, jumping down off the stool and charging at Luccia, who turned away.

"You're not...sick. You're...flawless," Luccia said.

117

"They need you!" Jacqueline said. "Where is your courage?"

"I left it...behind a rain barrel in Rome," Luccia said. "How can you love me?" Luccia asked tearfully, raising her eyes to Jacqueline. "I'm so...broken."

Jacqueline turned away and sighed, then looked at Luccia's frightened face and pulled her into her arms. "The shine, my dear," Jacqueline said in a whisper. "The shine."

Marcelle and Luccia reached a peace, leaving just enough time between them to cleanse the vision of them from Jacqueline's skin, to make way in her turbulent, ebullient heart for someone new. Yet they rarely coincided. One spring day they did, though, and they were both so elated over the end of the rain, so pleased to be riding or walking with sun on their faces, that there wasn't any room for what at this point wasn't true jealousy or even competitiveness, just a ritualized separation. Marcelle and Luccia threw their arms around each other's shoulders, comrades basking in new sunshine. Jacqueline, thrilled at their joint arrival and their new peace, pivoted and ran forward, then dared them to chase her. They took up the challenge and she sprinted forward, then whirled back to see them and fling her arms out with joy. But she kept her eyes on them, so unique to find them side-by-side, that she couldn't remove her eyes fast enough. She stepped backward, with too much of her spirit in front of her and not enough behind her, so she didn't notice the tree. She spun around and sprinted forward and they heard a bough crack, but it was Jacqueline, and the tree felled her with a broken collarbone and a severe blow to the chest.

Luccia and Marcelle carried her back, speechless, breathless, united again in their tending of her, and in the weeks that followed she put some semblance of a body back together. When she could walk again, she had a defensive, caved-in sense to her body. Timidity had entered her and Luccia thought that the fear she exhibited was even more painful to see than the damage to her body. Luccia and Marcelle fell over each other caring for her, and then sat silently together with Fiona by the fire circle drinking too much pear brandy, while Jacqueline, who had entertained them all with her fanciful stories and her peeling laughter, slept in the cottage. The silence held them, bugs in pinesap.

When the winter came, the cold settled in Jacqueline's damaged lungs and the three of them sat around her bed while she did her best to comfort them, coughing and laughing and trying to die beautifully, always with cats inhabiting her shoulders and her lap. Marcelle was frantic: she screamed at the cats and incurred Jacqueline's wrath for hurling more than one of them across the cottage. Fiona and Luccia struggled with tinctures and mixtures and Luccia even fled into the forest to ask the Wicca at the caldron what to do. Bloodroot and white horehound to produce a cleansing cough was followed by coltsfoot and comfrey to calm the cough. Luccia even gave her some of the Plague remedy in the hopes it might break up any infection. In the end, she brewed St. John's Wort for the four of them and outlawed the brandy.

The cats sent up a din the afternoon Jacqueline passed away and Marcelle pulled a side of pork from the pantry and hacked it to bits with her knife. Luccia sat in the dirt of the compound as if she had just fallen off a horse. Fiona, sweet Fiona, wrinkled and gray now, limping and not so prone to seizures as to relentless small tremors, rocked Luccia in her arms as if she was eight.

Chapter Twelve

*T*he death of Jacqueline left the five of them — the old lady Fiona, the madwoman Poulain, her little child Jean, and two middle-aged adversaries — as spokes, no hub; clan, no matriarch; rattling around uneasily in their lives.

Fiona stepped over Luccia for several days while she sat listlessly in the dust of the encampment and Marcelle wept in the bed. Still taller than the rest of them despite her being stooped over and shaking, Fiona took a walking stick and prodded Luccia up off the ground, pulled the vial given by Luccia's mother from beneath her dress and put it around Luccia's neck. When the pain was too great, her mother had said, and Luccia gripped the glass.

"You should keep it," Luccia said tearfully, and Fiona gathered her into her arms and cradled her head.

"You keep it, I'll keep you," Fiona said and Luccia held her tightly. She moved her hand up to cover the Celtic broach at Fiona's throat and clutched the vial in the other hand.

Fiona stroked her cheek and gripped her shoulders. "We're leavin'," Fiona pronounced to the group, as she beat the covers to make Marcelle come out of bed. "Call Poulain and Jean in from the woods."

Every move they made to leave cut them all — packing Jacqueline's shawls, gathering in one last crop, carting cats to the edge of the village and setting them out, bundling others to drop off as they traveled. But at least they were doing something. They packed, hitched up a wagon and helped Fiona into the passenger seat. "North," she said, pulling her blue cape around her shaking legs, and waving them on with her stick.

They arrived at Simone's village just as she was lumbering out of a barn with an oak barrel on her shoulder. She tossed it to the ground and it cut a three-inch scar into the dirt at her feet. Hands on hips, then crossing herself, she regarded the rag-taggle group of them and took charge. Jean was given another brutal bath, food was laid out, and they slept as if hoping to wake in another country.

The following morning, Marcelle and Luccia offered to tear down an out-building that was leaning over, and they flung themselves at it furiously, as if the building were Jacqueline's bones that had broken, the shell of her lungs that collapsed, the structure of their lives that had been destroyed. They yanked boards off with their bare hands and their raging muscles, while the stable hands leaned on their pitchforks in surprise. The two women hurled the wood, broke it under their feet, and Marcelle stormed into a barn, returned with an axe and chopped the building up.

But her fury turned into blood lust and whirling around, she looked at Luccia and snarled, as if Luccia had been responsible for Jacqueline's death. Luccia could have stepped aside, or cooled her down but when Marcelle lunged at her she took her on, full fist, drawing blood. If they hadn't been so selfish, Luccia thought as her fist knocked Marcelle's head back, if they hadn't both insisted on being with her, or if they had been more generous, Luccia growled as she grabbed Marcelle's hair and threw her to the ground, if they had been willing to be in the same place at the same time, not a tacit but an actual agreement, Jacqueline wouldn't have been surprised, would have seen the tree. They had killed her with their vanity and it was justice to draw each other's blood.

Simone and her youngest daughters Henrietta and Teresa, ran toward them, skirts billowing and hands flapping to pull them away from each other. Simone shoved Marcelle, who flew back several feet before hitting the ground.

"What have you done?" Simone screamed. "No one said you could turn it into firewood, for the love of God. These were going to be used in another building! Look at the waste. The waste of my property," she bellowed. She whirled around to Luccia and put her hands on her hips. "What could possibly make you fight like that?"

There was no way to tell her of Jacqueline and their love for her. Simone had met Jacqueline, had been in their encampment, but women who have had husbands don't see love beyond a beard. Even knowing that she risked her life and her livelihood shuttling herbs, they refrained from enlightening her.

Marcelle charged across the distance between her and Luccia, and the women around them flinched, at the ready, but Marcelle threw a muscled arm around Luccia's shoulders and drew her in, leaning her head on Luccia's shoulder. No one in the world would know her pain but Luccia. She cupped Luccia's head with one of her strong hands and, in turn, Luccia gripped her with all the power in her arms. It was their guilt, their love. Marcelle's blood was Luccia's — she could feel it on her lips as Marcelle spat onto the ground.

"You'll work it off, both of you," Simone said. "You'll cut the trees yourself," she said to Marcelle, then turned back to Luccia, "and since you can't peaceably be in the same place at the same time, you Luccia, you will head my first wagon going to Metz."

Teresa stepped forward in startled protest, "Mother, you can't send her to..." She received a wilting stare from Simone. "To Metz..." she said meekly.

"One day here, one single day and you've destroyed months worth of work. Get out of my sight," Simone said, and lumbered back into the barn. Her daughters shrugged their shoulders and wrung their hands: they all knew better than to challenge Simone's edict. But Metz was in Germany, and they all knew the burnings were more frequent, and more ferocious, in Germany than anywhere else.

Luccia didn't care, really, she thought as she stomped away. To be on the road again would be a blessing. To be away from Marcelle and the reminders of Jacqueline was essential to her sanity. It was tearing her stomach up. Her jaws hurt from grinding her teeth. Risk and danger, she heard Fiona say. Risk hurt so much worse.

In the morning, Luccia received terse instructions from Simone on the hiding places of herbs and other contraband that was hidden on the wagon, plus the destinations of the barrels of ale, the casks and boxes and bales. Documents were handed over on what should be traded for what in which town. She was reminded of the foibles of each of the horses and given the new locations of stables that could be trusted. Luccia was so sullen that she could barely speak, but she threw her bedroll and satchel into the back and mounted without even bidding Simone goodbye. Just as she picked up the reigns, Fiona came tottering out of the inn with her own satchel and insisted on being helped on board.

"Stay and rest," Luccia told her, but Fiona waved her on with her walking stick and stared straight ahead. Fiona knew it would be a long and tiring journey, mountainous, and her German was not up to the challenge, but Luccia was her talisman now, more than ever.

Luccia sighed. None of them had any fight left in them. None of them could articulate why they were acting as they were. Luccia slapped the horses' rumps and they rumbled out of the village.

One hectare away, Poulain jumped out of the bushes, spooking the horses, and she leapt on the back of the wagon. Poulain, as overcast as the rest of them, stumbled around the back of the wagon frantically looking for her son, until Luccia stopped the horses and they calmed her, explaining that he was back with Marcelle.

"Go home to your child," Luccia told Poulain, but Fiona touched her arm.

"Oh, let her come with," Fiona said, settling into her seat again. "Jean's in good hands with Marcelle and we could all use a change of pace, including Poulain."

So the three of them lumbered ahead, grave and crestfallen. They rolled into Avignon and bristled over the cheery self-importance of the papal court. Fiona kept the hood of her cape up and Luccia insisted that Poulain walk between them so they could keep her from wandering or attracting attention.

Along the Rue des Teinturiers beside the Sorgue River, the brightly patterned, freshly dyed cottons hung above their heads, and wrapped them in the comfort of women's work. Fiona bought a piece for Luccia but she smiled weakly and stuffed it into her bag: it reminded her too much of the festivity of Jacqueline. They drove on, trading, eating, and sleeping with an exhaustion that was beyond their task.

In Dijon, they negotiated so well with the spice merchants that they were able to buy another team, hire a driver and send the second wagon back to Simone. But none of them were willing to break up the trio, even though they would have been able to double-back and be home sooner. They were all they had left and though they worried about Jean and wanted him with them, they pressed on. Grief dulled their senses and slowed their feet.

Fritz Bremer did not heal well from his impaling and no one he consulted knew enough to diagnose his head injury. His arm withered from the infection in his shoulder, making half his body droop along with his face. He and Father Peter took to riding in carriages again because Bremer couldn't control his horse, and when the carriage hit ruts or jolted and Bremer bumped his head, he would crumple on the seat, unconscious for several hours.

Whenever Bremer slumped, Father Peter rolled his eyes and turned his attention out the window, trying to ignore the mutterings of the broken old man about a book, always some damnable book, and granite women and banshees. Peter had seen the two in the hospital who had attacked Bremer, and they seemed the same as any of the other pernicious witches he had encountered.

He didn't listen because he had other things on his mind. A sickly man and a misshapen youth were not welcome in many quarters and times had gotten very thin lately. He had spent his entire life with the professor and the Bishop (except for the years in the orphanage which were cold and lean but not as bad as those with the Bishop). And now that this slobbering imbecile was shortly to die, Peter would be on his own. The Bishop had supplied them with credibility and stature, and the professor had given them a task, foolish though it was. Soon he would have nothing. Attaching himself to someone else was of utmost importance, and it couldn't be done too soon.

He had been pondering this last night in a public house, staring into the gruel-like stew that their dwindling cache of money could afford them. Despite his priestly training, he had no real ability with it, could barely recite a psalm and hadn't been to confession himself since the rat-bastard Bishop had died. All he had known was the Inquisition. Following men hunting witches. He knew nothing about conducting an investigation himself, operating a trial, not even torture, really. He was at a loss. So unfair. Just when the bar maid was taking away his bowl of stew and he held up his stein for another ale, it occurred to him. He had heard a Dominican priest — a Jakob Sprenger — speak in Cologne. Dean of the Faculty of Theology, he was. The lecture hall was packed, and Sprenger had been very eloquent and specific on the methods of securing a confession from a witch. Sprenger was the man to get in with. Why, last year he had been appointed Inquisitor Extraordinary for the Provinces of Mainz, Treves, and Cologne. Now that was stature. So this morning, guiding the decrepit Bremer by his withered arm, he had clambered into the coach and ordered the driver to set their sites on Metz, where Sprenger was reportedly heading.

As Luccia, Fiona and Poulain drove on, nearing the border with Germany, the terrain changed. Poulain gave up her occasional wandering in the forest and huddled in the wagon nervously plaiting her hair. There were fewer women on the roads and Luccia decided outside the village of Nancy to hide her hair and travel as a man, since the three of them were beginning to draw attention. One man was all that was required to pass muster, and she preferred the garb anyway. She felt better in disguise.

Afterward, Luccia could only think that grief had clouded their eyes, that their preoccupation with Jacqueline and the days spent near her skirts had made it difficult for them to be in the present. Surely there had been signs to warn them as they approached Metz, Luccia had to believe, though she couldn't recount any of them. What other explanation could there be for three women, two of whom prided themselves on an ability to sense and dodge danger, who blindly rode into a trap?

They plodded across a stone bridge overhung with fragrant branches, well on the outskirts of the city of Metz. Luccia was reaching up to touch the leaves for solace, when six peasants scrambled up from under the bridge and overtook the wagon.

"Turn over your witches," the men shouted to her in German. "They're ours now."

"Get away!" Luccia snarled in German, trying to sound like a man. She kicked at them but they seized the horses so she couldn't flee.

Fiona, seeing the men holding the horses, convulsed with a seizure. Poulain started shrieking, making cat sounds, tearing at her hair and Luccia couldn't calm her, tend to Fiona and beat the men away as well. She grabbed the whip while several of the gang shouted about the mark of the Devil on Fiona and Poulain, about the price the two would fetch when they delivered them to the town square, and how Luccia would just have to capture more if she wanted the money for herself.

They pulled Luccia off the wagon and threw her onto the stones. They mounted the wagon, captured Poulain's hands and threw her to the back of the wagon, surrounded Fiona and rode off.

Luccia stumbled after them, screaming, then running into town as fast as she could.

In Metz the crowd was nearly impenetrable and by the time Luccia had muscled her way through the furious crowd, Fiona and Poulain were two of a hundred women being staked to a pyre. Luccia's screaming broke the inside of her head. She ducked behind a barrel, tried to be a slug on the wall. She hung back a moment before following. They saw a man, she realized as she emerged.

The fire was lit, but how could it go up so fast? Some of the women on the pyre begged for more kindling, for a fast fire rather than the torture of a slow burn. Who could heap a fire as an act of compassion?

Especially a fire holding Fiona. Luccia pitched and whirled to look for weapons, pushed toward the guard and shouted at him to let them go — ineffectual, hysterical, at her wit's end, charging the field, pulling the flame-carriers to the ground, receiving a sword-handle in her gut. Luccia was cordoned off by guards into a crowd of men who shouted for their wives, who wept and held their children against their legs, who stood horrified over being men among men. And on the other side of the square, a much larger crowd jeered and threw garbage at the women, spat at them and called them the Devil's instruments.

Through the thick air corrugated by the heat, Luccia saw clergy on a balcony and felt her stomach drop to her heels — two Dominican monks, a misshapen priest and a seated, drooping man in a German professor's cap.

Bremer, his head pounding with pain, saw the red-haired Fiona being tied and tried to stand, gesturing to her and shouting garbled words. The Dominican monks and the priest passively sipped from goblets. Seeing Bremer's sudden reaction, Father Peter had an idea.

"A book," Fr. Peter said to Sprenger.

"What?" Sprenger questioned over the shouting of the crowd.

"You should write a book on this," Father Peter said. "You're so very...efficient about it. The world should take lessons from you."

The second monk, Heinrich Kramer, leaned forward. "I have a treatise already composed," he said haughtily.

"More exhaustive than that, Heinrich," Sprenger said, considering the idea. "We need...a book like a hammer."

Luccia pressed against the spear of the guard, screaming through clenched teeth. Luccia turned back to Fiona to the Celtic knot at her throat, and as her eyes gutted her heart with the horror, a clean-shafted arrow clipped through the square and pierced Fiona in the heart. Fiona slumped against the ropes, motionless, before the flames reached Fiona's blue cape. Luccia took a breath with no release.

Luccia stumbled backwards, and then blessed the arrow, prayed to the arrow, thanked the archer who had spared Fiona the agony of the end.

Fr. Peter was not pleased over having his conversation with Kramer and Sprenger disturbed. Kramer had been the Spiritual Director of the great Dominican church of Salzburg and the right hand man of the Archbishop there. These were men who made his former guardian the Bishop look like a simple church sweep (though it was true that invoking the Bishop's name had gained him access to the group). These two worked together by order of Pope Innocent VIII himself. Over slabs of beef and glorious potatoes that he ate slowly for fear of displaying an unseemly hunger, they were pondering his idea. His idea. Well, Bremer's actually, with a new twist. And that's why it was so annoying to have a little snivel-faced novice tapping his arm. Bad enough to have this opulent room all closed up and stuffy from the noise and the smell outside but then to have an interruption to their celebratory dinner at this most critical moment in the discussion. He had established a connection, made a contribution. So when the novice implored him with a timid voice, he tried to brush it off.

"Father, your...friend is..." the child said haltingly, pointing to the square outside where the fires had burned down to cinders. Fr. Peter set his wine goblet down with a thud and went to the balcony windows.

Bremer was tumbling at the foot of the pyre where that redhead had been, blindly flailing and screeching to himself and the staff who had to sweep up all this mess. Probably searching for that damnable granite girl, as if there would be anything left of her. The fool tottered over to another post, then back. Suddenly Bremer clutched his head and fell into a heap on the ground. Fr. Peter laughed to himself, making Sprenger and Kramer turn in their seats.

"You sound like a bird," Heinrich Kramer scoffed and turned back to his plate.

"Or a cackling old woman," Sprenger said, suspiciously. "I saw monkeys at the window during this last trial."

"Monkeys?" Kramer questioned.

"Monkeys and goats screaming obscenities," Sprenger said, picking up a thin piece of toast. "It's blessedly quiet now, isn't it?"

Fr. Peter closed the curtains and smiled indulgently at his new friends.

Luccia walked out of Metz like the near dead. Three women hung from a single tree near the town boundary, children crying at their feet. Luccia collected their children and marched them away, sat at night by a fire with them on her lap, brushing their hair as if asleep. Why did they kill her? Because they are fools. Was she a witch? She was a wise woman. Where are we going? On a march through hell.

Eight women were butchered just outside their doors, twenty in a clearing in the woods, four tied to rocks and thrown into the river to drown. There were too many dead women to hang on to hope. Too many of the doctors, midwives and herbalists, too many old woman, too many good women carried off to the church, to jail, too many whose corpses now stood like blackened match sticks in what had once been the marketplace. The smell in the air said that all the medical knowledge of four hundred years had been extinguished, that the lessons of Trotula could not possibly make their way into the future. Luccia dropped the children off with anyone who would let them in.

Luccia wrapped her bare arms around her, unable to stop shaking, or moving west. Those women who were left after the slaughters will cower in their root cellars, picking at invisibilities on their aprons and wringing their hands. That's where we all will stay, Luccia thought. Cowering. Hiding. Careful of our words. Silent more than not. Money that we have stitched into the hems of our skirts or the boundaries of our lives as dangerous as sin. Our property hidden behind the names of our sons. Voices to be raised against our husbands catching in our throats. The smell of these fires will linger in our lungs for generations, she thought as she stumbled forward. It's a smoke that follows us down dark streets at night. We will smell it on the hands of the doctor, the priest, see it hanging over our weddings, our childbirths. Deep in our skin we'll remember. Luccia saw it in women — a sudden flinch around the eyes, a careful step, a whisper only just heard. We'll remember, somewhere in our bodies, in our dreams, in the way we hold our children. We'll remember that they have hunted us down like rogue pigs for the roasting.

Luccia dropped the last child off to a wife of a farmer who gave her some women's clothing just as the sky darkened and the child's soft little hand slid out of her like Luccia's last grip on hope. She walked on, and the wind pulled at her clothes, bent her double though she was already sobbing at her kneecaps. The rain lashed down in torrents, flooding ditches and moving across the parched dirt road. Animals brayed and trotted toward shelter, birds flew but were felled, bushes were uprooted and flung. She trudged into the wind with no destination, no concept of where she was, bending against the tribulation out of long habit of agony.

That's when Luccia decided that she could die. Lie down and give up. Marcelle and Jean were still with Simone. Jacqueline was gone, Fiona and Poulain killed in an instant that had been worse than any nightmare of Rome. Her mother was long since dead, the manuscript's survival an impossibility. They had won. In a world that was hell, who cared about health? Why should she bother about a couple of tinctures and poultices when they used racks and fire and the Plague?

Her mother's potion had made her stronger and healthier than most, and now that was a curse. But Luccia was stronger than her mother's medicine, wasn't she? She could just lie down and will herself to die. Why not? The wind pushed her backwards, made her stumble. She could lie down in this ditch, here in the storm that was shaking the fence-posts from their seatings. She could fall into the mud here and be done with the pain, once and for all.

The thought of it was such a relief that she collapsed into the trench, face down, listening to the howling wind and the brittle fury of the tree branches snapping. She felt the rainwater soak her hair, then struggle to roll over her, divert its torrent around her ears and shoulders. She could die here. She could be done. Leaves piled up against the crown of her head and the sand silted around her face.

Then the bulk of an enormous animal fell on top of her, blacking out the light. She was thankful that something had created a top to her dirty coffin. Whatever carcass it was, she felt badly that it had to die in the storm, but was glad it finished the job the trench had started. Bull, she wondered? Ox, perhaps, and she thought of her father and the ox of his death. She let the crush of this enormous scruffy animal seal her inside and she resolved to die.

Chapter Thirteen

The morning came. She knew this because the carcass was snoring. She found herself breathing in rhythm with the heaving wooly sides, her arms wrapped around its ribs as it snuffled and harrumphed. They had pitched around in the trench until she was pressed between the animal's back and the clay-cold sides of the ditch, the morning sun piercing into her eye. Furious that she was alive, she pushed the lummox aside and dragged herself onto the road, spitting out gravel and dirt, swearing at the break of an unwanted day. More of this damnable life, the pain of the recent past flooding into her. She gripped her head.

Then the animal stood, unwrapped enormous limbs, unfurled an incredible chest, and clambered out of the ditch. Luccia stumbled backward several paces and looked up, because it turned out not to be an animal at all, but an enormous man. He towered over her head on legs like oak trunks wrapped in hide. As he stretched out the night's knots his arms seemed to travel down the road to the next village and return, kicking up a wind as they swooped back, wrapping around him and raising huge puffs of dust off his shoulder blades. He was covered in the shaggy hides of several animals, which made a tent on the road when he bent onto one knee and drew close to her.

"So you made it." He poked at her chest with a stubby forefinger.

"To the devil with you!" Luccia shouted at him, and hit him on the shoulder with everything she had. He didn't even rock backward.

131

"Ah, yes, well, the Devil will have his way with me soon enough. But that's quite a way to say thank you," he said, scowling at her. "I probably saved your life."

"Who gave you the right? Who asked you to? I... I don't want to..." Luccia pummeled him. His beard was caked with mud and his hair was tied behind him in a long leather thong that reached his knees. His face was craggy but his eyes were as huge as river stones. This presumptuous lump of a man had saved her body, which condemned her heart to more pain. She couldn't take the thought of walking further and finding more women burned. And she'd lost her nerve to dodge it. Fiona, she thought, her mind reeling. She picked up a handful of mud and threw it at him.

He pulled a dagger, its steely sound sharp in the morning air.

She picked up a stick that was lying by her foot.

He smiled.

"A woman ready to fight is not a woman ready to die," he said, and put his dagger back into its sheath. Oblivious to her stick, he reached forward, cupped her face in his hand and scraped the mud off the edge of her cheek with his thumb. Her knees buckled under his touch.

"Never saw anybody shake like that," he said. "I thought I may as well warm you as warm the dirt. But my apologies for spoiling your plans to die like a dog in the gutter."

He bent down and picked up a log that had lain beside their trench and when he stood up he scowled and brushed mud off it with tender hands. It was a bow. The tallest bow of the thickest wood she had ever seen and it was elaborately carved down its entire length depicting stags chased through woods and elaborate pastoral scenes.

He whistled and four men clambered out of the bushes by the road, dusted themselves off, gathered bows that were less complex but treated just as tenderly. They stood beside him, regarding Luccia. Archers, each one of them, at one with their bows, their quivers, the fletches of their arrows jumping in the breeze.

"Did you shoot in a banshee in Metz?" she asked breathlessly.

Not a muscle on the men's faces moved.

"Did you? Did you kill her? I thank you," Luccia said, grabbing the giant man's hand. "I thank you for your mercy."

"Stop eating the bugs on the bushes — they're making you mad," he said, then turning and motioning his tribe to follow him south.

"What's your name?" she called, stumbling after him.

He turned. "I beg your pardon," he said with some reservation, but extended his hand. "I am Claude, the Bowman, master archer and hero for hire. Twice decorated, thrice shot. Friend to all, except my enemies."

Luccia shook his hand, then laid her left hand over his, her palm barely covering the width of his knuckles. If you had been in Metz, she thought, then shoot *me*. Shoot me now.

"My house is half a day's walk but there'll be food when we get there," he said to Luccia, then started down the road, each man falling in beside him.

Back from the edge of death, Luccia couldn't think of anywhere to go. She had no clothing or provisions, no horse and cart to take her to Simone, not as much as a blanket. She clutched the vial between her breasts. Worst, she had no will, belief or conviction left of her own, so she set off with the bedraggled men toward the home of the Bowman.

Sucked along on their current, following the arrows with their fluttering fletches like carrots before a stunned donkey, she followed, at odds with the men's easy camaraderie and their banter. To the Bowman's left loped an archer as tall as the Bowman but spindly as a birch, who seemed to be cut from the same tree as the bow he wore slung across his back. Flanking him were twins dressed in somber clothing, clutching their quivers and their bows for security. The entourage moved in unison as men do when accustomed to long lives on the road together, and dusting the ground behind them like a brood hen marshalling her chicks, was the strangest looking archer of them all, a half-bent man they called Malo, with no teeth, a bald head and flapping lips, who couldn't seem to keep step or stay up with the rest.

Claude the Bowman was acutely aware of Luccia straggling behind them and though he didn't turn to encourage her or check on her progress, he silently hoped she was following. Ragged, half-mad thing, he thought, like a part of himself. Like one of his nightmares, out there on the road limping along.

133

When they got to the house, the Bowman stepped over the threshold, bending low and sideways to accommodate his girth and then each man entered in turn, laughing and groaning over the delight of being home, filling the hut with arms and legs of divergent lengths shedding cow-skins and unwinding scarves, raising a dust cloud as they whacked at the cob-webs on stools and scraped off leaves that had blown onto the table.

Luccia was standing near the hearth in a stupor when Malo stacked wood on the grate. It went up with a vicious whoosh and it surprised Luccia, it brought her back to the life she had barely trudged out of and she turned to see the flames licking the smooth rounds of the logs. She backed up, ran into the short man, bumped into the table in a desperate search for a corner and she trembled and cowered against the wall, moving like a blind rat along the stone and sod of it, finding the farthest corner to collapse in, sobbing. Whether it was just her world or the hut in its entirety she didn't know, but the joviality turned to silence as she folded herself into the tiniest bug she could make, wishing to die once again.

Instead, enormous arms lifted her and rolled her in a blanket, put her in a darkened corner of a big bed and she wanted to drive herself through the tunnel of sleep into a place where black was all, the end was release, where death was a compassionate kidnapping.

"A face of flint," she heard the twig-man mutter. "Light the fire with it next time."

Once again she awoke to the sound of the Bowman, this time coughing.

The Bowman coughed in great wrenching spasms that made his four friends wince each time the rattle shook the big man's body. The Bowman sat upright in a huge log chair near the fire, shivering with such force that the joints of the furniture shook. Despite the fact that it was mid-morning (of which day Luccia wasn't sure), the windows were shuttered and the twins tended the fire, stoking it until the flames jumped up the chimney.

The storm he had saved her from had climbed inside his lungs. The twins and the twig-man named Guiseppe wrapped the Bowman in a blanket that had been heated in the coals and they poured him onto the bed next to Luccia, as life-like as a winter's grain supply.

Luccia could have gotten up and mixed salves to burn heat into his lungs, but she was done with medicine. Done with books and grand plans, or a struggle against the onslaught. If he died beside her, she would be jealous.

The cough subsided but the Bowman woke in the night, bellowing his rage at war, drowning himself and Luccia in sweat, moaning and calling the names of compatriots. The heat of his body took her to the pyre side and she shrieked in her sleep until they tossed together, sobbing and reeking. Waking again in the night, they made no apologies but whispered to each other. Cruelty, butchery, insanity, injustice — they had both seen them first-hand. There was no horror she described that he couldn't match. There was no squeamishness on her part to hear his tale. They translated snippets of terror from dreams, recounted tragedies that were all the more horrible because they were a tiny piece of what they had lived through — disjointed, grizzled visions of hers from the Plague, from the pyre, from the cats hanging in trees, and told by him, of men running toward him with bayonets covered with the gore of a good friend, headless bodies twitching as he stepped over them to kill another, the moment when the archers all let loose their arrows to whistle through the air, the eerie silence just before the thud of them into flesh and the screaming battle cries began.

As the night went on, followed by other nights, they mopped each other's backs and cradled each other's heads, held each other up. He offered her a willingness to let her into his weakness, to share a place where both of them were helpless against the visions.

He looked down the length of her body. "And what is this?" he asked, laying his hand flat on the vial still hidden between her breasts. His palm was wide enough to graze her nipples without moving.

"A potion from my mother."

"Are you a witch, or a magician?"

"I am the daughter of a great doctor, one of the Salernitas of Italy." But that life is over, she wanted to shout. There's no medicine that can save the damned.

The Bowman reached his hands inside her blouse and Luccia shuddered, but he pulled out the vial, tiny in the palm of his hand, and he kissed it, laid it gently into her cleavage again. Then he cupped Luccia's angular face in his enormous hands, pulled her towards him, and kissed her.

Could there be, especially in this world, she wondered, a place for a woman who has seen the worst of people, witnessed things done to bodies that made her wish she didn't have one? Are there arms strong enough, a body big enough or a heart open enough for a woman like that?

The Bowman held her while she sobbed, while she drank in the smell of his skin, while she nestled under him like a newborn opossum. She had wanted to die and he had sheltered her, and now when he pulled her into his arms, rolled her onto the sheets and crouched above her on his knees, the Bowman offered her another kind of shelter. She wanted to believe that a thousand arrows couldn't pierce him, a hundred storms couldn't move him. The shelter of his body felt like a home she hadn't known.

The Bowman loved Luccia with ferocious and tender attention. He loved her like an endless meal. And in return, Luccia loved him with surrender. Like death only better — falling into a well, happy for the descent. New skin, no time, drinking from an ocean of wine, the elimination of her body through the body's delight. Safety, she thought, more sacred than affection, scarcer by far than desire.

In the morning, Luccia sat in front of the fire struggling to write a halting note to Simone, breaking down then starting again, to tell her of the death of Fiona and Poulain, and after entrusting it to the twig-man Guiseppe who would take it to the village to be carried south, she rolled herself in a blanket as had been done to her the first evening there, and the Bowman held her.

Near dawn, and the months of dawns that followed, the Bowman moved his big fingers along the sharp edges of her cheekbones and chin, holding her face as if she were something precious. Surprising, she thought, for a woman who has traveled in a thousand disguises and none of them pretty. For a woman who has learned to hide from the body, to cover it and fear it and refuse to see it. He startled her with the peace and quietude of trust, and the willingness that grew from it. The abandonment of artifice, of distrust or disguise, of guile and wit, the Bowman loved her in spite of her fear. What did she know of love that grows out of gratitude? What did she know of love that grows from shared pain?

Still, she clung to the wasteland of grief, frozen in it, unable to act, with every mourning dove's song cutting her to the quick. She lay in the Bowman's bed, immobilized until one morning she heard horses outside the door, and the grumbling voice of Marcelle.

Helene, the oldest daughter of Simone, flanked by Marcelle and Jean, brightened at the sight of Luccia, and Jean, ten years old, jumped off the horse like a sprite and flung himself on her. His little arms slid down her shoulders and he started to cry. Marcelle, oddly disheveled in the first dress Luccia had seen her wear, descended and pulled him to her skirt, then encircled Luccia with rough affection. Helene joined them, then lead Jean away to tend the horses, and sit on her lap to cry for his mother.

Marcelle and Luccia crouched in the bushes beside the cottage and Luccia shook as she told Marcelle of the horror of Metz, of Fiona and the arrow, of her maleness and how it had spared her. How did she come to be here? Marcelle asked and Luccia told her of the storm, the Bowman, but not of her desire to die, not of her weakness, and her cowardice.

"Did you come to fetch me?" Luccia asked and at first Marcelle made half-hearted gestures, but then ran her hand over her road-dusty hair.

"To join you, actually," Marcelle said, oddly vulnerable over making a commitment to her former enemy. "I don't tend animals," she growled and Luccia nearly managed a smile at the thought of Simone bossing the ferocious Marcelle. "She had me brushing lambs, bringing them little drinks of water, digging the shit out of their wool! And Helene and her mother — two cats trapped in a box. The screeching alone would drive you mad. Jean is here because now he goes everywhere with me."

Marcelle had brought a bundle of Luccia's clothing and she regarded them as the costume of another woman. Taking the package, she put her arm around Marcelle and felt something of her old life pour back into her, and Marcelle fill the void that surrounded her.

She introduced the entourage to the archers: the twins bowed low but then picked up their weapons and headed toward the forest.

Malo shuddered behind Luccia's skirts but then fluttered about bringing beakers of water and loaves of bread for her friends. Guiseppe, on the other hand, sat on a log several yards away and regarded Luccia askance, chewing on a willow twig. He simply nodded when Luccia brought the clan over to meet him and they withdrew noiselessly.

The four of them bathed in a nearby creek with none of the frivolity of their past years and as the evening descended they held a wake for their dear ones, slowly chewing Malo's bread and bits of dried meat Marcelle had brought from the south. Marcelle, Jean and Helene set up an encampment across from the cottage.

Watching Luccia retreat into the Bowman's hut, Marcelle glared at Luccia. Luccia caught the glance but continued. Love of a woman, love of a man, Luccia had abandoned all of it, and now had found shelter. Marcelle hadn't seen what Luccia had seen, she hadn't trudged with children clinging to her with nowhere to go. Luccia had lain down in a ditch filled with sorrow and woke up a different woman, a woman who owed her life to someone else. Marcelle didn't know.

In the morning, Guiseppe announced that he would offer himself as part of the Duke's hunting team to supply meat to the castle, and Marcelle leapt up from her side of the encampment as if given a reason to live again.

"Women can't hunt for the Duke," Guiseppe said scornfully and mounted his horse, shifting a twig to the other side of his mouth. Marcelle drew the dagger from her waist and sliced off the plait that hung down her back. She walked to the middle of the encampment and, in broad daylight and full view, pulled off her dress and yanked on the leather trousers and tunic that she wore every day that she wasn't in the public eye. Guiseppe snorted, impressed, and waited for her while she saddled her horse and pulled up alongside him.

"Fetching," he said with a little sneer, putting his palm on her cheek, which she batted away with enough force to impress him again. They rode away with a wave to Jean, and Luccia was relieved when they returned that night, signed on with the Duke's staff, which would bring them money and give Marcelle a chance to be back among the wild things.

Helene busied herself between the two encampments, gleaming with youth, her skin rosy and clear, her hair shining. The twins turned away whenever they met her eyes, and kept their distance when she worked.

The Bowman decided that it was time for a feast. Guests demand a celebration, he bellowed, bowing to Helene. He and the twins hauled the table outside, and he sent the two-some off to find their friends. Luccia watched him carting logs for benches, heard him break into snatches of songs. He had the strength of four Simones and the joy of Jacqueline. When he laughed and stomped his enormous foot, the hut trembled as if chuckling with him, all things around him riding on the wave of his mirth. Luccia ran up to him and flung herself in his arms to absorb the warmth of it, and he gathered her up and spun her around, encircled her as he set her down and she was enveloped in the heat of his happiness. She shared his pain, she basked in his joy, and would fold herself into his vest if she could live hidden and protected.

The Bowman uncorked the spirits before noon and danced with Luccia in the dust to their own imaginary music. She stumbled around in his enormous arms as if music and joy were more foreign to her than the arms of a man. Neighbors arrived with their entire larders and Helene and Luccia chopped and cooked while the Bowman drank and sang, inviting everyone who passed to join them. Strangers on donkeys stopped, carts were abandoned before the farmer could reach market and a pig was slaughtered in the crossroads. Neighbors produced goblets and sweets and musical instruments. Marcelle and Guiseppe returned after sundown, and ate until the pork fat dripped down their chins, until the fish bones and the rabbit carcasses were piled high on a platter.

When the morning broke, the Bowman was passed out on the table, shards of pottery underneath him with Luccia on top of him, and the twins were slumped with their faces close to their plates. Guiseppe was sleeping beside the water trough spooned into the back of a young man they had never seen, and Malo, poor strange little Malo, was curled up with the stray dogs and their bones under the table.

Helene, Marcelle and Jean woke up in their encampment, tidy and disapproving.

After the smell of Helene's biscuits roused the clan, his compatriots decided to capitalize on the Bowman's hangover and challenged him to a shooting match. Guiseppe was solemn and precise about it, Marcelle ferocious and vocal, even Helene took a turn, while Malo delivered everyone's quiver and bows before realizing that he didn't have his own. He simply waddled up, shot and waddled away.

The Bowman was grandiose, noisy and expansive, despite his hangover and tired eyes. The twins chided him, tried to trip him or bump him at the last minute while he grumbled about seeing double. His first arrow overshot the mark and his friends howled with pleasure. Even severe Guiseppe managed a smile. But a man named the Bowman, twice decorated thrice shot, was capable of doing more, even with a hangover. He split the arrows of the others, his arrows shot through the straw bales and took off tree limbs on the other side. He whirled in a circle and hit the bull's eye. The Bowman shot under his legs, behind his back. He shot sitting down, and each time that his friends came up with a new way to handicap him, his arrows remained true.

The only one who could match him was Guiseppe, who made the targets smaller and smaller, the starting point further and further away. Guiseppe was cool and silent throughout the contest, chewing the end of a new twig, gleeful only with his eyes as he watched the Bowman squint. Guiseppe split the Bowman's arrows, shot behind trees, ran up behind the Bowman and shot underneath the Bowman's arms, making the big man bellow with humiliation. In distance contests their arrows flew perpendicular as if their fletches had reunited in the same bird. Finally, sweaty and flustered, the Bowman rumbled over to his cache of weapons and pulled out a metal disk pierced with five holes, stuck five arrows through the holes where they stayed as a single projectile, and shot with such force that the arrows exploded the hay-bale target, all five striking a tree next to the cottage and severing it from its trunk. It tottered for a moment, and then crashed down across the landing of the Bowman's own house. Only then did Guiseppe laugh.

Malo jumped around as if he had been struck by the tree himself, making sounds but no words. He tapped the Bowman's arms and his enormous back, as high as the half-bent man could

140

reach, bouncing up and down on his toes. Guiseppe encircled the Bowman's enormity in his long, birch-y arms. He bowed with a flourish, honoring the Bowman. The Bowman lumbered over to the spirits jug, muttering under his breath.

"Luccia," the Bowman bellowed, wiping a drop of spirits from his lips onto his sleeve. Standing her perpendicular to the target, the Bowman put his bow in her hand. When she started to drop it because of its weight, he grabbed her hand, stood behind her and they cocked the bow together. The arrow flew past the target, well off course.

"Doesn't bode well for your choice in women," Guiseppe guffawed.

But Luccia was stunned. She had never felt power emanating from her hands like that. The arrows of mercy. They sailed through the air in gracious slow motion and then hit their target with ferociousness. Luccia stepped away from the Bowman, her eyes wide.

"Teach me," she said hungrily.

The Bowman reached one hand out and grabbed her face, laughing like mountains rumbling.

Luccia tried Guiseppe's bow, she shot Malo's, her arms straining against the tension of their weapons. While the others told stories of women archers in the Hundred Year's War, Luccia shot every arrow in every quiver and then, amid their derision, collected them from the grasses far and wide. When she attempted to pick up the Bowman's weapon again, he smiled, pulled out a knife and walked into the forest. When he returned later in the morning, he had a bundle of twigs strapped to his back that he unloaded at her feet.

The Bowman measured the branches against her height and the length of her arms, selected two, and lashed them together in a rudimentary bow. He brought out an extra string, gave her a few of his worst arrows. He joined the Duke's hunting party the next morning, leaving her to spend the days shooting arrows until her fingers were raw, she had scraped her forearm bloody and whacked her breast sore while Helene watched, applauded, gathered the errant arrows.

One evening, after meticulously wiping the duck grease from his beard, Guiseppe leaned forward across the table.

"She could make arrows for the Duke," he said to the Bowman, who stabbed his hunting knife into the tabletop and grunted. "Take some into the village first and when she's good enough, carry them to the Duke. If we must have this entire clan here..." he said snidely, glaring at the Bowman for emphasis. Clearly the Bowman was harbor for Luccia but she was not the first harbor for the Bowman.

"Teach me," she said curtly, unwilling to allow the two men to decide her fate.

"Only arrows," the Bowman growled. "Not bows."

As it was the Sabbath for some, including the Duke, the Bowman began Luccia's apprenticeship in the morning.

The Bowman taught her to leave the bark on the shoots during drying, to build a rack so the air could circulate, to seal the ends so the moisture seeped out evenly through the shaft rather than splitting the ends as it fled. Luccia wondered whether the moisture could be captured, whether it had properties that could be used, and he listened to her, astounded at the question, unable to answer. She practiced straightening the arrows by pulling them through a hole cut in a deer antler, and running them down a grooved stone that had been heated in the fire. She burned her knuckles, she nicked her fingers, but she touched the shafts as if they were precious.

The following evening the Bowman brought home a turkey, and while Helene cooked, Jean tried to poke it with a stick and Malo chased him around the table, the Bowman taught Luccia to save goose feathers for winter hunting because of their oil and use turkey for fair-weather shooting. She split the base of the feathers, ground the inside edge, glued them to the shafts with spruce pitch, wrapped them with the sinew of a white-tailed deer. She was clumsy but as devoted as when she first became a scribe, when she was a girl memorizing the smell of herbs. The following day she worked without stopping until Malo returned from his foraging and she heard the hunters' horses in the crossroads.

Guiseppe, however, was not impressed. The first batch of arrows had the feathers glued at odd angles, shafts that were not of consistent size along their length, and when the men went to shoot them to test her work, they flew wild and haphazard.

"You can't mix right-wing and left-wing feathers on the same arrow," Guiseppe pronounced with disgust, and tossed the rest of her handiwork into the weeds. "I hope she serves her purpose well," he muttered to the Bowman, and proceeded to dinner. She wanted to pick up one of her arrows and pierce him, but he was right. She had brought four people into their lives and only one of them, Marcelle, was earning her way. Luccia's place in the Bowman's bed and his terrors was not contribution enough for her.

That evening as the others retired, the Bowman pulled Luccia to him and pressed her cheek against his warm chest. She pulled away and put her hands on her hips.

"Guiseppe won't tolerate extra mouths to feed in the winter," the Bowman said quietly and she stiffened over the thought of enough women passing through the Bowman's bed to make Guiseppe lay down a house rule. "He'll give you until the leaves fall but no longer."

"And you?" Luccia asked pointedly.

The Bowman shifted his weight, rubbed his beard. "Next day without work I'll teach you to cut staves from trees," he said. "The Duke won't take arrows from saplings."

Chapter Fourteen

he Bowman taught Luccia to send herself into the arrow, to run along the very edge of the creek while loading her bow and shoot with accuracy. He taught her to shoot apples that he hurled into the bushes and threw into the sky. The muscles in her shoulders and arms developed. The Bowman cut an arm-guard from a swatch of deerskin and strapped it to her arm, tried to kiss her neck but she moved away, refused any invitation.

September barreled through their crossroads, a chill wind with a warm sun, reminding them of hard times ahead. The entire clan was outside seeing the hunters off in the morning when a young priest, leading a procession of devotees, marched through their crossroads and stopped in the middle, Marcelle and Jean on one side of the road with Helene, Luccia, Guiseppe and the Bowman on the other. The procession prayed, and Luccia saw a number of the older women staring at them above their knuckles. Marcelle shielded herself behind the body of her horse and except for its anxious stomping, the clan made no sound.

The Bowman stepped forward and crossed his arms over his chest, towering over the priest. The procession moved on, but it had done its work with a two-minute prayer. Luccia carted her entire cache of drying arrow shafts into the woods behind the cabin where they could be concealed as kindling. A woman with weapons was not a sight a village priest would ignore.

Luccia paced in front of the table at the mid-day meal tearing at a piece of bread while Jean kept his distance and Helene nervously played with her hair. Now that they were living out of the privacy of the woods, close to a village, they had an untenable situation. Who is

Helene? The eldest daughter of a woman who shuttled contraband. Who is Jean? A wild child born of a madwoman. Who is Marcelle? A woman masquerading as a man because her best years were lived with a woman who had died from divided love. And who is she? A university woman recently lost, a scribe with more medical knowledge than is safe, now hawking weapons and making love to a man who pulled her out of a ditch. Even a shape-shifter would have difficulty making this clan palatable to a little northern village.

They had known the rains would force them to build a house, if they were going to stay, but now the question was, whose house? Marcelle, parading as a man, could not now live in a house with Helene without causing scandal. She couldn't live with the Bowman and Guiseppe because she was really a woman. The discovery of her gender would land the lot of them on the pyre. And poor little Jean had to have a lineage that would pass muster in a village. Luccia's presence in the Bowman's bed... well, it didn't bode well. These things weren't important in the forest or on the battlefield but none of them were feral anymore. Villagers liked orderly streets and orderly lives. They had to find a place for themselves, or leave. Guiseppe would love to have a reason to turn them out so he could go back to his men-only clan and the Bowman, Luccia thought, ripping at the bread with her teeth, could stand up to a priest with an entourage but not to his friend. Leaning on him, she presumed, would take them only so far.

"Right," Luccia said, tossing down her bread, and Helene stood, ready to face whatever challenge she laid out. "Today we trade."

They made up new identities for themselves. Helene and Luccia washed and dressed in their best, and Luccia gathered two dozen arrows so straight and exact that they would pass even the muster of Guiseppe. They wrapped them in Helene's shawl to look like a baby or a loaf of bread, and set out for the village.

"You are my goddaughter," Luccia pronounced as they paced down the path. "And Jean is... Marcelle's nephew."

"Son," Helene declared, and they clasped hands.

"Do you love him? The Bowman?" Helene whispered.

Luccia nodded, biting her lip. "Should we head south again?" she asked Helene. But where would they go? Italy held the ghost of her mother, north of Marseilles was the pain of Jacqueline and Helene's own problems with her mother, while all the points in between screamed with the Wicca who had burned.

Helene wrapped her arm in Luccia's. "There isn't room for me in the south. So, we trade. The merchant ladies of northern France."

Luccia kissed her hand, shuffled the arrows in her arm and they proceeded. There was a bird overhead, a shaft of sunlight, the babble of the creek near town, and Helene turned to her again.

"Marry him," Helene said with determination, and Luccia flinched, then laughed nervously. How could this be suggested by Helene who had been born of a furious coupling? "At least you love him."

Luccia sighed. The plumes of smoke from the village were visible now, and within minutes, the roofs of the houses. Helene threw her shoulders back, fluffed her hair and nodded curtly to Luccia. Their charade was to begin.

"First," she said, "to the church."

"The church?" Luccia said incredulously, but Helene looked at Luccia from the corner of her eye and so she followed.

Helene strode through town like a duchess, nodding and smiling to the baker and her customers who poked their heads out of the door to investigate the strangers and Luccia nearly crumbled over the smell of butter and caramel. Helene ruffled the hair of little children they passed and complimented their mothers. Luccia had taken on a hundred disguises in her life, but never one like this ladylike demeanor, this aura of privilege and entitlement. She had been skulking and invisible, hideous and impoverished but Helene charmed their way into the village. Clutching her arm as they glided down the lane, Luccia peered down side streets looking for a merchant who would take their arrows, until her eye caught the front window of a curio shop stuffed with scales and copper pans, braziers, quills and paper.

The sight of the quills and paper made her shudder. She lurched, and Helene took the opportunity to pull a scarf from her neck and cover her hair, then produce one from her pocket for Luccia and lead the way into the church. She urged Luccia to genuflect, and though Luccia stepped on her hem and nearly toppled over, she recovered and even muttered a few words she remembered from early childhood as she followed Helene into the pew.

"Did you see any place?" Helene whispered over her praying hands.

"A shop." She didn't mention her fear of the quills and paper.

Helene smiled as she had at the children in the street, then crossed herself, and lead Luccia back out into the lane.

As they stepped inside the curio shop, Luccia's nose was assaulted with the musty odor of old pelts, damp paper, pots still carrying the sweaty grease of their contents, rusted rulers and dusty bolts of cloth. Luccia turned aside and sneezed.

"*Ga zoonta*," a voice beside her said and she started, then smiled at a little man in a black coat, a yarmulke and prayer shawl, holding a feather duster.

From the back of the shop, Helene shrieked.

Both the little man and Luccia hurried through the shop, where Helene was standing beyond a curtain that separated the store from a back workshop. She stood in front of an enormous reflective plate, and on seeing it from the side doubling back a second Helene, Luccia's mouth dropped open. They had both seen mirrors in their lives, little hand-held things of polished tin, or convex rounds for decoration that made one look like a pig, but never one so large, nor as exacting.

"It's glass," the little man said with triumph. "Not really ready to be shown but since you have discovered it…"

"Glass?" Luccia said incredulously, moving a little closer to inspect it, while Helene stood transfixed over her own image. The only glass Luccia had ever seen was bubbled and thick, discolored. It took skill enough to keep glass a single color, let alone as smooth, flat and clear as this piece.

"From Italy. Smoother than any I've found," the little man said. "I'm trying to find the right amalgam of tin and mercury to coat the back. But see here," he said, bending to inspect it, "it has a flaw here at the bottom that throws off the reflection."

Helene bent down to touch the wrinkle on her skirt that was only there in the mirror. "Come here, Luccia," she said hungrily, beckoning her to stand in front of the mirror. Helene touched her own face, her hair, turned sideways in awe.

"No!" Luccia said, avoiding its revelations and scurrying back into the shop but avoiding the window because of the paper it held. She had completely forgotten the arrows cradled in her arm. Flustered, she attempted some of Helene's decorum.

"Your name, fine sir?"

"Moishe. Moishe Hornstein. What can I interest you in today?" he said, turning toward his shelves.

"I have something for you, actually," Luccia said, and laid her arrows across the counter. "Hand carved... with care and precision. Fletched at perfect angles."

"Not from a war, are they?" Moishe asked suspiciously.

"Certainly not."

"I won't take weapons with little bits of souls clinging to them," Moishe said.

"I carved them myself. These are of saplings, these are of ash."

Moishe pulled out glasses and inspected her arrows, nodding.

"Where are you from?"

Helene quickly returned to her side. "We're new to the area."

"Where are you staying?"

"Glad tidings will tell you soon enough," Helene answered brightly.

"Where are your people?" he asked Luccia, his eyes staring deep into hers.

Out of habit, she glanced around to be sure they were alone.

"Working alongside yours," she said quietly. Moishe had not expected her reply, and he walked to the other side of the shop.

"You want to trade arrows for paper?" he said, regaining his banter.

"No!" Luccia said, too quickly. "No paper."

"Perhaps next time," Helene said, slipping her arm through Luccia's. "Today, we'll settle for money."

Outside the shop with the coins in her hand, Luccia was giddy with triumph and Helene chattered about the mirror. Helene steered them down streets until they found the butcher shop and, though Luccia protested that they had no need of meat with the hunters in their party, Helene insisted, and ordered a small amount of pork and a strand of sheep gut casings.

On the walk home, she explained the casings' use.

"Put them on his what?" Luccia shrieked, and Helene howled and danced in the lane.

"Put one of them on his ... member," she said pointedly, laughing.

"Helene Tasse!"

"I learned it from the Wicca," she said. "That man's baby would kill an ox."

Luccia turned away, then slyly regarded the strand of casings Helene had jauntily tossed around her neck like a scarf. "Are you sure we have enough?" Luccia said, and they ran laughing the rest of the way back.

When the hunters returned, Helene and Luccia had a spread laid out to astound them. Four of her rejected arrows were stabbed into the tabletop, with the coins of their adventure laid out between them. The encampment was filled with the smell of fried pork and shallots, and Malo's foraged, late-season peas, a relief to Luccia after the gaminess of venison and wild bird. Helene and Luccia were cleaned up, even Jean was tidied, and Malo sat at the table in wonder.

Marcelle arrived first, jumped off her horse and strode toward the house with barely a glance at the table.

"Ready the bed, the bed!" she shouted breathlessly and they scurried around, thrown off their plan.

The Bowman arrived on his horse, leading Guiseppe's that was dragging a pallet behind it and Luccia rushed forward to find Guiseppe groaning in pain, his pants ripped, his leg bloodied and torn open, the bone protruding.

The Bowman carried him in, as drained of color as Guiseppe.

"They wanted to cut the leg off," the Bowman said.

"What happened?" Luccia gasped, moving to the bed where Guiseppe thrashed. Blood was staining the bedclothes and Luccia backed away, reaching out to the wall to steady herself.

"Boar. A pack of wild boar. It startled him and he fell off his horse, then one of them gored him before the rest of us could ride into the pack," Marcelle said.

"My God, Claude, what a break," Luccia said, turning away from the protruding bone and the blood pooling in the bed.

"I couldn't leave him with the Duke's doctors," the Bowman said, pacing through the hut. He grabbed Luccia's shoulders, and then let her go. "They kept looking at him as if they didn't want to dirty their hands."

Guiseppe moaned, rolled in the bed, hit his leg on the side and screamed. The Bowman grabbed Luccia by the forearm, and Luccia looked from his to Marcelle's expectant face.

"I'm not a doctor, Claude," she protested. "I can't…"

"Luccia," the Bowman said gravely.

"I can't, Claude!" she shrieked. She stepped away from the bed, frightened. She didn't know how to set bones. She had had to leave Salerno before being schooled in bone structure or surgery. Since Rome, Luccia knew only plants, but had given it up. She had hidden in her laboratory when the sick arrived. Now she had even walked away from medicine.

"Luccia," the Bowman cupped her head in his big hands and looked into her face. He knew what she had been through. He knew the size of his request. "You lived through the Plague!"

"But that was… known. It was…before…" when Fiona was at my side, Luccia thought. Before I gave it up.

Claude dropped to his knees and grabbed her shoulders, his eyes pleading. "It's Guiseppe," the Bowman whispered. "You have to try."

Guiseppe moaned again and they turned to him.

"Brandy!" the Bowman bellowed.

Build a house in the shadows, she thought. "No brandy," Luccia countered, stepping forward, uncertain of what she was stepping into. "It thins the blood and he needs his strength. Tie him," she ordered with a trembling voice. "He's making it worse with his thrashing. Marcelle make bandages. Send Malo for water."

Guiseppe wouldn't let Luccia near him, so it took the Bowman's strength to hold him while they tied him down. Malo scurried into the cottage squeaking and flapping and was sent out for water by a frantic Bowman.

Luccia crouched beside Guiseppe, sweating, wishing for the net mask of her Plague beak, for a subordinate position by Fiona's side. She stared blankly at the carnage of his leg, turned away. Helene crouched at her side, and opened her palm to show Luccia magic mushrooms. At least it would take his mind off the pain and whatever it was that she was going to do. Luccia nodded and Helene prepared a tea.

"Strong," Luccia said to her, "but warm, not hot. He's not going to be able to drink an entire cup." She cut back his pant leg, and stepped away. Marcelle ferociously stuffed bandages into her hands and Luccia tentatively strapped on a tourniquet. One step at a time, Luccia, she thought. The Bowman crouched behind her, shielding her with his bulk. Leaning forward, she could smell the boar on Guiseppe's skin. The bone glinted in the firelight. "Where's that tincture?" she barked.

"Coming, coming," Helene said, unnerved by Luccia's tone.

Luccia took the cup and she motioned inarticulately for a spoon.

"Hold his head," she commanded the Bowman. "Guiseppe, this is for the pain." He thrashed his head and pulled at his restraints. "Guiseppe," she said sternly, "you have to lay still."

They spooned the mixture into his mouth and he tried to spit it out. Luccia knocked him between the eyes with the spoon. "Stop it, just swallow."

They stood back and faced his accusing eyes as they waited for the mushrooms to take hold. Luccia turned away when Marcelle presented more odd cloths she had collected.

"Witch hazel will clean a wound," Luccia recited to Helene, calling up knowledge she didn't want to remember, "garlic will cut an infection and comfrey will knit tissue. A needle, a knife, gut to sew the muscles together, I think. I don't know! I'm an herbalist, not a surgeon." She didn't have any of those things, and she didn't know if they would be strong enough for a wound like this.

151

"I don't know where the Wicca are," Helene whispered desperately. They had seen no apothecary in the village, no doctor's shingle.

The Bowman was sitting dejectedly in his enormous chair, the jug of brandy on his knee. Jean hid behind the chair. Luccia strode to the Bowman.

"Take a big swallow," she directed and as he tipped it back, Luccia jerked it from his lips. "Now find me a needle and your sharpest, smallest knife. Marcelle, gut... something. I need gut thread."

"Luccia, we don't have anything here to be gutted," Marcelle protested, looking around the cottage.

"Luccia, the bleeding," Helene called, and she strode back to Guiseppe, whose blood was soaking the bed. His eyes fluttered closed, then he opened them as if he couldn't believe his eyes. Helene bit her lip but nodded. The mushrooms had taken effect, which would make it possible to tend to him, but the bleeding had to be stopped first, and the boar's essence would have to be purged before it made its way into his blood stream. Luccia set down the brandy and strode out of the cottage.

She walked into the crossroads, and held her head in her hands. Think, think! Mandrake and willow for pain; lavender, witch hazel, lady's mantle for antiseptic. Even simple little sage they didn't have. She thought of their meager attempts to build a life, as she paced toward the creek. The creek.

"Malo!" Luccia shouted. They ran to the creek and Luccia stumbled down its length until she reached a bend where the water flowed slowly. Choking the creek was sphagnum moss, capable of stemming bleeding and fighting infection. Luccia yanked it out furiously and, Malo, flapping and grunting, began to do the same. Luccia burst back into the cottage, her hands cradling the moss.

"Claude, get into bed with him and hold him tightly. Now!"

The Bowman lay down and collected his friend, who was muttering in his hallucination. Luccia poured the brandy into the wound and Guiseppe bellowed but the Bowman held him fast. She smelled for evidence of the boar, sat back, let the alcohol evaporate, smelled again, then with a nod to the Bowman, shoved a huge handful of moss into the wound, adding the putrid smell of stale water to the stench of blood. Just as Guiseppe screamed in pain there was a knock at the door. Luccia, still holding her hand in the wound, nodded her head to Helene, who ran to open it.

Helene backed into the room, followed by the little village priest.

"I've come to offer last rites," he said haughtily, but raised his eyebrows and crossed himself over the sight in front of him: two men entwined in bed, an unknown woman soaked in blood with her hand in a wound administering herbs. Guiseppe was muttering madness about animals that were flying around the room and Marcelle put her hand to her throat to shield her breasts from view.

"Woman, you are a doctor?" the priest sneered, "Do you know the punishment for witch doctors?" and Luccia glared up at him. "Have you unloosed his mind, witch? And you, Claude. Guiseppe's damnation as a pervert is well known, but you?"

The Bowman rose from the bed and the floor of the cottage shook as he barreled over to the priest and grabbed him by the throat. "What should I do, father, let him die?"

"Better than to submit to a witch's magic," the little man choked.

The Bowman lifted the priest off the floor with the hand around his throat, opened the door and threw him into the encampment. The priest hit the table where the coins jingled and, collecting himself from the dust, he shouted about the Devil, about fornication and pederasty and the madness of witches. He scrambled to his donkey before the Bowman could pace to his side and, kicking the animal ferociously, he headed back to the village.

The Bowman returned. Marcelle was facing the corner with her forehead against the wall. Luccia had changed the packing of moss in the wound and the discarded batch sat like bloody afterbirth on the floor.

"Marry me," Luccia said to the Bowman, her hand still inside Guiseppe's leg. For you, she thought, I'm up to my elbows in blood, for you.

There was another knock at the door and the Bowman flung it open with a violent force. Little Malo trundled in, his arms cradling enough moss to stop the wounds of an army, dripping river water onto the floor.

Chapter Fifteen

egarding their faces, Malo turned in circles, uttering nonsensical phrases. Marcelle grumbled and turned with protest, then leaned against the wall again. Helene railed against the priest, charging at the door and pacing back. Jean hid in a corner and Guiseppe moaned in his delirium. The Bowman alone was still, regarding Luccia in the midst of the hubbub. She turned away, leaned her head on the arm that was holding the moss pack.

Luccia was incensed by the priest's interruption, frightened over the prospect of setting a bone and sewing muscles, but she barked orders for more mushroom tea and ordered the Bowman back into bed with Guiseppe.

"I still have nothing for gut," Marcelle wailed.

The sausage casings, Luccia remembered. She ordered Helene to retrieve them, and watched them cut into long strings.

The night crawled by punctuated by a deafening scream from Guiseppe as they set his bone and moaning from all of them as Luccia tried to stitch the torn muscles, then silent weeping from Luccia that only the Bowman understood.

Claude encircled Luccia in his width to absorb her fear. She had faced the carnage for him and that was battle-worthy valor. That she would want to be his wife felt as if it reattached that ragged part of him that had struggled down the road behind him when they first met. It would mend them.

By daybreak, they left Guiseppe tied to the bed in a mushroom sleep and passed the brandy jug at the table. Jean and Malo were curled up underneath the table, asleep. Neighbors and a

154

few huntsmen, who had been here celebrating several weeks ago, had been standing watch through the night, and brought them hot tea from their breakfast fires. They patted the Bowman's shoulders in commiseration and nodded to Luccia.

As a small group gathered around him, the Bowman lifted his cup. "Next gathering will be for a wedding," he pronounced, trying to sound jovial and the crowd barked in muted celebration, and then turned to Luccia, who sat weary and dejected in her bloodstained dress.

Among the crowd who had appeared were the twins who regarded his announcement as treason and they argued with the Bowman out of Luccia's earshot until they packed their meager things and reported that they would look elsewhere for another war to fight: too many women, they muttered.

The twins were not the last to object. Marcelle, who emerged in the morning in a tightly laced doublet and her cape, her hair even shorter than before, paced in front of Luccia as if she had told Marcelle that she would cut off her arm.

"What are you doing?" she hissed into Luccia's face. "How can you do this?"

Luccia slammed her cup of tea on the table and, arousing the suspicion of the neighbors, lead Marcelle by the arm to the back of the cottage.

"What about you, Marcelle?" Luccia challenged. "This isn't the wild forest. Who's going to love you now? You make yourself a man you have to stay a man. You can't take up with another woman: who would strike such a bargain in a place like this? So what are you going to do, live without love the rest of your life?"

"I had Jacqueline's love," she shot back vehemently but Luccia could see that she had thought about the problem she had so nonchalantly made for herself by signing on with the Duke.

"The forest is the only place for you if you choose to live like this, but you can't raise Jean in a forest," Luccia continued. "He needs to learn to read and write, to be part of the world, Marcelle, not a forest creature."

"And so you become what?" Marcelle shot back, "a little village *haus-frau*? You think that will protect you?" she growled.

155

Luccia brushed at the blood on her dress. How could she explain about the difference between the hunt and the net?

"What about the herbs?" Marcelle said, seizing on Luccia's moment of weakness. "What about your precious manuscripts?"

"Don't you see it's over?" Luccia exclaimed. "They've won, Marcelle," she said, her voice shaking. "They've burned us out. They want to believe it's all from God, well fine, let them believe whatever they want. I can't... fight it anymore."

"So what's this," Marcelle sneered, waving her arms at the encampment, "a hiding place?"

Luccia charged at her and grabbed the front of Marcelle's shirt and tunic with one hand, the codpiece of her leather pants with another. "And what is this," Luccia growled, "a hiding place?"

Marcelle tossed Luccia away. With a ferocious but pained expression, Luccia turned to check on Guiseppe.

Luccia couldn't tell Marcelle what she had learned from Jacqueline about the rough hands of love. She and Claude had knit themselves a home in each other's fears. So what if it was a hiding place? Behind a rain barrel, in a disguise, in a big man's bed as his wife. Hiding was part of timing, and timing was the key to survival. If their timing had been different Fiona and Poulain would be alive. And perhaps Jacqueline as well.

The wedding two days later was an odd procession. Marcelle refused to attend. Luccia trembled in the dress she had borrowed from Helene, fearing the priest. The Bowman made Luccia wear a cross of his mother's on the outside of her dress, and it tapped against the vial between her breasts. The Bowman was relieved when he found an old monk in the church, a man he had grown up with, and who was so pleased that Claude wasn't marrying a camp follower or a whore that he greeted Luccia joyfully. There was a clumsy conversation about where Luccia had been born and the extent of her Catholic upbringing but the Bowman managed to joke and insinuate enough to get them to the altar. Jean stood by, cleaned up and shining, a smile on his little face, with Helene holding his hand.

They returned to check on Guiseppe's progress and neighbors came by with cakes and ale, relieved that the Bowman had been correct in his prediction and that this was not yet a funeral. The village priest was nowhere to be seen.

Helene and Luccia bathed Guiseppe's wound in sage water and brewed tea of wood avens against the bleeding. His pain was great enough to require more mushroom tea, and Luccia had to hit him between the eyes with the spoon so frequently to get him to take the medicine that when he finally healed and rode back to the Duke's, he had a four inch scar on his leg and a spoon-shaped bruise on his forehead. Luccia had to admit to herself that the bruise pleased her.

They built two other cottages, one for Marcelle and Jean, one for Guiseppe and Malo, and Helene moved into the Bowman's house with Luccia. Her bright spots were evenings sitting at Claude's side and the trips to see Moishe, who delighted Jean with his boisterous explanations of objects, their invention, their use and noble histories. Still, Luccia refused to develop medicine, had no interest in books, never touched quill and paper except to teach Jean to write.

One evening at the end of the following summer, Luccia devoured an entire pheasant by herself, not even stopping to wipe the meat grease off her chin. She looked up at the clan, staring at her, their hands resting beside their clean plates, because she had consumed the entire dinner without pausing between bites to even notice them.

The color drained out of Helene's face. "You're with child," she pronounced breathlessly.

A pall fell over the table. The Bowman put down his tankard, Guiseppe shook his head with sad disgust and Helene reached her hand out and touched Luccia's arm with concern.

Luccia started to protest, then remembered that she had been ravenous for days, that her sense of smell was strangely heightened. It hadn't occurred to her that she might be pregnant, and she tried to recall her last menses. Since the clock inside her body had been altered by her mother's potion, she had grown to distrust and ignore her body. It was something that could be mistaken for a man, for an old woman. She had grown more accustomed to believing in her disguises than to believing in her body.

The Bowman, occupying the entire breadth of the head of the table, stood, and paced out into the meadow that fronted his hut. Guiseppe, in his silent way, cut down a rabbit from its string by the side of the door, skinned it with an easy motion and began roasting dinner again. Malo, seated at her left, covered his eyes with his hands began to cry. His tears and his blubbering lips frightened her and she threw down a bone, wiped her hands and hurried to the Bowman's side.

He was immovable, regarding the setting sun that lit the meadow on fire, the silhouette of the tree break at the meadow's end. Luccia stood in front of him, refusing to be ignored.

"You cannot have my baby, Luccia," he said sadly.

"I can and I will," she said, not believing her own ears.

He turned to her with fury in his eye. "You cannot! Look at me." He stretched up his arms in front of her. "I'm a giant! The son of a giant cannot be born of a woman. It will kill you, do you understand? I thought you were beyond this, you told me you were too old." His eyes grew sad and Luccia turned away. She had seen women die trying to force out a big man's baby. Once past a certain point, there is no way to even starve the baby to a reasonable size: the bones alone could kill you.

"I thought I was," she stammered, "… too old."

"You will *not* have this child! Find something. Some way. Some herb," he said.

"You brought me back from death's door," Luccia said, but felt herself shrinking, "and if I walk through it this time…" But what could she tell him? How could she cling to this child so intently?

"Luccia," he whispered, grabbing her shoulders. "Please don't. Please…don't."

What could she say to him? Truly, women in love are fools, she thought. They think there is no such thing as physics. Nature. Gravity. Did she think it was an addition to her disguise, that a baby should shield her somehow? She had seen enough children crying at the feet of their dead mothers to know better. Did she think a child would turn their shared fears into joy?

She never knew because she grew very sick. She met the dawn by vomiting, watched her husband ride off to the hunt and vomited into the shrubs beside the cottage. She was too weak to make arrows, too sleepy to tend to her duties

"Listen to your body," Helene chided Luccia, crouched down and panicked beside her. "You can't do this, Luccia. It will only get worse. You have to do something before anyone can tell there's a baby in there or…"

She didn't need to tell Luccia the punishment for abortion.

When the Bowman returned in the evening, he found her weak and feverish in a chair, the smell of bile and vomit stifling in the overly heated cottage.

They lay together that night, sleepless, speechless, clinging to each other.

"Find me pennyroyal," she whispered to the Bowman in the morning. "Hide it. But bring it."

The Bowman bellowed to Guiseppe and Marcelle to go to the Duke's without him, and he set off on his horse into the village. Helene wanted to run into the forest to find the Wicca but Luccia needed her there: pennyroyal was effective but many women had died using it and Luccia couldn't spare her. Call it the insanity that comes with labor, the terror that arrives when one's body takes command of life.

She sweated into the sheets for two days, with no sign of the Bowman, or of Guiseppe and Marcelle.

Finally, on the morning of the third day, Marcelle came back disoriented, panicked, beside herself with the news that the Bowman had been caught by the little priest. The Duke was annexing land on the other side of the hill, and the peasants arrived in the village in protest over the theft of their land, and then the Bowman lumbered into town screaming for abortifacients. In his fear for her life, the stupid lummox had roared in the village, bellowing his need for the herb. Great bushels of it. The Duke and the priests took it as an opportunity and had all the protesters and the Bowman imprisoned.

Luccia never should have asked a man to fetch the herb, she moaned. What do they know about being stalked? Of being discrete — only the oppressed know discretion! Certainly not the Bowman, who charged into battle behind a cannon, seven-dozen arrows in his quiver.

At first, Marcelle related as she paced the cottage, he had put up a fight, escaped, but the Duke, charging him with treasonous support of peasants, ordered his guardsmen mounted and they had set out after him.

Claude held them off for miles, though, at first riding well, and then when they felled him, just dragging the men along as they tried to restrain him, two on each arm. Bellowing like a bull, he had called from a clearing, and Marcelle had been able to slip into the fray to catch an enormous muslin-wrapped bag and bring it to Luccia.

Helene snatched it from her. "There's enough to abort a whole flock of sheep here," she wailed, slopping hot water into a bowl and stuffing in mounds of it, burning her hands. She called to Luccia for directions, but Luccia was shaking Marcelle by the shoulders, and when they stumbled outside Marcelle pointed at the sky and Luccia could see the telltale sign of a marketplace pyre. Helene brought her the cup, and swallowing it and spitting it scalding from her lips, Luccia screamed out the Bowman's name. She pushed the others aside and whirled around the inside of the cottage for anything, any sign of what to do.

His bow hung over the mantle, enormous as a river-craft, with the disk for a mighty cache of arrows, and beside the fire, drying like little trinkets, were her arrows. Luccia grabbed them blindly, pushed aside the other women and she mounted Marcelle's horse, rode toward the village in a white heat.

The village square was catching fire, the peasants' rakes were kindling, and in the center of the maelstrom, either because of his size, the fight he had put up or his own enraged bellowing, was the Bowman, tied to the burning peg with enough rope to keep a ship moored. He was bloodied and beaten, his hands were crushed and his head half-shaven, and the flames were catching on his pants.

Luccia hid behind a cart of some sort that was to the side of him. Her trembling hands stuffed the arrows through the disk with one goal: to save him from more torture, to repay the debt of ushering Fiona out without pain.

Arrows, her precious arrows, but she couldn't pull back the bow. She strained her arms, the contractions of the pennyroyal twisting up her insides, but she had one thought. She took aim, pulled, and then a great strength entered her and the string pulled back and the arrows flew, all of them, to fell the tree of her Bowman.

The arrows severed his chest, tore his lungs from his body and his head slumped. An inhuman moan came out of Luccia's throat for the skin she had tended and now torn, for the blood that poured from him to make the flames below him hiss, for the flesh and fat that bubbled and charred on his frame, for the vindication, for Fiona, for forgiveness and mercy and the cruelty she had just committed for loving him, for her sweet Bowman, expansive and joyful now reduced to carrion in the town square.

But the arrows — the arrows continued. The disk that held them broke as it shot past the burning peg and it unleashed its arrows, one of which severed the arm of the priest watching the burning. Ripped it off at his shoulder and he turned, so surprised, before he fell.

An arrow lodged itself in the chest of a Bishop behind him. He held out his milk white, bejeweled hands, astounded that he, too, had a body, that he, too was as vulnerable as a peasant, mortal as a pig, and he fell forward as an arrow tore into the face of a priest at his side. Their lovely little vestments of velvet and lace were slopping in the mud of filth and their own blood and it was her arrows, from her shaking arms, her muscles infused with rage, her mouth filling with a taste she didn't know, eyes devouring their pain.

Not outwitting them by timid skulking, or surviving by the flight of the hunted but standing up, face front, Luccia thought, as her face twitched with the agony and accusations that a million dead women had longed to utter.

Suddenly, she wanted carnage. Damn the medicine and the nurturing and the silent little half-triumph of just living another simpering day, she wanted them torn. She wanted the Pope's miter on the rack and the Bishops screaming under thumbscrews and naked as the damned on a chair of nails. She wanted them to know what it felt like to live in relentless fear. Down to their blood streams she wanted them to shudder over an overwhelming force marching through *their* countryside destroying *their* love and *their* religion, stealing everything *they* had including a glorious pieced-together knowledge of how to birth and flourish. They wanted death, her swimming, flinching mind decided as the pennyroyal twisted her insides and the blood started running down her legs.

It was that moment — with the villagers fleeing from what they were sure would be the gates of Hell yawning to swallow them all now that a precious priest had been harmed, with the guards of the Bishop riding at break-neck speed out of town for fear of another arrow launch — at that moment, with her mind filled with the too-familiar smell of burning flesh, her own heart seared out of her body and the vision of every dead woman, every dead cat, every boil-spotted corpse flying in front of her eyes, every time she and her mother had lowered their voices as a priest had passed because there were some people who weren't allowed medicine, there were some kinds of medicine that had to be denied — that Luccia realized that she was all of those some kinds — a lover out of wedlock, an abortionist, an herbalist, a pagan, an educated woman, a testifier to injustice. At that moment she stepped forward to claim yet another damnable tag: Luccia Alimenti, assassin.

"Oh, Luccia," a deep voice behind her moaned, "now we've sealed our place in Hell."

Guiseppe tightened his arm around her waist. It had been Guiseppe who had pulled the bow with her. Her stomach turned at the carnage in front of her, and she moaned in grief, then snarled at the dead priests, unable to move from her archer's stance.

Guiseppe threw a cape over her and the bow, flung her onto Helene's horse again, mounted his own, and grabbing Luccia's reins, lead them running back out of the village.

She burst into the cottage looking for Marcelle, Helene and Jean but couldn't find them. While Guiseppe stayed mounted, turning in the crossroads as a sentry, she ran to the back and gathered arrows. Luccia heard Guiseppe calling and when she returned, Marcelle, Helene and Jean were already packed and on their horses. They had been hiding in the woods and returned when they heard the two arrive.

The clan of them sped down the road, then into the forest. They rode all day, terrified and witless, in a blind sprint to an unknown destination.

That evening, when they stopped to rest the horses and tend to Jean, Guiseppe paced a circle around them peering into the trees for signs of entrapment.

"Tell me it was you," Luccia challenged him as she stumbled forward, sweaty and delirious, blood soaking her skirt, her breathing heavy and sick from the miscarriage and the grief. "Tell me you spared Fiona."

"Alright!" he barked as he whirled around in her direction. "It was me. They kill the men's men, you know. They rape us and tie us together as faggots for the fire. I did it to spare them. Sneaked out of camp. Even Claude didn't know."

"Teach me," Luccia said.

"No," Guiseppe scoffed, turning back to the woods. "I won't teach you to become a murderer."

Surprisingly, it was Helene who stood up. "Murder for the crown you're a soldier," she said, pulling her shawl around her. "Murder for the church you're a saint. Murder for the rest of us, you are what?"

"Condemned to be hunted like a mad dog!" Guiseppe shouted.

Marcelle stood beside Helene. "And what are we now?"

"Hungry," Jean said, taking Marcelle's hand.

Guiseppe fell to one knee and covered his face with his hand, shaking his head and muttering the Bowman's name.

Helene pushed up the sleeves of her dress. "We eat, we honor the Bowman," she said, crying, looking at Luccia sick and unsteady on her feet, her face twisted with sadness. "Then we agree on a plan."

She took Jean's hand and they unwrapped provisions while Marcelle started a fire. Guiseppe tended to the horses but laid his forehead against a flank and stood frozen in grief. Luccia rolled herself in a blanket with a cloth between her legs to catch the blood.

They honored the Bowman by tearing little pieces of their clothing and, sending their prayers and praises into them, threw the scraps into the fire. But they waited until Jean was asleep to begin their plotting. Helene had brewed Luccia tea and she sat cross-legged in front of the fire, letting the blood and the tears flow from her. Despite her grief, though, Luccia's mind was latched onto the expression of the Bishop as he had tumbled over like a deposed statue.

"I'm through with running," Luccia snarled with a steely coldness in her voice, her eyes burning wildly and her face contorted like a battered tree trunk.

Marcelle thrust out her hand to make a pact and Luccia placed hers on top. Guiseppe considered for a moment and then slapped his on as well. Helene added her hand, too quickly, Luccia thought.

"No," Luccia said, withdrawing her hand. "Helene, you should go home. You've haven't done anything."

"What protection is that?" she stood in defiance. "They know I lived with you. I stood up at your wedding. They know who I am."

Luccia sighed. Guiseppe had already killed, as had she, and Marcelle was a hunter in danger for dressing like a man. She shook her head.

"No," Helene retorted, "don't dismiss me like a child. You don't know what I've been doing since you left my mother's place. I know more about the Wicca across the length of France than anyone other than my sister. I know more than my mother. I cannot be caught, Luccia. And you know," she said, pointing at Luccia with a angry finger, "that I'm not the compliant type. What they've done to Fiona, to Poulain... I could sit all night at this fire," her voice broke but her fists were clenched and her jaw was set, "and make a list of friends I've lost. That's why I came north with Marcelle. I barely got out alive the last time."

"Someone has to stop them," Luccia hissed, pointing at Helene as more evidence of their crimes. "Running just leaves them to kill someone else."

"Stop them?" Guiseppe asked incredulously. "What are you suggesting, a war against the church?" and Luccia thrust her hand out again. This time Marcelle and Helene quickly slapped theirs on hers. The grief and the rage coursed through them, binding them together.

Regardless of Guiseppe's decision, Luccia knew that this would be her course of action. Walking away from the struggle hadn't helped. Giving up medicine and manuscripts hadn't given her a life with love, a child, a home. She had thrown her life into a ditch and even suicide had abandoned her. So what did it matter if she took a few other murderers to Hell with her this time? What could they possibly do to her that they wouldn't have done for her being a complacent, timid little woman with a sprig of tansy in her pocket? Subterfuge would serve her well but this time, her disguises would hide not a book but a blade, not a tincture, but a poison. It was time that bridge was crossed. Luccia thought of the Bishop looking at the arrow in his chest.

"They won't be hard to track," Marcelle said.

"They have armies of their own, do you know this?" Guiseppe said furiously, pacing in front of the fire. "Every Bishop has his own armed entourage."

"Then you'll have to teach us to fight, army style," Marcelle said.

"You're not soldiers!" Guiseppe wailed.

Marcelle challenged him. "I'm as good a shot as you."

"You are, Marcelle, but Luccia can't shoot accurately. You can't just injure them, Luccia, and let them describe us to the Bishops. You have to kill them."

Luccia struggled to stand. "Then I'll tip my arrows with poison."

The others regarded her with startled silence.

Guiseppe hung his head. "God have mercy on us," he muttered then stood, thrust out his hand and joined them.

Guiseppe taught them the art of the ambush, to strike from a flank, circle and strike again to give the impression of a larger group. He taught them to wait until the enemy was vulnerable before striking, to take positions around an encampment and to shoot together at the sound of his owl's hoot. They practiced on stags. They plotted out strategies in the dirt around their campfire; they ambushed trees that he had marked with little bits of cloth. In a way, it comforted him to watch the women intent upon their task. He knew how to grieve for a fallen comrade but he had loved the Bowman, and these women were out to avenge his death. Their ferociousness was unlike a mercenary's. It was single-minded and untainted. It restored an honor to his profession, gave him camaraderie in his formerly secret campaign.

But he had known fighting within a great army that pitched tents in the open and plodded face-front across a country, so in return, Luccia taught him stealth, disguise, to live in a cave with bushes drawn across the front, to gather food, to silently stalk in a world listening for a twig snap. She taught him subterfuge and he taught them warfare.

Helene worried about Jean, though. The rest of them had willingly surrendered their lives to the slaughter. But Jean hadn't had time to formulate enough of himself before Luccia had whisked him away into this new life and he was too pleased with it, too easy in it. He began devising costumes and masks for himself, inventing a personae of the killer for himself. She insisted that he hide in caves with the food while they trained, telling him that he needed to guard the arrows so they could swoop in and gather up the supply for the next campaign. They spoke of Jean over the fire when he was asleep and agreed that he shouldn't be there, but they had no idea of where to send him unless Helene took him back to Simone. One night a solution presented itself.

A brilliant moon in a cloudless ski lit the tops of the trees. They had moved into hilly, wooded country and with the moon that bright, Luccia and the others were nervous and on edge. Guiseppe was standing watch and just as Helene was pouring broth into the cups, he cursed and drew an arrow. Luccia and Marcelle jumped to his side.

"What is that?" he whispered, pointing to the road below them. Silver light radiated from below as if a piece of a lake were traveling down the road. Marcelle squinted, then readied her bow. Luccia put her arms out to stop them.

"Moishe!" she said, careening down the hill toward the road.

As Luccia neared the lane, she crouched in the bushes and called to him, ran further and called again until he pulled his donkey up and peered into the night.

"Moishe," Luccia said stepping into the lane. "Moishe Hornstein is your mirror still not ready?"

He looked furtively around and beckoned Luccia to sit beside him. "My God, Luccia," he said, regarding her feral look. "At least you're not dead. And the lovely one?"

"Helene is safe, thank you. But you, you've left?"

"A Jew knows, my dear, that when they kill the peasants and the Duke's biggest huntsmen it won't be long before they come for him. I'm very sorry about Claude."

Luccia hung her head and clenched her fists.

"Besides," he said, slapping her leg, "I'm off to Paris where they appreciate scientific achievements. Come, look." He jumped down and beckoned Luccia to follow him. He flung open the doors of his little caravan. Amid the blankets, the black clothing and a little stove were the scales and rulers, the ink pots and braziers that she had seen in his shop.

"It's in here somewhere," he said, one foot on the running board, ready to hunt for his latest find.

Luccia backed away, disinterested. What was the point in new inventions? They couldn't restore lives or sanity. Why uncover more for the church to bury? She was growing a new skin and not certain what kind of animal it would make her.

"Luccia," Moishe said forlornly, holding out his hand to the bedraggled and wild-eyed version of his friend.

Guiseppe and Marcelle stepped out of the bushes, weapons ready.

"Jean needs a different life, Moishe. Take him with you. Take him to Paris. This is… no life for him," Luccia said.

"This seems to be no life for you, either," he said quietly. Luccia set her jaw and turned to confer with the others.

She argued that Jean could learn to read and write with Moishe, that the old trader would be kind to him. Jean could start again in Paris, where no one would know him, and grow up to be a gentleman.

"A Jew?" Guiseppe grumbled. "You can't send him off with a Jew."

"We're as good as dead," she whispered to them. "What right do we have to raise a child?"

So they sent Jean off, telling him he had an important job: to go to Paris, learn to read and write. Marcelle cried for the first time since Jacqueline's death. Jean clung and protested, but then took on his duties like a good little soldier, and believed them when they said they would join him in Paris. With the four of them crying in the dangerous moonlight, Luccia scrambled back up the hill, then plummeted down again and pressed the Bowman's weapon into Jean's hands.

With the little boy gone, they threw themselves into their revenge with no buffer between them and madness.

Luccia taught them to track the burning courts through the countryside as Fiona had taught her, only this time they didn't skirt them, they drew near. They sewed their dresses into pants and wrapped deer hide thongs around their legs. They painted their faces with marigold yellow and blue paste, different patterns for each excursion so they couldn't be identified. Helene and Luccia cut their hair and, in a frenzy, Marcelle shaved her head. They needed enough hair to make a wig so that Guiseppe could pass as a woman servant in the abbeys.

When they found a burning court and Luccia had killed her second cleric, not in the heat of her rage, not an accident in the mercy killing of her love, but cold-blooded and deliberate, she heard his blood pour onto the dirt of the forest as a howling wind.

Luccia focused on making poison for her arrow tips — the root of wolfbane pounded on a rock, put in a small cloth and squeezed for its juice. Obsessed, Luccia bent over her task, putting the juice in a dish in the sun, then at night keeping it under cover, so no water or dew could touch it. Sometimes she'd get up in the night, everyone stirring when she did, and putter with it, checking the moon, moving it closer to a tree, setting it on a rock, in the morning moving it in and out of the heat of the sun, then near the fire, until it was glutinous and formed like thickened wax. Everyone stayed distant when she handled it, making sure she kept the bowls separate from the food stores. Luccia spooned the wax in a tightly closed box, and hid that box inside the dark wooden box festooned with studs that Fiona had given her to carry to Plague remedy.

Luccia smeared it on the tips of her arrows with a sloppier hand than she should, nearly letting it lay on her skin in her wild nervousness, jerking and twitching with the rage that tore her.

Guiseppe watched the progress of her madness, calculating. He'd watched men unravel and he'd even seen entire troupes follow them into battle as if their insanity would be some kind of buffer or a talisman. But he and these women were a small band, and a woman gone mad could jeopardize them.

Even on nights when the others huddled in the shadows, sickened with their task, Luccia prepared for the next slaughter. She didn't want to just kill the head cleric; she wanted to murder them all. Every time they found a court, she tried to increase the number she killed. The next time she butchered one of them while still on his horse, the time after that, she rode past them screaming, and when she shot them they fell into their own fires. Luccia learned to use a knife and which artery to slice, her fear of the body colliding with her rage and she screamed when she cut an Inquisitor with a shrillness she didn't know. Luccia opened a priest up like a melon and left him for the crows, only regretting that he didn't die in a more humiliating way, in the town square, screaming for mercy. The others hung their heads with remorse, while Luccia plotted a new way to kill. She had no soul left. No heart. She could have sat in the sleet and felt at home.

It's not actually difficult to kill a Bishop, Luccia decided. They're slow moving and gullible. They ride in ostentatious convoys that can be spotted miles away. Bishops are easy to stalk, and as Luccia had taught her clan to be shape-shifters, they followed them like smoke through the alleys. They were women in men in women depending on the cloak and the breeze in from the sea.

In the evenings, she paced around the fire circle, grunting, shaking her hands and swatting at bugs that didn't actually fly behind her head, making sudden exclamations and moans while the others warily glanced at her as if she had grown fangs. Luccia's eyes lit up when her arrow found its mark, the corner of her mouth curled up when the blood spurted onto the ground, when the pasty faces of the priests were sprayed with blood. She had seen the body as a target before and it was again. It bubbled and charred, it stank and oozed, and now it bled for her. Pustules or wounds, what did it matter? Gruesome demise, that was the body's lot, and she would exact it, she would inflict it, not hide but run screaming, face twisted like a stone gone mad, into the core of butchery. The arrow was too merciful, too neat so she seized a sword from the body of a guard she had killed. She slit them open, hacked off their arms, she sliced their heads at the tonsure, she reduced them to pulp on the roadway.

The blood caked on her skin, the paint on her face and she paced the encampment swinging the sword, fighting an invisible enemy. She checked her bow, fashioned more arrows with jerky, slicing motions, breaking them and flinging them in rage, beginning again, almost never sleeping.

The others derived only small comfort in the revenge. Helene wept behind trees when the sun started to set. Marcelle threw her dagger into the loam by the fire pit in a repetitive game played close to her feet. Both of them were lost in the evening flames, reliving the fall of a cleric, the part of a body that an arrow pinned to a wagon full of women. They replayed the moment of their own first kill, or the killing just past, the instant when the skin was pierced and they crossed again into criminality. They felt the heat of whichever fire it was in their life that made the screams of their loved ones garble with the murmurs of their lives and the whispered warning signs of a impending snare. Only Guiseppe knew how to return home from a battle without falling apart.

The days wove themselves into a macabre pattern as they traveled northern France, comrades barreling up the roads then cutting into the back woods when the courts looked for peasant women to steal.

One night, Helene threw down her dish and put her hands on her hips. They should just rescue the women, not wait until the burning was done and butcher the priests on the road, but to ride ahead and seize the entourage, freeing the women. The others took on the idea as a solution that was long overdue.

"But we kill the court, afterwards," Luccia growled and the others turned back to the fire without speaking.

In backwoods rescues of two or three in a village, or a single woman who had been plucked from a wooded well, they saved them. They veered into little towns dressed as nightmares and whisked women out of dark alleys as they were being lead to the pyre. Dressed in black, they joined the processions, then threw blankets over the women's heads to dive into creeks and run through the forest with them. They sneaked into villages at night and broke the locks on public cages, tore apart dunking stools, left butchered bits of pigs in the stocks where women had been kept. Luccia and her clan chopped down a hundred burning posts in the countryside. They crept into campsites, drugged the priests and spirited the women away. They tied up all the priests and attendants, blindfolded them, then stole the carts filled with women and drove them miles from their homes. The women embraced, they prayed, but frightened by the look of their rescuers, stumbled away.

Helene was straight-backed and triumphant over their new rescues and Luccia didn't notice that Helene killed fewer and fewer clerics. Marcelle looked the women over as they fled, yet maintained her hunter's eye on the task.

Sometimes Helene would attend to those who had been injured in the dungeons. Often they only had time to give everyone water before the rescuers had to flee again into the forest, pivoting in their saddles to see the women diving into bushes and caves.

On one foray, the women huddled together in the middle of a meadow, whimpering and dazed.

Marcelle, whose face was painted in wild colors and her weaponry strapped to her arms, tore at her clothing as her horse paced under her.

"Why don't they run?" she growled. "They are sheep! Why are we saving people who can't save themselves? Go," she shouted at them. The women stayed clumped together. "Flee into the forest, for the love of Mary!"

"What is your first name?" Luccia barked.

"Gretchen," a woman whimpered.

"You don't have to shout at them," Helene said, dismounting. The women stumbled backwards at her approach. "It's alright. We're not here to hurt you. You're free now."

The women stood.

"Think!" Luccia shouted. "Think of who you can be!"

Still they didn't move.

"My God, even a rabbit would run under a bush," Marcelle growled to Guiseppe, who pulled his horse alongside hers. Luccia turned to him for advice, but he waved his hand in bemused acquiescence. Helene tried again.

"You can't stay here," Helene said. "You can't go any place where anyone knows you." A few women started to cry. "You have to…start a brand new life."

"Switch first names with the woman standing beside you and invent a new last one," Luccia barked.

"But my children!" wailed a woman in the back of the throng.

"Your children are gone!" Luccia turned in exasperation, turned back. "You hurt them more than help them to go back," she growled, then heard her own mother's voice. "You have to leave here." Tears gathered in her eyes.

"You are innocent," she shouted, holding out her hands to them. "You have done nothing wrong." She wished she had the power to absolve them, absolving her own mother. "Nothing!" Luccia dismounted, then clasp the first woman's face, brought it to her and kissed her on the cheek. "Go," Luccia whispered. "Into the forest."

"I'm going back to my child," a woman cried.

"No!" Helene ran to her, as the woman stumbled back toward the village. "You'll die. They'll hunt you down again, and do worse... to you. You can't tell them about us!" The woman pulled away from Helene, and ran.

Luccia was incredulous, watching the woman as if she were a wandering lamb.

What Luccia didn't expect, though, was that Guiseppe would stand tall in the stirrups, watch the woman running across the meadow, and shoot her in back.

Helene shrieked, turned to Guiseppe horrified and ran to the woman's body, fell to her knees. The other women in the entourage moaned and cried, dropped to the ground, huddled together in fear of them.

Chapter Sixteen

arcelle drew a dagger point under Guiseppe's chin, their horses dancing underneath them, but he bellowed into her face about war, and prisoners.

Luccia faced the women who pulled themselves into tiny balls. "Stand up!" she growled, and they stood. "No, no, sit, sit," she barked, and they sat obediently. They were too close to a village to stay here. They had always struck and fled.

Helene returned to her side. "Tend to them," Luccia said. "Make them switch their clothing and their identities."

Luccia paced over to Marcelle and Guiseppe, who sat looking expectantly at her. She glared at Guiseppe. "We have to burn it. We give the horses to the women to get them out of here, and we burn the priests in the wagon. Maybe the villagers will think it's the end to it and that the priests have moved on."

They dragged the priests into the wagon, and put the woman Guiseppe had slain on top. Helene, who wouldn't look at Guiseppe or speak to him, said prayers for the woman and they lit the pile ablaze. The women wept at the sight but Guiseppe and Luccia stood shoulder to shoulder, eyes open, jaws locked.

Helene broke their stupor. "I'm going with them," she said resolutely. "They have no idea what to do. I can serve them better by going."

"Where?" Marcelle asked incredulously.

"Into the forest. We'll drop off little groups of them when it seems right. Some of them can join the Wicca," she said.

Guiseppe and Luccia crouched around an unlit pile of sticks. Thunderclouds were amassing over their heads, and it was uncertain whether they would eat before they were drenched. Luccia ground her teeth with worry about Helene and her wandering flock.

Marcelle paced in front of them.

"How long are we going to continue doing this?" she said.

"As long as it takes," Luccia said, standing.

"Takes to do what?" Marcelle said angrily.

"To stop them."

"Have you ever known a time when they stopped, Luccia? Ever?" Marcelle challenged.

Instead of acknowledging her, Luccia paced behind Marcelle, looking her over, then reached from behind her to snatch her knife from its sheath. Luccia slipped it into her belt and, stung, Marcelle disappeared into the darkness, sleeping alone in the dripping bushes that night.

Guiseppe slept beside her with a skin tarp pulled over the two of them, but they glared suspiciously at each other in the morning. Guiseppe had shot a woman in the back; Luccia had disarmed a member of her own clan. Luccia's head started to spin. She gave the knife back to Marcelle, ceremoniously but without a word, as they neared an entourage of clerics on the road several days later.

The rain settled in Marcelle's lungs and robed all her fluids of their vitality. She started shrinking in sickness, and Luccia brewed her medicine with clumsy hands but Marcelle knocked the steaming bowls to the ground.

Marcelle had just been a nubile wild woman from the forest and now she was withered and sick. Increasingly, she was a liability to them, but they had nowhere to send her. She should have stayed behind and tended a pot of stew but they couldn't afford to risk having a home base. They had to keep on the road, keep hiding, as the Bishops sent more troops to look for them, more guards to protect the burning courts. It strained Marcelle to run and on more than one occasion Guiseppe had to pull her up a wall when her muscles gave out.

But they kept on their campaigns. Luccia and her clan stalked a caravan that was heading south. The entourage included a

Bishop, which meant that the fires would be big and the protection around him would be thick. This caravan was exceptionally long, with a surprising number of carts of impenetrable construction. Surrounding the carts were ornate carriages for the bishops and priests. How many women did they have captured there? How many lives were hanging in the balance, Luccia thought, very on edge.

At the front of the line, on two shiny horses with fancy tack, were two Dominican monks and a misshapen priest to whom young novices rode with plates of fruit and foodstuffs. Hiding by the side of the road so close that the wagon wheels blew dust into her face, Luccia saw the priest pick up a morsel, bite into it, spit it out grandly and knock the plate into the novice, then laugh with the sound of chickens being killed. It was Fr. Peter, and it took all the strength Luccia had not to jump from the roadside and slaughter him right that moment. For Fiona. She gritted her teeth.

The clan tracked the entourage for another two days, while Luccia was so edgy and furious that she drove them on until after dark and had to be restrained several times from attacking. The Bishop's entourage stopped at an abbey. That night around a meager fire, Luccia, Marcelle, and Guiseppe agreed that the plan had to be well developed and sophisticated and so they would investigate the abbey in the morning.

Luccia was up before the rest, pacing at the base of their bedrolls, wringing her hands, her bow across her back, quiver poised.

Guiseppe woke and put his hands behind his head, stretched as if it were a summer morning. "Are we going to storm the place? Just the three of us?" he asked sleepily.

"Get up. You saw the carts. You know the size of this one," Luccia snarled.

"I suggest we try another approach," he said.

Dressed as a woman with no visible weapons, Luccia hid in damp bushes, circled the encampment, slipped behind the gilded carriage, then became a camp servant with an empty platter that she picked up beside a dying fire and proffered whenever she reached a doorway. A guard chastised her and shuttled her down a hallway. She slipped into a room behind a curtain, went to the window to see the lay of the building. Where were they keeping the women? Where was that goat's ass Fr. Peter? Luccia had to figure out a way to move through the house without detection for at least a half hour.

Instead of moving through the abbey, though, she was immobilized by what she saw. If someone had come in behind her they could have cut her throat without a sound, without struggle. It took her several minutes of watching a monk grasp a short handle on one end of which was a leather sack, like a sporting ball. He took the ball and rolled it in ink, which made her only faintly remember that at one point she had loved a quill more than she now did her arrows. She strained to see above the window frame.

The monk rolled the ball across the tops of a plate, but it wasn't a plate. Individual letters were locked in a frame, but what astounded her then was the paper that was laid onto the frame, then off, up into the air to dry, covered with lettering. Like magic. First a blank sheet, then an entire page appeared in an instant. A page that would have taken her five hours to transcribe was onto the paper and off before it seemed to land.

She had briefly heard of this, hadn't she, she wondered, mesmerized? Something about Guttenberg, and a few towns now that mechanically made a smattering of books. Life on the road didn't bring her news very often but she had heard that they had printed the Bible. Moishe would be so pleased to see this. More paper than Luccia had seen in one place — the pile would have lasted them a year at the scribe's office in Salerno. Stacks of it. The carts must have held the paper.

On the one hand, Luccia was happy that they hadn't contained women, grateful to find an abbey without dungeons filled. Instead, it was paper with four pages on each side, black squares that instantly appeared. The scratch of two-dozen quills on paper rose into her ears, the slow dance of her childhood, the smell of the sea and lemons in her nostrils. Luccia looked around furtively, moved to another side of the window to see more stacks of paper, the creaking of pulleys as the paper moved from press to hanging line to delivery on a huge pile of such whiteness as she'd never known.

Young boys straddled benches and sewed the books together with hands that chased one another with thread. The books flew together, tiny and compact, something she could have held in one hand, not requiring two arms to hold as *Trotula* did.

So many books stacking up, a plain black cover, not the Bible, she could see that far. What book? That's when a block print on the one of the hanging pages caught her eye: three women hanging by their necks, a dog barking hurrah. The death of women. A book on the death of women? And that cackling priest in the building. What book was this? Was the professor near? Luccia had to know.

She had to get a copy of the book but a guard rattled into the room so she slipped down the corridor and outside. Pressing herself against the stone wall, she heard a heavy side door creak open. The first thing that came out the door was a copy of the book, then the arm of a monk. She heard his soft laughter as he read the pages. Luccia lunged out behind him and slit his throat with her knife, catching the book before it hit the ground. Why had she killed him for a book? But she did, and the dogs would find him in the morning. Her shirt suddenly smelled of vinegar. She dashed into the woods, flagging Guiseppe who leapt into the spot behind her like a new buck.

At the fire where Marcelle had been left, she and Guiseppe were relieved that there was no carnage ahead of them, no women to rescue, but Luccia turned the book over in her hands as if it were a hot coal. *The Hammer of Witches*, by Jakob Sprenger and Heinrich Kramer.

Reading the first few pages, it seemed like the usual lament of a husband against a nagging wife, and Luccia sat back, somewhat amused that two Dominican monks whose order was wife-less should take an interest.

But then she read Sprenger's instructions on the methods of torture of 'witch midwives.' She read, throwing log upon log onto the fire, soon with a violent arm. Torture upon torture to be brought on them in waves. She read about the rack, the red-hot pinchers tearing off women's nipples, about the collars of spikes and the raping, the ways to break a woman bone at a time to make her confess, the test of virtue from her tears, for the book told them that a witch could not cry because the devil had stolen her tears.

The pages said that all witches had sex with the Devil and that his member was cold and shaped like a goat's. Luccia saw the stacks of books, then the number of women who would be tortured as a result of each volume, saw the women stretch out from her fire in the forest, a line of near-dead women cascade over more countryside than she had ever walked.

Here was an instruction manual, the book to teach the monks to murder. Stacks of them sitting inside the abbey, and as the flames of her evening fire jumped behind her, she wondered how many more abbeys were producing these books. They had been trying to stop the burning courts one by one, Bishop by Bishop and here they produced instructions to train an army of killers faster than Luccia could ever hope to hunt them down. 'Here we must reference witch midwives, who surpass all other witches in their crimes...And the number of them is so great that, as has been found from their confessions, it is thought that there is scarcely any tiny hamlet in which at least one is not to be found,' the book pronounced. How many volumes of this, she wondered, were ready to be transported across Europe?

Marcelle and Guiseppe couldn't read, didn't understand what she was saying when she railed at the book, charging up and back across the encampment.

"'And what," Luccia read to them, nearly shouting, "of those witches who collect male organs in great numbers, as many as twenty or thirty members together, and put them in a bird's nest, where they move themselves like living members, and eat oats and corn."

Guiseppe stopped his eating and leaned forward.

"A certain man," Luccia continued, "approached a known witch to ask her to restore his member to him. She told the afflicted man to climb a tree, and that he might take which he like out of a nest. And when he tried to take a big one, the witch said: You must not take that one because it belonged to a parish priest."

Guiseppe laughed and slapped his leg.

"Burn it," she shouted. "Burn it to the ground."

"Burn the book?" Guiseppe laughed through a mouthful of food. "Does it have directions to the nest? Now *that* I would kill for!" He turned in a circle to laugh into the trees.

"Burn the entire... the entire abbey," Luccia stormed. "Burn the process. Stop them. We have to... stop them."

Marcelle looked at the book over Luccia's shoulder, recoiled at the prints.

Guiseppe tossed a piece of gristle into the bushes. "I'm not risking my life for... a book."

"It's not just a book, it's an instruction manual," Luccia said.

"I don't fight... books," he said.

Marcelle looked from Guiseppe to Luccia, as Luccia tried to explain the importance of the volume, showing him the pages, telling him of the torture. Marcelle moved away from the conversation, loathe to discover something else to hate them for. Guiseppe, however, was unmovable.

"We have to do things differently," Luccia said. "As long as the book exists there will another monk ready to take the place of those we kill. We can't kill them all."

"Now you're seeing the light," Guiseppe said. "Besides, it's nearly winter and too damn cold up here," he said tentatively. "I say we move south, back to Italy. Or to Spain."

"But this," Luccia said, shaking the book into his face, "this is where the battle lies."

"Not my battle," he said.

He turned away from the two of them, and opened his pack. "There'll be a Duke somewhere who needs a solider. A real soldier."

Luccia furiously slammed the book closed. He was leaving them now when they needed him the most.

But Guiseppe had known enemies as other men on horseback, victory through bloody combat. He had given up the prowess of an established army to vindicate his friends and to help Luccia and Marcelle. But wasn't it too much to ask him to give up combat as he knew it? As a man, he had a chance to build another life, to be part of an army with banners, food, sleeping quarters and status. Despite her anger, she couldn't fault him for it, really.

Guiseppe and Luccia turned to Marcelle. Would she continue to fight with Luccia for women, or choose to pass as a man and go with Guiseppe? Looking at Guiseppe with a furrowed brow, Marcelle put her hand solidly on Luccia's shoulder.

As he packed up his roll to go, a light snow began to fall. Both Luccia and Marcelle clung to him. Luccia felt his strength behind her on the night they had killed the Bowman and begun this madness.

Either for companionship or against the snow, Marcelle and Luccia curled into each other's arms. Now there were just the two of them, and it seemed a paltry number to Luccia, who could see the doubt in Marcelle's eyes and feel the wildness in her own.

"Alright, what's the plan?" Marcelle asked.

They knew that monks go to sleep early and Luccia and Marcelle decided that it would keep them warmer to strike at night. They gathered their bows and quivers, tore up some old cloths to make balls for the end of their arrows and soaked them in animal fat.

There was only a sliver of a moon that night, and they crept to the side of the abbey, struggled to find the print shop again, opened one of its creaking windows with the tip of an arrow, struck the flint and shot the burning arrow into a four-foot high wall of paper. Marcelle stood in awe of the amount of paper, and Luccia was surprised to see how quickly the fire jumped up the stack.

The fire overtook the room, and Luccia was pleased when the scores of pages were gobbled up as they hung vulnerable from pegs on rope through the room. The fire was bigger than any they had ever seen: abbeys have tapestries and drapes and straw for animals but they are mostly stone structures. This abbey, however, being filled with paper, went up like an inferno and the two women had to run hard to keep ahead of the flames.

Just as they cleared the last door, there was an explosion and Marcelle took Luccia's hand as they ran, neither of them knowing what they had unleashed.

Marcelle commandeered one of the abbey's lambs on the way, slit its throat and dragged it bleeding into the hills, then hauled the carcass on her back. They feasted, tearing at the meat before it was cool enough to touch. Marcelle's eyes were bright. The fire was so enormous that they could see it from any vantage point on the hill.

"Now *that* is the way to fight!" she chortled triumphantly, regarding the fire and then turning back to tear at another piece of lamb. "Look at that! We did that," she shouted, jumping around the encampment. "Luccia, I could really love this. We stopped them!"

Luccia put her arm around Marcelle and saw how bright her eyes had become. "Fire!" Marcelle said with delicious breath.

They slept better than they had since before the Bowman died.

As dawn broke, Luccia and Marcelle watched the abbey from the hill. The monks lined up the dead, shrouded, in the new snow and Luccia counted them, shivering, hoping Fr. Peter was among them. Marcelle nudged her arm, and pointed to the far side of the abbey.

"What are those?" Marcelle asked.

Luccia pointed at them but had no words. The two watched as monks brought out big lumps of metal and presented them to Sprenger, who looked at them and then heaved them into the snow. Luccia turned to Marcelle with the first sign of delight that had crept into her furious eyes.

Sprenger, Kramer and Fr. Peter were frantic, pacing across the snow. Luccia hungrily watched Sprenger kick the metal frames, hold his head in his hands. All the type had melted into blobs of metal, ending their printing operation. He was still alive, but the type had been destroyed.

Luccia staggered back from the hill's crest as if released. They had done it. She fell to her knees with exhaustion, the scent of lamb heavy in the air, the coldness scorching her lungs, and she slowly rubbed her face with snow. It was enough to stop the book. When she opened her eyes, Marcelle was chortling, and welcomed her cleaned and renewed *visage* with the offer of a lamb shank.

They watched the chaos all morning. "We should follow," Luccia ordered and Marcelle packed their few items.

Luccia rolled up her blanket and paused over the studded box containing the poison. She opened the box and dumped the cloth and pottery container into the fire pit, heaved the circle stones on top of it. They had done it.

When they arrived at the next abbey, they expected to watch a defeated Fr. Peter and his cohorts. Luccia wanted to investigate, so she strapped a bundle of twigs to her back and limped through the rooms as an old man, replacing kindling on the hearths.

Luccia heard the thud of metal against metal down the corridor and she followed the sound, keeping the bundle of twigs on her back, stooping low to shield her face. She paused at the top of stairs that spiraled down. Dungeons? She wondered if she had found the presses or the rack and thumbscrews. But she smelled ink and didn't hear moaning so she stepped tentatively down the stairs.

"Fourteen," Sprenger said, as Luccia lumbered through the door, her eyes averted. She crept to the fireplace and began taking the twigs out one at a time for fear of removing the bundle and her disguise. "Imagine that, Peter. We are the first to be mass-produced. After the Bible, of course. Presses here, in France and in Italy. Fourteen presses spreading the word, Heinrich. Our word."

"And that of the Pope, Jacob," Heinrich admonished.

"Of course, of course. We shall be on the bench of every judge, the desk of every magistrate. Like a hammer," he hissed.

"Yes, do light that fire," Heinrich commanded Luccia, who bent lower over her task. "I don't see why we have to suffer through this cold by moving down here."

"You saw the type," Jacob sneered, as the presses began clanking again.

"It was an accident, Jacob," Heinrich said, inspecting the pages that were already fluttering over their heads.

"I saw goats dancing just before it happened," he said, striding over to the fire and standing just inches from Luccia. "Several of our brothers perished."

To have a blade, Luccia thought, recalling the Bishop's visit to Simone's when Luccia was just a child.

Fr. Peter limped to his side. "Goats," he said with weighted seriousness.

Heinrich Kramer shook his head in disgust. "The insane leading the enraged," he muttered to himself.

"We kill them," Marcelle growled, when she was given a report of the conversation.

Luccia shook her head, and Marcelle was taken aback by Luccia's sudden disinterest in murder. They had to follow them to discover the 14 locations of the presses. They would burn everything in their path, but they would follow.

They rode hard, they rode in stealth but in relative safety because this trio had no army, no fortified carriages or Bishop's company.

In the middle of the night, they burned the next abbey, and watched the fire while lying on their bellies in the snow.

In the morning, instead of bodies, the monks carried flat black trays as if they were sacred objects and laid them on tarps in the snow. Jakob Sprenger, Heinrich Kramer and Fr. Peter scurried up and down the line, directing them.

Luccia scrambled across the hillcrest, alarmed, watched as the monks calmly reordered the platens.

"What are those?" Marcelle asked.

"Our demise," Luccia said forlornly, and turned away. They had burned the paper, burned down the abbey but the type must have been sequestered in stone rooms for precaution. They should leave immediately. Luccia watched a young monk saddle up and ride out, surely to get soldiers from the nearby town to hunt for them. They were on to the plan.

She watched as another caravan arrived and left the monks to suffer through their rebuilding, carrying off the trays of type, with Kramer, Sprenger and the cackling Fr. Peter.

Riding deep into the woods before cutting back to follow, Luccia tore at branches as she passed. In the world of the scribe, if the paper, the ink, the quills, the wood cut illustrations and the original manuscript were burned, it was over. Natural fibers fall in natural disasters. And the scribe himself, a scholar, an honored craftsman, was vulnerable as well. If the town scribe died, there were no books, no letters produced. But what was this? Any child who could turn a handle could suddenly produce a book. The people were interchangeable and the machinery was impervious.

When Luccia explained it to Marcelle, Marcelle still wanted to continue, to follow the type through the countryside and burn it from its new home as well.

"They take it elsewhere we burn that one as well," Marcelle said with her hand on her hip.

Luccia sighed, but agreed. She feared the lack of a plan more than a plan she knew wouldn't work, for now. Besides, Marcelle seemed more alive than Luccia had seen her since Jacqueline's death. Maybe this new plan was easier on her soul.

"Look," Marcelle said, turning Luccia back to the abbey. "They can't pray, they can't torture, they can't make books. They have to live out in the open like us, Luccia. They finally have to face the flames."

Luccia was even less convinced as the days went on. They managed to reduce the operation to lumps of metal when it stopped at a wooden abbey, but when they caught up with the entourage they were busy at work melting, pouring, reassembling and then back in production faster than she would have imagined.

She watched *The Hammer of Witches* appear over the landscape like mushrooms, in every church, in the saddlebag of every ragged priest they saw on the country roads. They didn't burn one abbey, they burned five, then the wagons with the paper as well.

But Luccia knew it was fruitless. Where were women being kidnapped, Luccia wondered. In what country town were the courts working? Shouldn't she be there, instead? She struggled with her desire to destroy the presses and the itch to find the location of the courts that were putting the book into effect. They tracked Sprenger, Kramer and Fr. Peter, and Luccia kept an eye out for the professor. She would hunt Fr. Peter off the edge of the earth for a chance to kill him, she thought, clenching her fists. More than any of them, he was the one whose entrails should be on the road. But stopping the book was now just as important. Which would make it stop, the trio's demise, or the destruction of the machinery? Both of them seemed impervious.

Marcelle, on the other hand, was driven to burn, with a new spring in her step and a hunter's glint in her eye. Her health returned and she ate ravenously every night, gnawing legs of rabbit and downing pots of cleansing tea. Marcelle was enlivened while Luccia flagged. Either Marcelle ignored the fact that the type frames were not being affected by their campaign, or she didn't understand their importance, Luccia thought. Marcelle was ebullient, ferocious, up before Luccia in the morning and ready to move on. Watching the abbey fires from afar, she was giddy.

By the depths of the winter they had to frequently seek shelter in caves with the Wicca because of unusually deep snow and they were given seats of honor at the campfire. Women told stories of bands of midwives who, hearing of the fires, were able to march west with renewed vigor, who had the strength to pack up their children and leave before the burning courts rolled through their village.

Marcelle reveled in the attention, brandishing a mug of ale and embellishing on the stories while Luccia sat at the edge of the encampment feeling like a traitor, unwilling to tell the women of the futility of the effort. They needed good news. They fed on it. But Luccia could barely eat. She sat despondently staring at the fire.

One evening of the following spring, a member of the Wicca dug into her bag and produced a book. Luccia shuddered that the Wicca would see the extent of what lay ahead of them. When she took it in her hand, though, she saw that it wasn't *The Hammer*. The book was written by Ulrich Molitor, called *The Archer Witch*.

The archer witch shot with enchanted arrows, read a young woman who took the book from Luccia. They bewitched the weapons of the church. The Wicca applauded. The archer witch burned cities to the ground, the woman recited, and, Marcelle stood up and raised her arms to the sky. She peered at the woodcuts of abbeys on fire and Marcelle and Luccia on the outskirts of town with their bows.

"Didn't know I looked so good in a dress," Marcelle joked triumphantly and the women at the fire circle laughed. Luccia was not amused.

"Let me join you," a young woman with bright eyes knelt in front of Luccia.

"No," Luccia said and tossed back the remainder of her ale.

Another woman younger than the first crouched down as well. "Let me join you."

Luccia looked warily at Marcelle, who danced in place holding the book in her hands. Luccia shook her head, stood up and walked around the young volunteers, then took another seat.

An old woman on the far side of the fire picked up her broom and laid it at Luccia's feet. Another woman beside Luccia did the same, then another, until half of the encampment had circled past Luccia depositing their brooms and she had to stand to avoid being hidden by the towering stack. Luccia searched their faces for the meaning of the gesture, and then the first old woman came back, pulled the top string that held a broom together. The twig skirt of the broom fell away and inside, the staff of the broom was an arrow with a bulbous head soaked in fat, waiting to be lit and used on another abbey. Women throughout the encampment pulled the strings on all the brooms and they tumbled out in front of Luccia, enough ammunition to burn down the Vatican.

Marcelle seemed to float over from where she had been standing, keeping her arms in the air and drawing the women's gaze. Luccia didn't hear what she said to them, she was so stupefied by the sight of the brooms turned to arrows. How could Luccia give them hope by taking up their weapons when she knew the arrows couldn't stop the metal frames? There is a book impervious to fire, she wanted to shout, but she still didn't have the heart to break it to them. She hardly had words to describe it, herself.

Marcelle strode through the crowd, now holding her bow aloft, and the women cheered. They picked up arrows and shook them at the moon, flung arms around each other and raised their fists.

Luccia felt a cold hand on her arm, and turned to a woman who had just joined them. Close into her ear she was told of the death of Simone Tasse.

Chapter Seventeen

uccia saddled up in the morning and rode south while Marcelle stayed behind to continue the work. Before she left, Luccia watched her wrap Molitor's *The Archer Witch* in a shawl of Jacqueline's, and tuck it inside her bags. Luccia wished that Fiona could see the book, sit with a glass of her brandy and laugh over their descriptions—little Luccia and Marcelle terrifying the countryside.

When Luccia arrived in the village of Tasse they had built a stone obelisk honoring Simone in the middle of the crossroads outside her business, and her enormous family, colleagues and friends spread through the village like spokes. Helene was there with two thin women who looked around them suspiciously, friends whom Luccia assumed had joined her after being freed.

Helene moved through the crowd, the eldest, in command, her skirts kicking out with the same force that had propelled her mother. Isabelle and Luccia stood with their arms entwined, weepy and resigned. Simone's younger daughters who had stayed home to run the shipping business had grown to be sizeable, more bulls than women.

When Luccia returned north she was more crestfallen than before. She sought out the Wicca's encampment where she had left Marcelle, and was greeted at the edge of the forest by a young boy who stepped out from behind a tree and grabbed the reins of her horse.

"Who sends you here?" the child demanded as if he had some authority.

"Marcelle," Luccia said, surprised, her horse dancing under her.

"You know our Marcelle the Archer?" the little boy said in awe. Several other children popped out from behind trees and the little one with her reins muttered to them about Luccia's knowledge of Marcelle. They turned their faces back to her, impressed.

"There's still space to the far right of the circle," one of them commented.

Luccia dismounted and yanked the reins from the child. What was taking up so much space that she needed direction? French peasant women sat with their daughters making arrows, a cluster of Gypsy women who wore daggers like necklaces sharpened knives. Luccia walked her horse past enormous Nordic women who cautiously stood up from their lone undertakings. Luccia could see through the trees to an encampment of fairy men and a clan of warrior women in tartans, small bands of male mercenaries and now and then she thought she glimpsed the face of a woman whom she thought had tumbled out of a burning-court cart. Marcelle had assembled a battalion and Luccia, at first in awe at having company, couldn't explain the nervousness in the pit of her stomach.

She found Marcelle on the hillside, leading a bedraggled group through fighting maneuvers. Luccia could tell that they weren't tactics for a quick-strike force, for subterfuge, they were the movements of soldiers fighting as Guiseppe had, face-front and marching, in hand-to-hand combat with straw men set up in the valley.

"You've come back," Marcelle said, and clasped her around the shoulders. "How is the family?"

"Holding up, under the circumstances," Luccia said. "Helene has risen to the challenge and is the matriarch now."

Marcelle nodded without taking her eyes off the foot soldiers in front of her.

"What are you doing?" Luccia asked Marcelle.

"Preparing to win, Luccia," Marcelle said, her eyes full of fire as she pulled away.

"Marcelle," Luccia scoffed as Marcelle walked around her and shouted orders for a squadron to ride around the far side of the straw enemies. "Marcelle you can't fight them like this. You've seen the armies of the Bishops. You can't... march these people to their deaths."

"What would you suggest, Luccia, more...skulking?" Marcelle said derisively.

"Yes. Split them into small bands and send them into different areas. Or send them back where they came from, for God's sake. How did all these people get here?"

"The Wicca," Marcelle said brightly. "They sent the word out and they came, droves of them. Ever since you left. My God, Luccia," Marcelle lowered her voice, "there are people here who make us look like little lambs in a pasture."

"Lambs before the slaughter is more like it," Luccia said. "Send them in as... charwomen or... camp followers."

Marcelle strode away from Luccia in disgust. "These people are sick of hiding, Luccia," she growled when Luccia caught up with her. "They're sick of sniveling little backwoods victories. And so am I."

"Leaving like Guiseppe?" Luccia protested, "There's no man's army waiting for you, Marcelle. Subterfuge is our best weapon."

"No! No, it isn't. Don't you see what we've done?" She swept her arms in an arc around the countryside. "It was the abbey burnings, Luccia. They could see them for miles. *The Archer Witch.* It's inspired people to fight back. Troubadours are singing about us. It's given them hope," Marcelle said turning to watch her recruits.

"False hope," Luccia said. "I forbid you to do this."

Marcelle whirled around and her eyes were daggers. "You forbid... me? You're not the captain here, Luccia, I am! Maybe that's what the problem really is. You can't stand that this is my operation. Mine," she growled, pounding her finger into her chest. "Like Jacqueline was mine."

Luccia charged toward her in fury but Marcelle drew her dagger and with its point a hair's breadth from Luccia's chin she didn't move, but saw out of the corner of her eye two Gypsies and a mercenary step out of the woods. Luccia heard the steely threat of three swords pulled from their scabbards.

"Either find your own war, Luccia, or take a place in the right flank," Marcelle muttered, then replaced her dagger.

Luccia took her place in the flank, never volunteering for the front. She kept quiet and thought of ways to protect Marcelle's soldiers from being surrounded. She camped alone, ate alone, made arrows as if praying.

But she had to admit that Marcelle was spectacular, alive like she had been when she strode out of Jacqueline's house ready to hunt. In Luccia's love for the Bowman, and her mad revenge, she had hardly noticed that Marcelle had been steeping in her grief. Now that she had thrown off the sorrow that had made her follow at Luccia's heels, Marcelle had stepped back into her own life. She spent her time walking among the troops, holding the hands of grateful women, making jokes with the men. Marcelle ate off their plates and they felt honored. She saw to the food supplies, to the arrows, the strategy, the horses, the camp layout, water and plan of action. She walked among the tents late at night; she was up first in the morning as if she feared that her entourage was water that might have seeped into the ground by morning.

If Luccia had been younger, less seasoned, less bitter, she would have been inspired by Marcelle, too, with her grown-in rope of golden hair, her deerskin pants, her tunic festooned with the little bags that her followers presented to her of amulets and their children's hair. There was something magical about the way Marcelle seized power like a man, Luccia thought. You trust her because she a woman; you want to follow her because she dares to grab life by the throat. She lived in the space above her waist, where ordinary women had fled, elbows in, arms to their side, hands passive. If Marcelle didn't like it, she tore it down with her bare hands like the shed at Simone's. If she disagreed, she charged chest out. She grabbed halters, she hauled boxes, she described a life beyond the reign of the burning courts and her coterie lived off the light in her eyes, embellishing on her attributes to the newcomers who arrived every evening.

Luccia had to admit that it was refreshing to ride with an entire battalion whose heads were held high. It helped with the loneliness of life without the Bowman, or Guiseppe and Helene. Marcelle taught them what Guiseppe had taught her, and several of the mercenaries took Marcelle aside in the evenings and taught her what they knew as well. But every plan was blind to the size of the

Bishops' armies, and to the very real possibility that if several Bishops joined forces, they could be outnumbered twenty to one.

Besides, Luccia knew that every day they spent practicing was another day that a mountain of paper was turned into witch-burning manuals. Another day that she was unable to create a way to destroy the metal type frames.

But Marcelle made the plans of a hero, and who is a hero but someone who inspires people to take up their own lost cause with pride, who rides face front to take an arrow rather than skulk in shame and success?

In their first campaigns they were magnificent, swooping down from hillsides and routing the Bishop's army in ferocious hand-to-hand combat that thrilled Luccia. It felt vicious but sane and honorable. Afterward, watching Marcelle in the encampment, striding triumphantly and rousing shouts from her army, then bringing them to solemn respect of the one mercenary they had lost, Luccia wondered if Guiseppe would have been pleased.

Their following campaigns freed enough women and involved enough back woods maneuvering to convince Luccia that this plan of Marcelle's might actually work. She tended to the arrow makers with a new urgency and hope, and took time in the evenings to be soothed by the scent of pine and cooking fires.

But their enthusiasm overtook them. On a moonless night Luccia sat on her horse waiting for the order to charge and she could have sworn that she saw the glint of Moishe's mirror. The troops were enough of a force to encircle a burning court as it made its way through a valley. Hundreds of Marcelle's warriors on horseback, imperceptible in the darkness, lit their arrows one after another in an ominous circle around the ring of the hill. The wagons stopped, the priests dismounted and looked in slack-jawed disbelief. First the priests' staff fled and Marcelle's army held their position. Then the monks fled down the path to the next town and Marcelle still held her ground. She had only to dispatch a quartet of riders to open the cages and assemble the women in the meadow. Luccia thought she heard the creak of Moishe's caravan but none of the wagons had moved, and that's when it dawned on her that if there was someone who would know about a new invention like the type frames, it would be Moishe. Paris, she thought, as she held the burning arrow tight in her bow.

A Bishop and a priest tried to march back and address them, as if they couldn't bear to give up a chance to speak to an assembled crowd, but Marcelle's troops were a precision corps, and she only had to whistle twice for them to turn the burning arrows, with an *whosh,* toward the Bishop. Wisely, he turned on his heel and tottered off.

Unwisely, Marcelle let him go, ordered the arrows extinguished in the dirt at their feet and then they whooped in celebration. She lead the entire battalion into the meadow in triumph.

"No!" Luccia shouted to those around her. "Hold your positions!"

But it was like a grand party, and Luccia, furious and shocked, rode the line of the hillside to protect the flank.

"Check the forest," she shouted. Her horse jumped underneath her as she called to others, rode into their path to stop them, but they waved her down into the meadow.

The thrill of victory must be intoxicating, because the mercenaries knew better than to set an enemy free and then congregate in the very place where they had been vanquished. Marcelle knew better. When the Bishop's soldiers marched back and let arrows fly into the crowd, Marcelle kept on shouting encouragement, brandishing a sword and egging her soldiers on before taking an arrow in her chest and falling.

When the Bishop's army marched into the valley Luccia could only imagine what they did, or how long Marcelle's dream of victory held her troops up. Luccia was not a hero, as Marcelle had pointed out, and she fled into the forest, down the hills, turning frantically to see if anyone was either joining her or in pursuit. Perhaps some had fled in the other direction. Perhaps some had survived and run into the woods. She rode back and forth trying to find them, to protect them or join them.

Luccia sat on her horse as it stood motionless in the forest all night, her shoulders sagging, her head bent, pounding on the saddle, her forehead, weeping into her hands. Marcelle dead, Jacqueline, sweet Fiona. Luccia was flooded with remorse. Fiona would have been ashamed of her butchery, but the Bowman would have understood. Men know about revenue, about giving up a piece of their soul to exact justice. And he would forgive her for not dying with the rest.

She jolted awake in the morning by falling off her horse and she lay in the duff, unwilling to move. Alive again. She felt her mother's vial cold against her skin. She hated the body, had willed it to die, and yet she sat here strong and younger than her years, having set bones for love and slit bellies in retribution. Fiona was the strongest woman she had met but her body belied her. Luccia's mother was brilliant but refused to see danger. The Bowman knew danger but only the kind presented to men. Jacqueline believed in the power of love but died because of its weakness. Marcelle took up a noble cause but was slain by her hunger for ignoble glory. What in the name of the sun and the stars did she know that was keeping her alive?

Luccia rolled face down in the leaves. Oak, poplar, loam rich in potassium, her nose told her. She sat up, scooped the leaves up, crushed them into her chest, her face. Plants change the landscape by thriving. Any rock will yield to a healthy tree. Suicide had failed her, homicide, warfare, marriage and motherhood. The books of Trotula had seemed pointless and yet the carnage that she seized upon instead was ended by the appearance of a book more powerful than any she could have foreseen.

She opened the vial, and held it over the weeds, her hands trembling as she considered dumping it. Her mother had given her a body that hardly aged and Fiona had given her the knowledge of when to hide it. She passed the vial across her lips and at the familiar licorice taste, she closed her eyes and shuddered. She was a mandrake broom. Wrapped in a willow skirt of fear and cowardice, she possessed a potent core.

Plants change the landscape by thriving. And yet they impassively regard the life and death of wolf and rabbit, the tromp of troops and adversaries that swirl around them. Stationary, resolute. Feeding their core of strength with one objective: to grow. She struggled to her feet, mounted her tired horse and rode west to Paris, to Moishe, to Jean, to take on her enemy — the metal book — though in what way she wasn't sure.

Among the Wicca who sheltered Luccia as she headed west there was endless talk of Marcelle and her army, of their bravery, and how the soldiers had been consumed in a fire so large that it arced and lit the trees on the hillside. Luccia listened to stories of Molitar and *The Archer Witch* but added nothing to the conversation, did not identify herself, nor correct their wild embroidering of the truth.

As the years went on, there would be another truth she wanted to set right, but did not. It was said that Jakob Sprenger, with his friend Fr. Peter, died suddenly and mysteriously in a beatific state in Strasbourg on December 6, 1495, after receiving a letter from the Pope applauding his work against the witches. That Heinrich Kramer died in Bohemia in 1505. The truth, however, had more to do with a small coterie of Luccia's, of a charwoman and a late-night call for a compress, of locked doors, of the tea of digitalis that stops the heart, and in the end, of the futile gesture of killing authors whose book was seized by a machine. Luccia received no comfort from either version of the story, because she heard the screech of a dying chicken in her dreams.

Chapter Eighteen

*L*uccia rode into Paris as a man with a shaven head, relying on the disguise that had saved her in both Rome and Metz. Cities, to Luccia, demanded manhood.

Paris surprised her with the delicacy of its buildings, its light, the stench of its river, the lack of vegetation, the sheer mass of people. Resting over a piece of bread, cheese and a tankard of ale, Luccia asked the barmaid where one would find an old Jewish tinker. The barmaid looked at her as if she had asked for the lodging of frogs but directed Luccia across the river into the swamplands where the Jewish part of Paris was growing.

Luccia walked her horse through the narrow streets, drawing stares at her forest attire, at the bow that was slung across her back, her bald head and her weary eyes. She peered into each shop and lost her way several times in her excitement over women in the streets in their odd dresses, butcher shops with seven kinds of fowl and fourteen types of sausage, and the intoxicating smell of the bakeries. Several times she had to stop, lean on a hitching post and ask a passersby. She was accustomed to villages where there was only one curio shop run by a Jew and while she was tired and bewildered by plodding from shop to shop, she hoped it meant that Moishe had company and finally felt at home.

The sun was setting and Luccia was staring at the way it was caught on the cornices of the buildings and the puddles in the road when she looked up and saw an expanse of brown wood that made her utter a moan that was the most feminine sound from her in recent times. It was the Bowman's glowing weapon, mounted high on the wall behind a counter, with the sun catching the intricate carvings. It shone so warm that Luccia felt the Bowman's skin against her, his arms around her, his enormity a combination of play and strength. Tears poured down her face and the sun on her back that had seemed so warming now just made her feel unprotected and vulnerable without him. The world had become so ugly since she had lived in the warmth of that man and that weapon. She pulled the vial from inside her skirt and held it against her cheek.

Moishe, behind the counter, saw her framed by the window, crying, and he hurried to the door, tied up her horse and brought her inside, pushing past the crowd of customers who moved aside with curiosity and revulsion. He guided her through a curtain to his quarters in the back. She didn't registered his exclamations or respond to his words as he set her in a chair, put a bowl of soup in front of her and, apologizing, returned to his customers.

At the end of the day when he returned to his little rooms behind the shop, Luccia was still sitting in the same place with the cold soup in front of her. She didn't move until a young man sat down beside her and she looked at Moishe for an introduction.

"Luccia," Moishe chided gently, "it's Jean!" Startled by the long, lanky 16-year-old boy in front of her, Luccia clutched his hands and started crying again.

She spilled out the details of the time since she had seen them, the tracking, the killing, the downfall of Marcelle. Jean put a shawl around her trembling shoulders with the same tender attention he had lavished on his mother, then jumped up like the little wild boy he had been and pulled together dinner.

Moishe paced the room, wrung his hands, and signaled Jean to ladle more food onto her plate, as Luccia described her battle with metal, lamented the appearance of the printing press and how *The Hammer* was overtaking the presence of *Trotula*.

"Yes, yes," Moishe muttered. "They're using it against the Jews as well."

But when she raged over the new machine, Moishe turned abruptly and leaned on the table, his lined face and bright eyes close to her.

"Oh no Luccia, the press itself — this not a thing to fight, it's a thing to hire!" Moishe said.

"Hire?"

Moishe, still close to her face, took her sharp chin in his hand and turned her face from side to side. "How is it that you still look so young, after...all this. And all this time."

She pulled away from him and said nothing.

Moishe straightened. "Luccia, welcome to Paris," he raised his hands wide. "Welcome to a new age. Books aren't sequestered with monks any longer. Anyone with money can print a book — salacious, foolish, entertaining, erudite, entirely personal. Anyone can publish on any thing. Tomorrow I take you to a bookstore, then a printer, and we will see about your *Trotula*."

Moishe found a simple dress in the back of his store and Luccia covered her head with a cloth but as they walked the streets toward the printing shop, she stopped outside bakeries so frequently that Moishe relented and sent her in for sweets. When Luccia and Moishe entered the printing shop, the sound of the presses and the smell of the ink made her head swim.

Luccia set her jaw and looked at Moishe with fierce determination. If the stack of paper in the back was now something available to her, she wanted every last sheet of it. To fight metal with metal, she would need a lot of paper to catch up.

Luccia took as many jobs as she could stuff into a long day. She rose in the middle of the night and trudged across the river to be swineherd for the city, marshalling a dozen pigs through Paris as they ate up the previous day's slop in the gutters. Home, she cooked breakfast for Moishe who went off in search of items for his shop while Jean and Luccia worked the counter.

She used the money she made to pay for the printing of *Trotula*, and insisted on standing by as the first sheets came off the press. She clutched the first copy as she slept and wondered if her mother would have been pleased.

Soon, she sold so many copies to midwives that *Trotula* took up as much of her day as when she had copied the book herself with a quill. Moishe put it in the window of the shop and when he and Jean brought Luccia outside to see the display, she was shocked. She pivoted and frantically looked around her, expecting to be seized for their brazenness.

But Paris seemed to be all about brazenness, about the freedom that accompanies anonymity. There were no great tracts of land to seize by rounding up the population: all the land had already been divided. There had never been a mass burning here and the courts seemed to confine themselves to rural areas. And there were just too many people to keep close tabs on the suspicious activities of a few. Luccia had never felt so free, so safe.

Moishe put his hands on his hips. Jean threw his arm around Moishe's shoulders. "Welcome to Paris!" they laughed.

Books bounced on the cart of every peddler. Women could be seen though the windows of their rooms, reading with their cheeks on their hands. And not just books, but single sheets printed up and posted to trees all over Paris, given out to passersby as if they weren't the most precious thing. Paper and messages were everywhere, floating down the streets like settling birds.

Luccia was introduced to the midwives of Paris who brought her requests for herbs, for mandrake, and though she first looked at them with resignation, she gathered and sheltered herbs in a tiny closet by the back door, where the women would congregate with their baskets of laundry and news of someone soon to be in labor, the puzzle of someone's rash. *Trotula* sold out the front door every day without anyone's subterfuge or coaxing.

Moishe, Jean and Luccia were an odd family — an old Jewish peddler, an old maid scholar, and the wholesome son of a feral woman. Eclectic, Luccia liked to think, but they were a family, ladling soup together on a Sunday afternoon.

Jean had Poulain's fair skin but he had become Moishe's son. He was content with the hum of the merchandise and the day's conversations around him, the warm firelight across his clean woolen vest, a soft, youthful beard curling on his cheeks. The sparkle in his dark eyes and verve in his voice held a touch of his feral childhood and the wildness of his mother. He spouted information about the trading routes North, the daring life of explorers, the wonders of the new inventions that came in to the shop. He chattered in the streets at Luccia's side, a colt, then an energetic and determined young man.

As Moishe aged and Jean matured, the boy took over the front counter of the store, encouraged the old man to read in a chair by the fire, and then Jean infused the business with his own lively, lawless flare. One of the first things he did was to move Moishe's enormous mirror to a prominent position against the wall just inside the door, and it drew crowds of young women who giggled, then slipped into the shop and were seized by its magic. Wide-eyed, they turned, stepped forward to inspect their face for the first time, to regard their dress, their waist, the unnoticed prominence of their ears. Businessmen who came in pretended to ignore it but hiked on their codpieces and adjusted their hats as if by chance.

Inventions and *Trotula* through the front door, herbs through the back door: it was a good life and Luccia felt blessed to have it.

She wrote to Isabelle to tell her that there was a market in Paris for her herbs, now so easy to post a letter that it nearly flew to the south of France. In no time, Isabelle was at the door, her magic mushrooms and opiates sewn into the hem of her skirt and her cape. Dogs clustered around her when she first appeared at the door, entranced by the mere vapors of her clothing. She stayed three weeks for business, and returned soon after without an invitation.

Isabelle came through Paris regularly, fell in love with Jean, and they were transcendent, one wild and brightly alive man and a deeply joyful woman, surrounded by success. Their love made Luccia ache for the skin of the Bowman, for just one more chance to curl up against his strong back with his ass in her lap, which had made her the happiest wolf pup in the den. It made Luccia ache for Jacqueline and her thighs, her breasts in Luccia's hands. Sweet woman, sweet beginning, Luccia smelled lavender and cried for the touch of a Gypsy scarf on her cheek.

There was still the butchery of Luccia's past to contend with, though. The sight of priests disemboweled on the forest floor had seized a part of her brain and rooted there. Her new life was a blessing, a peacefulness she could hardly have imagined, but distrust, suspicion, lived in her core. She woke in the night with the carnage possessing her dreams. At first, she fought the visions and sweated with fear, but the nightmares didn't change. The motive, the action, however, had drained out of them, and with it, the fear. They weren't dreams of murder, they were pictures of the inside of the body. In Salerno, the body was sacred, not to be opened on a whim, examined only by the few surgeons the school produced.

Soon, the dreams infiltrated her waking thoughts and she developed a fascination with gore that she couldn't shake. Butchered pigs, chicken legs and the muscle structure of a dead dog fascinated her. She wanted to know everything she could, not about herbs this time but about musculature, about the internal organs of the body. She wanted to travel the length of a muscle and see where it ended, to touch the place where the throat met the belly.

In Paris during the spring and early summer months, there were dissections of human cadavers, conducted in public, on platforms that were otherwise for political speeches, traveling musical shows, and the occasional merchant who would put on a public display. Luccia was drawn to them, wandering from dissection to dissection throughout town on a Sunday after her soup.

A good dissection was conducted in Latin, and frequently held near the university. The more popular dissections were conducted in French and held near a market, by someone who had just rolled into town. After a short song and a fear-inducing introduction, the huckster frequently mislabeled the body parts, chopped intestines out of a body and flung them to the crowd as if conducting a sideshow. These dissections drew women carrying vegetables into town and men with hay rakes over their shoulders, a boy urging a donkey and cart to the market. The dogs would go wild and the women would scream, the boys would guffaw like the men near the front.

Luccia, carrying a sketchbook, a quill and a bottle of ink, would stand and shout back at the hawker, then pack up her things in disgust.

Still, returning home, her sketch of the intestines had improved. Jean explained some new invention to Moishe as he sat under his shawl and Luccia laid out her papers on the dining room table, received a kiss from Isabelle without turning from her work, and sketch until she heard Jean blow out the last candle in the back room.

One summer, Luccia was selling lungwort out the back door to battle a sweating sickness that had come over from England. Morning business done, Luccia set out for a dissection, hoping to study the neck. She set up easel and quills, inkpots at the ready. Luccia had a leather binder of all her sketches with her, because while she wanted to sketch the neck, she had other diagrams that were unfinished, and whatever part he chose to examine, one of the sketches could improve. The massive speaker, in striped clothing and worn shoes, his long beard caked with blood, strode to the edge of the platform and called for the crowd to turn to him.

He started shouting about the mysteries of the body, and then flung his hands out, each one clutching an organ that shot blood and offal on to her meticulous illustration. Right on cue, the women screamed, the huckster smiled and Luccia leapt up, furious that his showmanship that just cost her hours of work.

"Get a little stomach juice on your pretty picture, lady?" the huckster shouted back at her.

"Idiot, that's the liver," Luccia growled at him.

"The liver, the lady says, and how would the witch know?" he asked the crowd.

A gentleman's voice rang out from behind the crowd. "Through a better education than yours," he said, and pushed his way toward Luccia.

The man was short, thin, dressed like a gentleman but filthy and disheveled, as if he'd lived in his clothing for a month. He picked her illustration off the easel and the others from beside her chair before Luccia could stop him, and motioned her to step back from the stage. She gathered her things furiously, stuffing them in pockets and trying to avoid getting blood all over herself, while this stranger pawed through her drawings.

"Those are private papers, sir," Luccia grumbled at him and tried to take them from him without losing her grip on the easel and little chair. He stepped further away from the stage, out of her reach.

"And very expertly done papers," he said.

Luccia knew better than to show any sign of medical knowledge to a stranger, even here in Paris where it seemed that freedom was the watchword.

"But you shouldn't work here," he scoffed. "You should be associated with the medical school."

Luccia looked at him as if he had recommended that she crown herself queen, and grabbed for her papers. What degenerate was this, with his filthy but ostentatious clothing and his conviction that he could tell her what to do? He backed down the street.

"Here," he said, "I'll show you where they at least pretend not to be providing a side show."

"Come back here," Luccia shouted, indignant and threatened.

"Mind you, they're brainless wind-bags as well but at least they know the body parts," he called to her and he paced backwards down the street. "I wouldn't let my horse submit to their knife, but …"

"Sir," Luccia growled, lunging for her portfolio, "at this point you are guilty of theft."

"And you shall thank me for it."

"Only when you return my drawings!" Every time Luccia tried to seize her drawings again, the easel and chair tangled in her skirts and made her stumble, increasing his lead down the street.

"Your excellent drawings, that is," he called to her in a chipper tone as he perused them and kept his lead. "Do you speak Latin?"

"Of course," she scoffed, then regarded him suspiciously.

"And where were you educated in the medical field?"

"I do not provide personal information to thieves and braggarts. Where did you receive yours?"

"The University of Turbingen," he said, as he leaned up against the door of the Sorbonne, "and I'm on my way to Vienna." Then he ducked into the door of the University with her drawings in hand and closed the door behind him. When she tried to follow, a guard blocked her way so she had to wait outside the door for the possible return of this little man and her hard-earned drawings.

Finally, the door opened and the filthy little gentleman stepped toward her.

"You have my drawings?" she growled.

"This way," he said curtly, and led her by the elbow, past the guard, into the University of Paris.

He ushered her into a room and she stopped, frozen, just inside the door because her illustrations were on individual easels around a wood paneled room, being studied by eight professors in black robes and caps. They looked at her cautiously, and she looked at them suspiciously.

"You have a fine hand, madam," a Don said.

202

"Thank you," Luccia said curtly. "Now if you'll excuse me, I'll be going."

"Where did you receive your education?" another asked.

"A subject best left for me and my maker," Luccia said quietly, then moved to retrieve her drawings.

"Gentlemen," an older Don said, stepping forward, "we are being far too coy. Madam, we need another illustrator. We've been naming parts with no record of them, which won't do, of course. We'll pay you, most certainly, and provide for all your supplies. In return, your drawings go into the private collection of the Sorbonne. Paracelsus here tells us you speak Latin, which will be essential to following the conversations. Would you like to try your hand at it? Contribute to medical knowledge?"

Hide, Luccia, she thought to herself. Illustrator to the surgeons, was it being an accomplice to the oppressor?

"Now Don Michous," another professor interrupted, "we generally have no women doing this. They have delicate stomachs, become squeamish. I suggest we wait to find a man."

Luccia suppressed a snort of derision and demurred. They agreed to let her go from assassin to a surgeon's illustrator. Her interloper, this Paracelsus, bowed to her with a smile and slipped out the door before she could prove him right by thanking him. He left her to begin a new life.

Luccia dressed in black, a headdress shielding her face from the students as she took her place at the side of the dissection table. She was the faceless illustrator, as still and indispensable as the leg of the table.

Luccia would sometimes see the young students shudder over the sound of the tearing tissue, over the smell of preserved flesh. Sometimes a student shed a tear for the toothless wretch on the table, whom Luccia knew had died a poor man and was now having his cheeks removed for the benefit of a surgeon. But she was transfixed, and while aware of the lamb chop nature of it, she watched the professors saw through bone and then without a word, she spent three days burning the knowledge of the spongy bone layer into her brain and sight of it into her drawings.

The first month she came home exhausted, and then took on the extra task of duplicating the sketches for her own collection, drawing until her hands were cramped and she fell asleep at her table.

For seven years she devoted herself to recording the constructs of the internal organs, and trying her best to keep silent when the professors proclaimed that mice were generated asexually from decaying earth; that wasps emanated from the carcasses of dead horses and that the only way to prevent the Plague was to wear wide-brimmed hats against the moonlight. Luccia let her headdress protect her when she recited the rose tincture under her breath.

As her private collection of drawings expanded, she began writing down the surgical procedures as well, first in slim volumes dedicated to specific parts of the body, then a large volume that was an exact replication of the course, then a study of the body by layers, each one cluttering a table and growing as the years went on.

Luccia still spent her wages on the printing of *Trotula* and offered the herbs and mushrooms from the back of the shop, though Isabelle took over many of her duties, just as Jean had taken over for Moishe.

Isabelle gave birth to two children and it seemed their little family was bursting out of the walls of their Jewish-quarter home, and then their family began to shrink. Moishe, who sat all day wrapped in his shawl at a table behind the counter, grew more and more feeble and finally passed away in the fall. Jean grieved, the good son, sitting despondently in the evenings until called to bed by his wife. Luccia suddenly felt very old and fragile and dug into the backs of her bags for the vial of her mother's mixture.

A month later, Jean came downstairs as Luccia was finishing her late-night tea. Amsterdam, he said, the spice trade was bringing opportunity into Holland and he needed to be part of it. Inventions, discoveries, they were flooding into Europe and his eyes lit up when he talked about it. He wanted Luccia to come with them, of course, and Isabelle, who joined them after tucking in the children, tried her best to convince Luccia. But she insisted that her work would keep her in Paris, it mattered to her, she would be fine without them and yes, she would visit, though she knew that she wouldn't. And Luccia knew she couldn't stay in the shop after they left: the shop front had to pay for the house and with her at the university there would be no shop. Besides, they had been accepted in the Jewish quarter because of Moishe and with him gone, it was doubtful they could even keep the house. It was right that Jean and Isabelle were leaving. After they climbed the stairs to bed, Luccia set a chair on the counter and took down the Bowman's weapon, held it to her, fingers tracing the hunting scene, looking for answers.

It came the morning after they packed and left. She had lied to them again, told them she was moving to a little room closer to the university, that she had plans. Instead, after she saw them off, Luccia threw open the curtains between the now-empty shop and the living quarters and she sat at the kitchen table, crushed by the silence of no children, no muttering old man and his chipper daughter-in-law. No more honey-butter son. There were marks on the wall where hard to sell objects had hung, where portraits of unknown people had stood in for their clan's heritage. The silence was frost on Luccia's ears.

What should she do now? For the first time, she didn't have people chasing her, hunting her. People talked about the burnings as if they happened in another country. *Trotula* sold itself, paid for its own printing. She was free, unencumbered. What was her task? Who would give it to her?

She walked through the shop, running her hand across the dusty counters, digging her fingernail into the scratches and grooves. She paused before reaching Moishe's mirror, as she always did, preferring to come into the shop through the back door to avoid it, averting her face whenever she was forced to walk by it. Tonight she drew near it, grasped the edge of its frame and inspected it, seeing her reflection in the corner of her eye. Slowly, she raised her eyes. How old was she now? Seventy-five? She ran her hands over her lightly wrinkled brow, her smooth cheeks, along the edge of her sharp chin. She took off her cap and her hair tumbled down around her shoulders, black as night and shining. She looked like a very healthy woman of forty. She seemed to have mastered survival but what did thriving look like?

She smelled fennel, mint, coltsfoot, and she turned back to the empty shop. Tansy, fenugreek, shepherd's purse. Stinging nettle grazed her leg, her hands felt the fur of sage. A laboratory. She would turn the shop into an enormous laboratory. She paced through the room, excited over the prospect: one side she would cover with her drawings of the body, and the other would be devoted to restoring her manuscripts — the Trotula she had augmented with the secrets of the Wicca.

She turned a circle in the room, her skirts flaring out. She walked back to the mirror and grabbed it with both hands, touched her face and smiled. Her own bidding, her own course. She ran her hand down her throat, pulled open her blouse to inspect her neck, her chest, stripped off her blouse and regarded her breasts. She turned back to the shop.

She wrote as if possessed. The memories of the Wicca's advice flooded into her and she scribbled to keep up. The pages stacked up beside her, the candle butts mounted in a bucket on the floor, and then an idea would seize her and she would get out of bed, re-light the candles, reorder all the papers, find some connection that had never been made and she would sketch out an idea, then grab her cloak and tromp through the district to find the herbs and build an experiment on the table. She followed her curiosity, abandoning the herbs mid-chapter to reproduce her drawing of the spinal cord that she had just begun at the University. She not only had to capture each detail as the days at work progressed, but to record what they said about the dorsal nerve root, the dura mater, the filum terminale.

She hardly slept. The pages mounted up on each side of the room and the plants littered the tables in between. Vials boiled over little flames, leaves soaked in potent mixtures while their vapors were trapped, branches stripped of bark lay abandoned on the floor and quills and paper marked the beginning of each new inquiry. She ate ravenously, bounded out of bed, cheeks flushed, eyes bright.

One night, standing with sprig in one hand, quill in the other, she regarded the two sides of her divided house, mirroring the two sides of the medical world, old and new, herbal and surgery, woman and man, and realized that, in fact, neither side should win the battle. And that, in fact, a battle was still being waged. Not just the battle against The Hammer, which she had turned her back on, but a battle that had become internalized within medicine. The Wicca were wise but they didn't understand the complex physical properties of the body. They treated a general area, not knowing that there were specific nerves attached to a unique artery or muscle that could heal by being treated in isolation. They didn't deserve the persecution they suffered, clearly, but they didn't know everything, and their reverence of the body, gracious and honorable though it was, would prevent them from gaining it.

The surgeons, on the other hand, who refused to learn anything from those they were bent on destroying, would wallow in their ignorance. But their disregard for the sanctity of the body, their insistence on treating the body as a machine that could be dismantled, had made it possible to make some startling discoveries, she thought as she looked at her drawing of the pulmonary artery and the root-like nerves that encircled it.

She dropped the quill and tossed aside the sprig. Unity of two sides. She set a drawing of a body part at the front edge of the table, then dashed across the room and sorted through her papers until she found the section on the herbs to treat the body part. For two months, during every moment that she wasn't at work, she sorted and re-copied chapters, transcribed. The surgical procedure, the herbs to treat the ailment, united, comprehensive, both university and Wicca knowledge, together for the first time.

Late at night, with the volume expanding and her drawings at work deepening, she leaned back in her chair as if fat with the knowledge. Unity. How to foster the unity? She couldn't teach the Wicca about surgery: they were hounded enough and if caught with a knife in their hands would be strung up even faster. The new male doctors wouldn't listen to anything that had come from a woman. So what was she to do?

Pretend it came from a man. And what do men value? Something they can steal. She chuckled to herself and poured a goblet of dark red wine. Then they would steal it from a shape shifter, on a breeze in from the sea. She leapt up and found a pair of Jean's old trousers, a shirt, a floppy hat, a cape.

In the weeks following she emerged late at night dressed as a man and frequented the pubs, the inns, the dining places and the herb shops where the doctors congregated, acting the flustered medic.

"Now where did I put that?" the man who was Luccia said, patting his chest, digging into his pockets. "My god, the formula! It was right here. Mother of God, my fortune rests on that remedy! The wife will have my head." And tottering out, muttering to herself about the riches that would have been made, she let a little piece of paper with the formula drop to the floor from her pant leg and whirled in a circle in front of the closed door just long enough to hear men dive onto the spot where her lucrative formula had dropped.

She attended meetings of medical guilds and asked leading questions from the back, (all in a deepened voice, sometimes sporting a goatee she had fashioned from her own hair), and didn't stop pursuing a line of questioning until she saw furtive glances thrown her way, until she knew that at least four medics were thinking hard about her words.

Each time she went out, she wore a unique disguise and she acquired costumes from different countries. As a man, she was invited to laboratories, to speaking circles, dissections and study groups. At first, she slipped in wearing a long cape, face somewhat shielded, muttered her secrets, interjected, then disappeared. Then she became bold enough to question the presenter from the back of the room, to stride forward as she informed the listeners of the connective tissue in the calf and how to improve its elastic properties.

The first response, when she spoke to a crowd, was to be questioned on the source of her education.

"Salerno," she intoned proudly the first time, the word on her tongue like the first bite of cake. "The University of Salerno," and it filled her with longing for the coastal air, for fried anchovies and lemons. She longed for a task as simple as running through the streets to see herbs in alphabetical order. Heads nodded throughout the room, acknowledging her hometown's stature, still. But she would only claim her homeland once, dismissing the question with the name of a different university every time. There couldn't be an entire troupe of doctors from Salerno in Paris.

Luccia walked through Paris with her shoulders back, and her head up, pride and strength infusing her step. Not skulking or clandestine as she had been when young, not rageful and violent when avenging Claude and Fiona, she, herself, had become united. Confident in her disguise and sure of her knowledge. She bought padding for her costumes, emerged as broad-shouldered men, and grew into her clothing. Forthright, articulate, expansive, Luccia engaged in lively debate. She taught, cajoled, and was surrounded by an eager crowd by the end of each meeting she attended.

She felt full from the inside, content and secure in her place. So this is what it meant to be happy, she thought one night after speaking at a study circle. She rested her manly leg on the edge of the table at an ale house and stroked her goatee as a barmaid leaned over her and set down a mug. To be free, to feel safe, to speak aloud and be honored, to do a job well. She reached out and cupped the woman's breast with her gloved hand.

That year in Paris it was said that there was a tremendous flowering of knowledge, brought in by a sudden influx of medics from all over Europe. A Bavarian with a limp, an Italian with a long beard, a Greek who knew the remedies of the ancients. Stories abounded as to where they were going but no one questioned why they were there: it was Paris, after all.

Her medicines appeared in shop windows marked 'unique' and 'here exclusively' and a few locals even stood up in their professional clubs and professed to have conducted extensive experiments that had yielded these remarkable results.

The thefts pleased Luccia, though the appearances began to seem minor compared to what could be done. Her studies were piling up in the shop and these little thefts seemed like droplets leaking out of a very full cistern. *Trotula* continued to make its way through the world, thanks to a small group of Parisian women who took on the task with the zeal Luccia had mustered in the past. As a book containing information on women, though, it didn't infiltrate the university curricula. Not enough was getting out, not enough was being adopted.

But it was something, Luccia thought, walking through Paris late one night as an elderly French doctor, her walking stick thudding on the stones. Unity on a small scale. She was going to attend a small study group and she had several recipes in her pockets, in preparation for tonight's topic.

An unusually bright light caught her eye and she turned to the apothecary shop, a particularly good one that specialized in importing herbs in from Palestine. Luccia gripped the windowsill, stunned, as she had been the first time she saw a printing press.

The shelves were bare, the counter had been removed and in its place was a huge copper cistern, pipes like a snake nest, glass vials and a cluster of excited chemists. Indignant, Luccia burst into the doors.

"How can you turn such a fine practice over to the making of beer!" she growled, tapping the cistern with her cane.

"Beer?" a member of the excited crowd admonished. "Gold, old man. Gold."

"That's enough, Francoise," the apothecary said and lead Luccia out by the elbow. "This place is no longer open to the public. Have a good evening, sir."

Luccia stood outside, leaning on her walking stick, heartsick. Thwarted once again by metal. And in the months to come, the unusually bright light of the hot fires of the alchemists began to dot the Paris night sky, every one a sign of defeat. Fritz Bremer was long dead; the authors of *The Hammer* rotting in the ground; there were no burning courts in Paris, but danger lurked nonetheless. It wasn't any longer that one body of knowledge was being lost while the other rose, it was that the knowledge that was rising had incorporated antithetical ideals: science for profit, money above medicine.

But she had her work; she had her subterfuge, though she began to feel old and stiff from the long hours.

Luccia was sketching the esophageal flap when a professor's assistant appeared at her elbow. Her presence was requested in the President's chambers. Luccia swallowed hard, straightened her clothing and followed him.

He opened a door and guided her into the President's chambers, where she had never ventured before, then closed the door behind her, and left her staring at her own illustrations, and the backs of a group of Dons, in agitated debate with someone in front of the fire.

"Well, that's an outlandish statement in keeping with your reputation," grumbled the President of the College, as he raised a hand to the fire. "Don Guilliame, meet Philippus Aureolus Theophrastus Bombastus Paracelsus von Hohenheim, who graces us with his presence and his… fiery opinions."

The man seated in front of the fire didn't rise from the chair in which he was sprawled, but instead, removed an old stick from an inside pocket to pick his teeth. It was the ragged gentleman who had gotten her the job. The fire raged behind him, showing off the dirt on his clothing, the holes in his shoes, the way he carelessly dangled his leg over the arm of the chair. The Dons kept their distance.

"Here obviously from less civilized environs," a Don said icily.

"But certainly no less educated," Paracelsus said, hauling his leg back over the arm and sitting forward, elbows on his knees and his gaze driving into the Don. "Even the Gypsies know that if the skin has a bruise you don't cut it out or bleed it with leeches, for the love of God, you treat it with a poultice of comfrey, brusewort or arnica until the next moon. A common cabbage leaf would be better than leeches!"

"The Gypsies!" the Don scoffed, while the other professors crowded around Paracelsus, derisive and challenging, frightened and disgusted.

Luccia heard it as din, because her mind locked on Paracelsus, reciting a Gypsy cure within the walls of the university. Luccia had recently heard his story during one of her forays into the all-male study groups and she stepped forward to get a better look at him. His father was a well-known country doctor and his mother had been a hospital administrator before she took her own life, Luccia had heard. The best friend of his mother, an old woman who had tended to her as a child, had gotten odd in her old age, was accused of witchcraft and burned. In her despair, Paracelsus' mother had thrown herself off a bridge. Here was the son, reciting the names of the medical universities he had attended, and been thrown out of one of the Dons pointed out, as he paced in front of the fire deriding the stupidity of those who thought they could teach him. Te infamous Paracelsus had gotten her the job.

Paracelsus hadn't grown into a handsome man in the years since Luccia had seen him. His blonde hair stuck out above his ears, accentuating a bald spot as if he had been a monk. He had a scraggly blonde goatee that crept into wisps of curly jowl hair. His gray eyes were like the coldest Dutch day and he had a flaccid pallor that suggested a lack of sun or fresh air. But Luccia caught his eye.

"Ah, the illustrator," he said, pacing over to her and grasping her hand. "I never did get your name."

"Luccia," she said reminding herself to act the deferential woman rather than the learned man she was at night. "Luccia Alimenti."

"Madam Alimenti, excellent work," he said, still holding her hand. "The University barely deserves it." He lowered his voice. "Pock-faced fools." Then he turned back to the Dons, and re-addressed Luccia. "And what would you say, Madame Alimenti, would be appropriate for bruising?"

To display herbal knowledge, could be more dangerous here than anywhere except perhaps in a church.

"Speak to me," Paracelsus whispered.

She owed him that much in return for seven years of employment, and she was so struck by his knowledge of herbalism that she couldn't hold back. "Your tincture is correct but the moon cycle is unnecessary if you cleanse the blood with a daily brew of sage tea. Or comfrey. Three times daily for stubborn cases," she recited Trotula's knowledge, clenching her fist that she had drawn into her sleeve.

Paracelsus dropped her hand and strode back into the midst of the Dons, then leapt onto an upholstered chair beside the President's desk. He thrust a finger into the air.

"You see!" he shouted, "the hair on the back of my neck knows more about medicine than you."

Luccia was unsure whether the Dons reacted to his insults, his herbal cures or to the sacrilege of his dirty shoes on the upholstery but the room broke into angry denunciations and shouting while Luccia laughed out loud at his boldness, then looked around the room to see if someone had noticed her mirth.

"This illustrator," he shouted, pointing at her, "knows more medicine than all of you chicken-brained professors combined!" He jumped off the chair and grabbed her hand, pulling Luccia out of the door and across the courtyard. Hand in hand, they ran into the streets of Paris, birds above danger.

Chapter Nineteen

"I do, you know," Luccia said to Paracelsus, stopping to catch her breath as they careened down the street.

"Do what?" he panted, smiling beside her.

"Know more medicine than they." She pulled off her headdress and ran her hand over her hair.

"Who are you, illustrator?" he asked quietly.

Luccia looked away, back to him, wanting to be seen. Wanting this strange, dirty little man to know her as a compatriot. She stood tall, but couldn't stop the shake in her voice. "Daughter of a medical professor from the University of Salerno, a scribe who is an archivist of both herbal and surgical knowledge, who has recorded the wisdom of Trotula more than one hundred times." She wanted to tell him the rest, that she was an assassin, a smuggler, the legion of doctors who had converged on Paris.

"The wisdom of whom?" he said, suddenly serious, and she lunged at him, grabbed his elbow.

"Someone who can tell you medicines that could heal all these things— the ailments of the organs, not the just the muscles and bones."

"The surgeons can't do everything, and they're fools to think so," he grumbled.

"They are criminals to think so, to insist upon it," Luccia said, braving her fury and gripping his arms. Perhaps he could spirit the information into the new universities. Her tactic of one thieving doctor at a time was too slow. Maybe if the knowledge was carried by a man — a gentleman — there was hope of it not disappearing altogether.

213

"Teach me what this someone has to say," he said.

Luccia took him back to the little shop in the Jewish quarter and he stood just inside the door, spellbound, hat in hand. The walls were lined with tables, stacked high with papers. Books stood in pillars from the floor to the tabletops. The illustrations circled the walls. An enormous oak table ran down the middle of the room, dotted with mortars and beakers and baskets of herbs. Potted plants, clippers, chopping blades, scales, and beside every object sat a sheet of paper, a quill, the results of a recipe half concocted, of an experiment partially completed. The room was a jumble of smells. Stacks of paper spewed slips with numbers, a coding system that seemed to connect disparate piles. Notes and charts sat beside the piles as deciphering systems and whole manuscripts were jammed half into a stack, a new idea not yet integrated.

Paracelsus walked reverently down the aisle, shocked by the density of knowledge. He regarded Luccia, who stood with her hands on her hips at the end of the aisle, this sharp-faced woman whose skin wrinkled slightly over angular bones, whose eyes were fireworks in her face.

"This is yours?" he asked tentatively.

"Yes," Luccia said. "Mine."

"All this is your work?"

"Well, no, certainly not," she said, turning to the tables. "It's the work of thousands."

"Thousands of whom?" Paracelsus was incredulous.

"Of the Wicca," she said, moving to the end of the table and sweeping her hand over the pile, "of the herbalists." She turned and charged forward to another area of the room. "Of the surgeons. And the alchemists and the professors."

He picked up the Bowman's weapon and Luccia gently took it from him, and set it on the sideboard, then escorted him to the end of the central table where a copy of *Trotula* sat splayed open like the Bible.

Her manuscripts, more constant than family, more reliable than love. Sometimes she was comforted by dreams of them as a forest that spread across Europe. She imagined the little huddled cluster of women who gathered around each one as if at a hearth-fire. Sometimes, when Luccia couldn't sleep at all, she would conjure the

214

image of these clusters of women, their hay stalls, their chicken coops, the little girls playing on the way to the well. She imagined the smell of their oxen at night, cataloged the herbs that would be drying in their eaves. It comforted her, as if her manuscript were the big old tree in the village square and she had many places to belong. That day in Paris, she spread it out in front of Paracelsus as a sacred offering.

Luccia and Paracelsus talked of medicine, and he startled Luccia with the speed with which he absorbed Trotula's teachings.

But Paracelsus was the one most startled. He stood gripping the edge of his hat as Luccia darted through the room, describing the course of her study. He had never met a cultured woman who didn't sit hollow as a cup. The few Gypsy healers he had met moved and muttered over their remedies without being able to articulate the properties or destination of their brew. This woman's mind worked like a scientist — and a damn good one at that. She had that passion that he could feel inside his own chest. She had that hunger. He could tell as she lifted a stack of paper at the mid-point, talked of how it correlated to the top of the stack, then crossed the room and related it to an illustration.

She opened wine, gave him a glass, moved to the center table and stood in front of her collection of mortars, the bunches of herbs on either side of her, with the clusters and branches hanging from the rafters above. Paracelsus turned to see if another log had been put on the fire, or an oil lamp lit. When he turned back, she was staring at him, one arm nestled across her chest, the other hand cupping her chin and those granite eyes staring at him as if judging his worth.

He drained his glass and set it on the table, resting his hand on its rim. She was radiant and astounding when she was surrounded by paper, but here, she was at home, as if she didn't study the herbs, but was of them. The plants seemed to sense that she was there, the leaves quivered and the stalks stood on end. Powders in their beakers turned over, as if premixing themselves for her ease, and the mortars vied for her attention. What witch was this? What sorceress?

"Why did you help me at that dissection?" Luccia asked him, the tips of her fingers resting on the table.

"Leeks," Paracelsus said simply, with a small smile, and he ran his hand over the sage in a basket on the table. "An herbalist who taught me about plants when I was very young. Smelled so much like onions and herbs that everyone just called him Leeks. Dear man."

Paracelsus gripped his wine goblet and took on a stern tone. "He died a poor man, however, and was dissected in the village square for the amusement of the townsfolk. My sweet Leeks. First teacher after my father."

He looked at Luccia, expecting her to wilt with horror over his story and when he met her stone-still eyes and chiseled face, he set one hand over the other on top of the goblet and regarded her.

"I fled the University of Tubingen when the professors proved themselves more interested in the sport of debate and the status of their plumed hats than in medicine," he said firmly.

Still, she was unmoved. "Of course," she said, simply, and gestured to the room. "Where would you like to begin?"

Paracelsus was unnerved, looked quickly around him. "At the toes," he said as a challenge but Luccia simply nodded her head and lead him to the front of the room.

Within an hour Paracelsus had stripped off his coat and rolled up his sleeves. Within two he had unbuttoned his vest and was scribbling with a quill.

Luccia watched him rummage, shake his head, take notes, as she stood at her table combining herbs, then making an oil-based ointment, abandoning her task and hurrying to his side to answer questions, interjecting. He challenged, they debated, he went back to his scribbling.

In the middle of the night he sighed, straightened his back and stood in front of her, looking again into her eyes to find out who she was.

She pressed the linen bag of herbs into his hand. "Bathe in these, then rub this ointment into your skin. The skin is our largest organ, after all, and yours has the most amazing smell of... horse bile and rotting grass."

He snatched the packages from her angrily.

"Will you come back tomorrow," she asked. "I'd like to give you a recipe against the Plague."

"You have something to battle...the Plague?" he challenged.

"John of Liege. Will you come back M. Paracelsus?"

He looked at her inquisitively, then set his jaw and bowed. "Call me Theo. It would be my honor to return, Madame Alimenti."

She beamed at him, her breath rising from the bottom of her lungs. She rested her hand on his forearm. "Luccia," she said, quietly.

Night after night they stood beside each other at the polished counter of the shuttered shop, at the long center table with their fists full of herbs, sitting shoulder to shoulder pouring through the manuscripts, crouched over the floor sketching out processes.

Theo listened intently, and then challenged her. She was adamant, but her eyes lit up when he tried to block her. She breathed deeply any time he stopped and stroked his goatee or quietly shook his head in concession. And in turn, he would sniff slightly and wiggle his toes in his boots when he said something that made her stop. "Really?" she would say, her eyes growing wide. "I must write that down."

Each evening, Luccia rushed home and bathed, changed into one of her best dresses. Theo arrived with great ceremony, presenting a loaf or a cake or a chop for them and she stoked the fire and they drank mulled wine.

Theo watched Luccia collecting a set of leaves from her table, all the while chattering about her love of herbs, the smell and feel of them, how she felt their oils and unction even when they were miles away. She was like an adoring mother.

"Even their gnarly, hard-to-know-roots," she said with happy eyes, shaking a bouquet in his face.

She had never been to university, had no degree, but she wasn't a witch, he thought, despite her prattling on now about how herbs were a form of protection sent by the earth, her ancestors, she said as she drew close to him. She described how she ground roots during the Black Plague, nearly falling asleep on her arm. Like a lover, like a mother, she sensuously described the crush and ribs and rippled leaves of them, the petals that had to be carefully removed and blanched on just the right day of the moon. Theo wanted to roll in all the knowledge, wanted to rub it into his skin like the ointment she had given him that first night, he wanted to reach inside her mind and possess what she knew.

And yet there was something dangerous about her, something threatening about being a woman with so much knowledge. He wasn't sure if he despised her or admired her.

Theo gobbled up the pages of *Trotula*, and he was so voracious that Luccia brought out one of the original manuscripts that she had copied herself as a girl, this one with drawings by a fine old woman named Sophia whose ability to render the herb was so exact that Luccia could tell the dosage content by the veins of the leaf.

Luccia was dismissed from her post at the University for her scoffing, for her display of knowledge, and her work became another gift whose faceless giver is forgotten. She revitalized her herb trade, met with Theo in the evenings.

Luccia stood over a tincture pan, brewing something that Theo leaned in to see. Now she had someone in the house that was a colleague. Even the chatter of Moishe on his brightest days was a buzz about mechanical inventions, and the companionship of Marcelle had had nothing to do with herbs. Finally, someone to talk with as she hadn't since Fiona. She moved closer to him. Theo moved away and Luccia looked down at the table, embarrassed.

The next night Theo carried in a small satchel and Luccia could see that his tethered horse was laden. He had a formal air to his walk.

"I've been offered a post at the University of Basel," he said stiffly. "I leave in the morning."

Luccia held two goblets of wine in her hands, felt foolish, set them down. "What happened to 'they're swine-faced idiots'?" Luccia protested. "We haven't finished, Theo!"

Men and their prizes. He had no regard for their knowledge but he would leave his studies undone for the chance to be one of them. She paced across the floor, her skirts slapping against her legs. She slammed her book closed. Its angry sound made her realize that she was also unhappy that he was so willing to leave her. She had no one left in her haphazard family but she hadn't noticed it in weeks because she had the wild conversation with Theo. That night they had dinner with a lot of wine. She refused to open any of manuscripts and when he leaned on her table, his lids half closed, she put her palm against his cheek.

"We are better...together," Luccia whispered, tentatively, braving her feelings.

He took her hand tenderly but set it on the table again. "I don't function... as other men," he said quietly, swallowing hard. Luccia leaned toward him but he stood up and looked away. "I had a very serious infection as a child," he intoned as if he were giving a lecture on clinical facts, "in my... testicles. They have been removed."

A eunuch? Luccia was stunned. Theo was a eunuch.

But she stood beside him and kissed his face, the thin jowl hairs, rubbed her cheek against the side of his nose. Every scar he had made him more of a compatriot.

"They are not necessary," she whispered.

"Of course they are," he said abruptly, pulling away. "What man can service a woman...when he is not whole?"

Luccia smiled incredulously, thinking of Marcelle. But Theo thought Luccia was scoffing at him and he flew around her room, gathering his cloak and slapping his gloves into the palms of his hands, making pronouncements of how long he'd be gone, and how she should take care of herself.

He went to Basel in 1517 and Luccia felt left in mid-step. She tried to work on a new set of illustrations but abandoned them mid-way, cheek muscles suddenly vaporizing where the nose should have been. She had only known him two weeks, she admonished herself, and she should soldier on. She lost the desire to move among men as a man, disgusted by their egos and the smallness of their games. She tried reorganizing her papers to map herbs by their point of origin but decided it was a foolish endeavor, pointless now that trade routes circled the entire globe. She left her papers in an incomprehensible jumble.

When she began pacing her room as if caged, unable to do anything, she heard of a need for a midwife, or more accurately 'an attendant at births' which meant that the doctors hung out the windows to plot the horoscope of the child and the women plied the actual medicine. The position Luccia took involved working for a drunken doctor, but Luccia didn't mind, because he would pass out shortly after arriving at the lying in and leave the midwives to the birth. When he came to, he felt guilty enough to grandly share his profits.

Luccia's laboratory gathered dust, except for an experiment in the middle of her herb table: the seemingly endless search for the contents of her mother's potion, now nothing more than a faint odor from the vial and a remembered taste.

Isabelle and Jean wrote letters of their children's successes and their own prosperity, Luccia wore her mother's bottle of tincture to bed every night, and shielded her slowly aging, lonely face in the street.

Several years later, Theo knocked on her door. His arms were filled with sweet cakes, flowers, candles and incense from India, bags of herbs she had never seen, cloth for new dresses. He acted as if he had been gone a week and this time, as they invented and created and exchanged, he insisted that she write down their creations, that she chronicle what he had learned on his journeys and he talked about what they would do together as the years went on.

She had never known companionship like this: even the Wicca couldn't match her because they were unschooled in the university curricula and knowledgeable only of the local lore. The university educated, at this point, knew nothing of the rich herbal knowledge held by the Wicca. Even his size and his fragility made him her companion: not a hulking, man's man like the Bowman who had comforted her with the difference in their size and strength, but a tiny, homely man who seemed as uncomfortable with the body as she had been.

He stood at an oil burner, watching leaves swirl in a mixture, explaining how they would extract it in the weeks to come.

And then in the morning, he bowed stiffly and announced his intention to leave.

He couldn't be contained, couldn't be committed to a place: just when they were in the midst of a grand discovery, he chased down the rumor of a remedy by jumping onto the back of a traveling cart and riding off to Asia with as much forethought as going to the well. He had nothing with him except his thin bag of surgical tools. God knows he didn't have any clothing, Luccia thought, watching him wave from the back of an ox cart, promising to return.

He returned shortly, turning a solemn and tasteless meal into a wild celebration. Animal magnetism, he spouted, electro-magnetic therapy, the healing properties of mineral hot springs, the concept of re-birth. It was heresy, she shouted at him, laughing, it was genius, she said as she threw off a tattered shawl and re-pinned her hair.

Deep into the experiments, he insisted that she walk out for supper with him and en route, introduced her to the greengrocer in a northern quarter whose vegetable stand served as the neighborhood pharmacy.

"Theo here tells me you'll join on as the herbalist," the greengrocer said, and she looked over at Theo with sadness. It meant that Theo was leaving again, and the new job was a trinket for her as some give music boxes to their mistresses.

She worked with the greengrocer for two years while Theo was gone. In the evenings, she transcribed their work, continued cataloging what she had learned of surgery at the Sorbonne. During the day she sold herbs but she had insides of clay when he was gone.

When the pain was too great, she remembered, but the potions she created to replicate her mother's strengthened her back, gave her new vitality, but didn't stop the ache. Of course, she thought, sadly shaking her head over another failed batch: there's no tincture against lost love.

When he returned, they doubled the size of their laboratory, until her bed was shoved into a small corner of her rooms. They paced the shrinking floor together. Following the Neoplatonists, and the Wicca, he insisted, it would be logical that there were three suns in the solar system: one physical, one astral, one spiritual.

He taught her what the Parisian law requires of pharmacies and got her a position with the city inspecting them. He disappeared again afterward.

One year when he returned, he burst into her chambers, with an side-kick assistant stumbling in behind him, both of them laden with copper kettles and piping, drunk and tottering, laughing like ale-house fools.

"Gold!" the assistant mouthed through blackened teeth and Theo shoved him in the ribs.

"Sweet Luccia" he said, sweeping low to the floor but staggering, the pipes clanking around him. He was honestly pleased to see her, she could tell. Luccia was suspicious, though, of his assistant.

He introduced her to Oporinus, and she nodded but kept her hands on her hips.

"You're not after gold, Theo," Luccia scoffed. "Another metal overtaking the real work of medicine!" By what she could see during her walks through Paris, the alchemists now chasing gold outnumbered the medics. "Suffering and death to line someone's pockets," she grumbled.

"You're developing deep furrows in your brow, my dear," Theo retorted, and Luccia turned away.

Furrows, she scoffed. If she looked her age she would be a withered old hag. When he and his drunken assistant had left her for the evening, she cautiously approached Moishe's mirror, which she had covered years ago. If he only knew how old she really was, she thought, touching the wrinkles in her once-taut cheeks.

Theo moved on, lured to another position at the universities he despised, another attempt at fame and stature, while sacrificing the medicine, the doctors and Luccia in his dash.

The midwives Luccia worked with spread word of Theo's travels, which started to skirt the outside of the fool-infested universities, much to Luccia's pleasure. In England he ignored the doctors at Oxford and worked with miners in Cornwall. In Russia, he joined the Tartars invading Moscow and invented a lice powder to ease their saddle chafe. He traveled with the Gypsies in the Hungarian provinces; he treated the aging Queen Mother of King Christian in Copenhagen. Eighteen princes had Theo to thank for their health. He traveled with the Moors through the fantastic lands of Northern Africa to the Nile. He learned from magi and yogis and when he burst into her rooms in Paris again he was festooned with turbans, silks, German leather and an enormous sword tethered to his waist.

She opened her inkpot and began recording again. Shoulder to shoulder in identical shawls, they were scholars together. Tinctures and powders and burners jumped up and did their bidding. Investigating, extrapolating, they became so entwined in their thoughts and the papers in front of them that their words overlapped, synchronous, harmonic. Luccia was enthralled with him and he was inspired by her. Better than with the Bowman, for whom she had been all surrender, with Theo, she surrendered and yet was inspired to grow, to shine, to fall back and spring ahead both, full of power and confidence, to create in an ebullient chatter, to clink beakers, chuckling over the joy of their projects.

A list of what they knew separately would have toppled a tower of books, but the recipes they created — remedies, identification of herb families, tinctures weaving East and West, increasingly south past the Moors into North Africa, and of course all the wildness that shipped in with the herbs from India and far China — would fill a library.

At this homecoming, though, he also made reference to another type of learning he had received, and he kissed Luccia, cupping her angular face with his small hands. Theo ran his hands up the folds of her skirt, up her legs to her thighs. He laid her back across the desk, in defiance of all their papers and she inhaled the smell of the herbs in the written tincture. As he knelt on the floor, she moaned with the joy of body and mind being in unison, finally.

When he reached for his cape and gloves, her stomach turned over.

"Sometimes my love is like a fur coat you don't know you have on," she whispered in his ear, half devotion, and half venom. She drew her lips behind his ear and held his thin shoulders between her hands. "It warms you, Theo, but you don't notice. Feel my love warming you."

Theo knew that if he walked out the door he would be gone for weeks, and though her pronouncement made him want to run, he set down his cloak and his gloves.

As the days and weeks went on, they took long walks in the forest to find herbs, and then through town, Luccia on Theo's arm. She felt like Jacqueline, languid and feminine in her movements. She imagined the two of them, she and Theo, making love to Jacqueline, loving her and Luccia at the same time. It brought Jacqueline near. It made Luccia herself. She lay in Theo's arms, against his hairless chest, both of them pondering their medical puzzles and reveling in each other.

They made love sometimes in the middle of the day in rooms he had taken nearby, while bending over a list of remedies and tinctures that they were studying.

Within two weeks of his arrival, though, he sought the company of the university dons again, much to Luccia's dismay. The first day he spent with them, he returned to her crestfallen and exhausted.

"I'm too tired from all their idiot questions, Luccia," he said wearily. "They are ignorant as slugs and this is the University of Paris. What can we expect from doctors who can cut but not heal?" he said with resignation.

"Butchery," Luccia said.

"Indeed." He unscrewed the top of his sword, bent over it as if he had just walked in from Constantinople.

"Other than you, Luccia, this is why I came back," he said, showing Luccia his sword. "I got it from an executioner who couldn't stand his trade any longer."

He expected her to flinch but she remained placid, reliving the moment when she had given up her own butchery.

"The pommel is hollow," he said. "I've filled it with something special, Luccia. A pain-killer like none you've known."

"Mandrake?"

"No. Far better than mandrake. From Asia. Laudanum. I heard the surgeons were at it here. Half the patients of these idiots die just rather than withstand the pain of being cut open. But this, Luccia, it's sleep. It induces a sleep like none you've had," he said. He poured a powder into a glass, added water and tossed it back. He made a glass for Luccia, his eyes drooping.

His last effort before lying down on her bed was to pass Luccia the glass and as his head hit the pillow, his breathing slowed, and he talked in a dream. Unwilling to abandon him to even this digression into another world, Luccia drank, and minutes later as the room swirled around her, she lay down beside him. Theo, his long leg hanging over the side of the chair, one boot flat on the ground, started talking about Asia, describing the yogis and acupuncture, his speech disjointed and delirious. As the drug overcame her, she thought of her killing spree, Fiona's death, and the mayhem of the Black Plague.

224

Hours went by, she imagined. Luccia thought of childbirth; imagined a black crow flying from between her legs. Jumbled images, Theo droning beside her. Then all was dark, and when Luccia woke, Theo was sitting up, a cup of mint tea in his hand, staring at her.

Except for his trips to the university, Theo and Luccia went everywhere together, ministering to the sick: to the poorhouses, under the city bridges, onto ships, into the swamps on the edge of the city, then into the ale houses, always in lively conversation.

The debates at the school raged on, and Luccia thought that Theo touting his wisdom in the university was a fresh, open window where none had been. Theo said that he caught a few of the Dons scribbling notes on his remedies that they stuffed into the pockets of their robes.

Luccia wondered how they tolerated Theo Paracelsus. He was a man, a gentleman born of means, yet continually insolent. But he had discovered an element he called hydrogen, and then one he dubbed nitrogen. Who could ignore a man with a mind like that, even if he put boot marks on the chairs?

Now, however, he started forgoing their study sessions to swagger with Luccia into the pubs, drink and sing, then stumble home to make love again. They lay and smoked his laudanum on a Saturday morning that turned into a Sunday night.

Rolling over under the covers, running her foot down Theo's leg, Luccia couldn't remember a time when she had allowed herself to do nothing, accomplish nothing, work at nothing. When had she ever lived without responsibility or a task that directed her day? She pulled the blankets higher and smiled.

Sitting in front of a roaring fire with the laudanum coursing through her veins, she thought there was something fantastic about it: to be so deep into one's mind that the body seemed to fly. To leave it behind. To follow the course of one's imagination, reveling in the images themselves, not the outcome or output. Just to be free. Not the sacrificial lamb sent away, not the draft horse on the road delivering books, or the terrified assistant struggling to save the damned, just a body naked on a clean bed with visions dancing above her. A private Bacchanal.

Free and yet successful: their book *Greater Surgery*, encompassing everything she had learned at the surgery table, plus what he had done ministering to countless armies, was published in 1536. It had no mention of Luccia of course, but astounded her that it was published and when Theo came to her laboratory with the first two copies, they danced down the aisle between the tables, stumbled drunk through the streets of Paris and lounged around with the laudanum and brandy for two weeks. Medicine, companionship, success, freedom.

Sitting in her robe late in the afternoon, Luccia was drawn to her center table and drew a mortar to her. She ran her hands along the leaves and branches clustered on her table, old friends.

"What shall we work on now, Theo?" she said lightly, enjoying the easy feel of it, the sense of accomplishment and noting the stillness in her, the lack of the gnawing hunger that had inhabited her chest for more decades than she dared count.

"A cure for the hangover," he said groggily as he clambered painfully out of bed, pissed in the chamber pot and padded naked over to his sword. He opened the top with trembling hands, threw the powder in a splash of water and tossed it back. He crumpled into a high-backed chair facing her and pulled a shawl around his thin shoulders, his ball-less dick laying limp down the upholstery.

"A cure for the French disease," he said, his eyes starting to roll back. "The end of syphilis — now that would be a contribution."

"A voluntary disease if there ever was one," she muttered disapprovingly.

"Suffering is suffering, my dear," he said groggily. "Mercury presents great hope."

"Metals do not belong in the body," she said disdainfully, as much because of his state as his statement. His head fell back against the chair and his mouth dropped open.

He would be out for hours, she knew, and she cinched her robe tighter, feeling a chill along the floors. She drew the leaves to her nose, and took out a blade for chopping.

That night he went out drinking without her and crawled into bed at dawn, stinking of vomit.

The next day he disappeared until nightfall when he returned with several new-found friends who stumbled in and drank up all their wine, tipped over an organized stack of papers and had to be forced out with a broom by Luccia.

She was up early the next morning, banging the teakettle and the ash bucket with irritation. Theo had all that mental fire, parts of his brain working that others hadn't even awakened or been gifted with, and instead he lolled around drunk, a stranger's drool on his shirtsleeves. There was so much to do. So much worth doing.

The shine, she thought, poking at the fire with rage. He wasn't living up to the shine.

Chapter Twenty

Theo woke up and watched her slamming around the laboratory, got up silently and dressed in his most severely formal outfit though she could tell from his stiffness that every movement hurt. He pushed past her and left.

That evening when he returned, he was without his vest and hat, and Luccia had stripped every leaf off every branch on the table, chopped every shoot, packaged all the greenery into tightly wrapped bunches, boiled them into essence, trapped them within bottles and burned the stalks with a vengeance.

"Why aren't you doing your work?" she growled at him.

"And do what, Luccia, be alone with it all?" he wailed drunkenly, his cheek flat against the tabletop, his words slurred. "Do you know what they're doing to Copernicus? Is that what a genius has to look forward to?"

"I've seen worse," she snarled, twisting her skirts up over the floor as she paced. And since when is being with me considered being alone, she wanted to shout, but didn't.

"All of this...foolishness of the Church. Driving all the good minds out of Europe," he said. "They're migrating, Luccia, to North Africa, to India. To Ireland. Luccia, ever since that Magellan bastard came back alive, there'll be no telling where we could go."

"Look," he said brightly, staggering but standing and digging in his pockets. "It's called a pocket watch. Look how small," he exclaimed drunkenly, "a whole clock, right inside my pocket. Oh, those Germans!"

Luccia stood with her arms crossed over her chest and her shawl tucked tightly into her waistband.

Theo looked down at the table, then back at Luccia's sobering stare. "Luccia, there isn't a good doctor north of Salerno anymore." He tapped a knife-point on the table. "The women are all dead and the men are making gold."

"Then God help us if another Plague comes through," she said ferociously.

"God help us." Theo stumbled around the table and took her in his arms.

In the morning, Theo cleaned himself up and donned a gentleman's jacket, announced his intention to return to the university, and was sent off with warmth and relief.

He carried Trotula's knowledge and their own discoveries into meetings with the professors, and would come home at night laughing over their incredulous denial and exposure as brainless fools.

It seemed to be a game to him. He bore it with more aplomb than any woman would or could, Luccia thought to herself. He brushed off their fury as if he had special armor against their rage. Their reaction was a brief topic they discussed in the evenings before settling into their latest project, in the pacing around tables and the hungry scribbling that would take over their evenings.

Now Luccia didn't have to force him to work, she had to force him to eat, pull him from across the room to get him to come to bed. And in the morning, enlivened by their latest conjecture, he would dash off to the University.

But Luccia could feel the tension building at the university, through the tenor of the conversations at home. She didn't understand why Theo couldn't. Did men really think they were that invincible? The Dons argued with him, refused to speak to him when he came into the halls. Hearing it second-hand from him, Luccia could only imagine what plans were being hatched behind his back. He told her that one Don threw something at him in the President's chambers but Theo laughed it off as the actions of a man up from the farm, displaying harmless and crude behavior. Luccia had seen crude behavior and it may not hold weight in the eyes of the gentry, but it was anything but harmless. He laughed that the Dons were so infuriated that they argued with him as he walked down the halls, and just to aggravate them further, he broke into ungentlemanly farting. Still, every morning, he returned to cajole and instruct further.

Finally it was the issue of the laudanum that convinced Luccia that Theo had no concept of the rage of the new medicine man. He talked to them at length about the humane use of laudanum, actually broke down and cried in front of them describing the pain that is suffered on the battlefields that none of them save himself had actually seen. Safer than other alternatives, less long lasting, he said, describing its properties, its use, its collection and preservation. Childbirth, alone, he concluded, demanded the use of a tiny humane drop of laudanum. Think of the women we could save, he pleaded.

He was utterly unprepared for the response. When he described it to Luccia, she sat back in her favorite chair, swirling a cup of tea and biting her tongue.

"Suddenly we were talking about the Bible!" Theo said incredulously, pulling on the thin shock of hair that stuck out above his ears. "We descended from learned men espousing science, to the rabble-jabble of the country friar!"

Luccia sipped and sighed over the rare display of idiocy on his part. Tie your medicine to the fate of women and they'll throw it headlong into a well.

From that moment on, they fought ceaselessly. She railed at him when he acted as if it were a new development that medicine men cared nothing for women. He shouted that the introduction of laudanum was worth the fight and Luccia screamed that his insistence on this one remedy would jeopardize all their work that now even surpassed the work of Trotula.

He tried to pretend that everything was the same, making flippant remarks about the Dons when he came home, but the quips had lost their light-heartedness. They were tinged with sorrow. He smelled of fearful sweat. His face was smudged when he came home as if he had perspired during the day and walked home along the dusty streets rubbing his forehead. Still, the two would work, though the pace had slowed and his insights were fewer, as if he were afraid to follow his mind along its path.

A sense of resignation overcame them, and one night Theo stood beside her in the light and placed one of his hands against her sharp cheek in appreciation. Luccia turned to kiss his palm, poor disillusioned fool, poor brilliant mind in danger he couldn't grasp, his fate thrown in with the Wicca and the Gypsies and the medicine women. Luccia took him in her arms, lead him to the bed and made love to him as if he were a woman, with tenderness and mastery. Poor, little broken man.

After that, he would come home night after night and just sit in one of the chairs smoking the laudanum in a little pipe he had purchased. At first Luccia would join him, and they would drift off from their pain. Then she refused, would watch him start to slump and struggle him into bed, help him dress in the morning, but finally she left him to his own devices and he would pass out in front of the dying fire, rise stiff and miserable in the morning and go back to the university in the same clothes.

One night they sat face to face in their favorite chairs, talking, and Luccia popped up to put the kettle on. When she returned to her seat, his eyes were starting to glaze over, his pipe in his hand and his conversation became disjointed.

"Isn't that right, my dear?" he demanded after making no sense at all, and Luccia cleared her throat against the rage building in the pit of her stomach. How dare he drag her into his nonsensical logic, leaving her alone in reality? What right did he have to hide himself in his drugs and his quest for recognition when legions of women had marshaled more courage for less? Faced down more frightening enemies than silly teachers in black robes and plumed hats? How dare his heart bleed for himself that he wasn't a famous doctor with an exalted position when women died in childbirth every day because no one knew what to do anymore? How could he be so selfish as to not know that Luccia was a woman worth staying in the world for?

She sat night after night watching him drug himself into a stupor. She walked the streets of the Jewish quarter and along the banks of the river. She waited. By the window, by the fire, by the desk that had held their work and their sex. The only sound in the room was Theo's snoring, and Luccia's aimless shifting of papers, the thud of a teacup against the table, the intermittent shuffle of her chair legs on the floor.

Luccia felt the loneliness that plagued her as a little girl struggling across the plain toward Rome.

During the day she continued their work, testing their new combinations of herbs, recording the findings. Documenting, archiving. But the task had lost its spark, its chase.

In the evenings, she took to throwing little nuts at him in an effort to rouse him, then little pebbles, finally hurling things at him that left him with bruises that reminded her of Guiseppe and the spoon-shaped mark on his forehead. He rose in the morning, oblivious, and returned to the university, leaving her desolate and protesting in her morning dress.

This was worse than being alone, she decided, as he shut the door on her as she pleaded with him. The work was the same, the rooms were the same, but the presence of a person who didn't want to be present, who couldn't be coherent, made her feel unseen, insignificant. And worse yet, he arrived to share her fire, to receive her comfort, but couldn't bother to be awake most of the time. Her rooms had been colonized. She was the charwoman. She stared at him, slumped in his chair, still clinging to his sword, and thought it was worse than catching him in some wench's bed, worse than when he had ridden off to see the magi.

She struggled to get him to bed, threw her dress off and curled in beside him, pulled his arm over her shoulder, but the loneliness grew worse. This wasn't the shelter of the Bowman's body, or even the togetherness of shared nightmares. She wept into her pillow, feeling sorry for herself, and ashamed of her self-pity.

When his head hit the chair back yet another night, Luccia looked around her laboratory in panic. Luccia knew demise when she saw it. And the first order of business was to save the medical knowledge. She wondered what sort of woman would consider that more important than saving the man she loves? Heartless, she surmised again. Sitting in sleet, feeling at home.

But how to do it? With *Trotula*, at least it was a single volume to be spirited. She looked around her own laboratory, at a loss as to where to start. *Greater Surgery* was already in its second printing, embraced by the medical establishment and so safe, to an extent. His theories of the three suns, of animal magnetism and others were too foreign to her, too unclear. But the medicinal lore, the herbalism from around world, now that needed to be saved.

232

She looked around the room, calculating the number of stacks that would have to be bound, the volumes involved, and plopped on a stool in defeat. It would take a donkey cart the size of her first to just carry a single set. How would she print it, bind it, hide it from him?

And then it occurred to her. The old scribe would do it the old way. She would copy the papers, but not with huge margins and fine illustrations, she would copy them onto the old-style pages but in a hand that was as tiny as she could make it, so small that she could fit a dozen volumes into a single book. She threw her shawl on a chair, and frantically dug through the rooms, gathering every blank piece of paper she could find, unearthing single sheets at the end of a manuscript, a chapter break, a little stack hidden in a drawer. She lit not a single candle but an entire row of them and sharpened a half-dozen goose quills to extremely fine points.

Perhaps it was because the rest of her life seemed so hollow, or because, at this point, she had spent eight decades in the relentless pursuit of medical knowledge, but during those evenings, Luccia disappeared into the point of her quill. The world seemed to drain down its shaft, and reappear as lettering as small as ant tracks. Tiny writing, so small it didn't look like writing. It defied the properties of the quill. And in fact, Luccia demanded it be even smaller, and so tied a needle to the end of the quill and wrote with that, lettering as thin as a spider's strand, words as tall as a grain of sand.

Whole towers of manuscripts disappeared, moved word by word from their place, into the book, and then discarded into jumbled stacks that grew up the far wall of her room like a fence.

Her arms cramped and her shoulders bent. She aged as she sat there, her face contorting over the task of squeezing two lifetimes of study into a tiny, safe space. She ate nothing but bread. Her hands became gnarled. Her skin wrinkled and hung off her bones. When she got off her stool she was stooped and stiff.

Whenever she looked up and saw him out cold on the bed she threw a piece of crockery against the wall. The silence that met her violence sent her back down the quill shaft. She copied the wisdom of the wicks, with the discoveries of Theo and the ideas of the Gypsies, united, compiled, reduced to miniscule characters tight up against each other, blackening the paper with the density of the words, filling every square inch.

In the mornings before Theo rose, she secreted her growing volume in the wall behind loosened bricks, then brought it out again after he had gone.

Luccia couldn't keep him from returning day after day to the university, couldn't protect him from the verbal abuse of the Dons. One afternoon he stormed into the room without noticing her flank of candles or the enormous book that was blackened with her miniscule writing. He immediately set to preparing the laudanum, his hands shaking so hard that they knocked into the candlesticks and the fruit bowl.

"For the love of God, Theo, at least have dinner first," Luccia admonished. And then more to the point, she lowered her voice. "At least say hello to me."

He turned to her with eyes that she had seen before, in women a thousand times but not in a man since the Bowman on the pyre. The look of the hunted. Filled with the sorrow of a sentient being the moment before they become a victim. Just before they move from consciousness to carrion. Luccia grabbed the back of her chair to steady herself as his eyes burned through the space between them.

There was a knock at the door that startled them both.

"Paracelsus!" they heard.

"It's the Don," Theo moaned, and turned back to the table to rid it of his secret stash of laudanum. The name of the Don made her freeze: he would recognize her as the illustrator, especially since she was standing there with her manuscript and medicines in front of her.

What was the Don doing on this side of the river? The pounding increased on the door, and the Don's voice was joined by others. She frantically closed her manuscript, knowing the pages would smudge. She didn't have time to get the manuscript into its makeshift cupboard. The door hinges rattled from the pounding and Paracelsus strode to the door. Luccia could only put the enormous book on the stool and shove the stool under the table, then grab a bucket of water. On her hands and knees, she scurried into a corner and began scrubbing the floor.

Their swords clanked as they walked in and Luccia wondered what kind of professors wore swords but she was afraid to look up for fear they would recognize her. Shape-shift, Luccia, become a bed bug, she thought, but wished she could shape-shift the manuscript instead. The guards paced through the room.

"What are you doing, Paracelsus?" the Don asked.

"Working," Paracelsus said shortly, with as much disdain as he could muster.

"Working with your precious opiate?" the Don said, looking over the contents of the table, the collection of mortars, the dusty chopper, and the work Luccia had yet to complete. "Working with the witches, are you? Oh no, you said the Gypsies, that's right," the Don sneered. "There are two goblets on the table, two plates. Will she fly in through the open window?"

The Don grilled Paracelsus on the papers along the back wall, noticed Luccia scrubbing the floor but stepped over her as if she were a dog. He demanded to know the origin of the herbs they had written on, quizzing him, shouting at him and tearing at the papers.

"I don't have time for this! Speak your peace and be on, Don," Theo growled.

"Where did you get this, Paracelsus?" the Don said, holding up a fist-full of papers.

"From the Sorceress," Theo sneered. "The sorceress taught me everything I know. Now get out!"

The Don shouted about the Inquisition, pointing his finger in Theo's face. Proof now, they had it, his own confession. The fire would be hot, the Don sneered, and there was no point in running. He'd be back with the Inquisitor soon. Theo shoved them out the door, locked it behind them. He paced quickly to the side of the bed and drew Luccia off the floor, held her head against his chest.

"You have to leave, Theo," she said. "They've killed others for less."

Theo dragged a chamber pot from under the bed, put it in the center of the room. He took the papers from the table and ignited them in the flame from the burner.

"No! I haven't copied those yet," Luccia shrieked.

"Copied?"

235

She stood defiantly, trying in vain to throw her stooped shoulders back, cradling her twisted writing hand in the other palm.

Theo turned and clawed at the papers on the table, threw them into the fire, which soon spilled over the pot and began charring the floor.

"Don't do this!" Luccia shouted, grabbing at his arm, which he shrugged off.

She hit him with her fist and he shoved her aside.

"We can run," she cried. "We can leave town. We have to take the work with us."

"They'll kill me, Luccia."

Luccia grabbed his hair but he flung her against the wall. "Then let me take the manuscript," she said.

"Burning it all is my only chance of living," Theo wailed.

"The work is more important than one man's life," Luccia growled, and Theo suddenly stopped.

She turned away while the smell of burning paper filled the room.

"They won't spare you, just because they can't find your papers," she said. "Let me take them." Luccia grabbed his arm as he turned away, pulling papers from the far wall. The fire threatened the bed curtains so Luccia pulled the blanket off the bed and started beating the fire to put it out.

"Give them to you?" he hollered. "You're the reason I'm in this mess. Childbirth," he scoffed, "they're going to burn me for it!"

Luccia dashed to him and grabbed him by the collar.

"It's the laudanum," she said. "They'll kill you for the laudanum."

"I'll never give it up," he said, and Luccia knew it was true. But he spoke from his personal hunger, not from his belief in medicine.

"You have to go," Luccia said. "Go now. Get as far away as you can. Just don't let them find you."

He took her in his arms and kissed her, and she smelled fear, pity and desire.

"Go, go," she said, turning away from him, facing the wall where her hidden cupboard was lodged. She heard the door close and lunged for the stool, limped over to the secret cupboard and dug out one copy of *Trotula*. She hid the books on her as she had when she was a child, and ran.

He fled out of the city and she followed at a distance, convinced she could track him and be reunited, that they could re-make themselves into a country doctor and his wife somewhere. But she was old now. She moved like an old woman.

And Theo, the great Paracelsus, was not accustomed to hiding, and he was inept at it. If Luccia had shown herself, he would have been in more danger, and he probably would have forced her to leave, so she couldn't help him when the carriage pulled along side him as the sun went down, and the henchmen of the Dons clambered out, forced him in. They drove so far, so fast, that she didn't find him for two days, finally locating a spot where the carriage tracks stopped suddenly at a cliff side, where there was evidence of great commotion, and the tracks began again.

Peering over the side of the cliff in the fading light, her heart sank and she lowered her chest and belly into the dirt until she was prostrate on the road. Luccia Alimenti, now an old woman oozing so much grief that her legs were too sodden to stand, stretched out on a promontory over an ocean cliff. She gripped the precipice that crumbled in her gnarled hands, her sharp nose filling with the smell of salt water and kelp, the wind slapping her face in mockery over the sea's possession of her lover laying broken on the rocks below. Theo's body rolled in the waves, a hand catching on kelp and twisting him sideways, a foot lodging among the rocks and dancing him rudely, then the bulk of him rolling back as the tide played with him. The water tossed him as if he were a bag of unwanted cats, as if his sword, secret container of a secret campaign, was just another twig tossed aside by a tree that had many.

The planks of her two books were strapped to her back under her dress.

She lay there for days, watching the tide try to carry him away, watching his sword break on the rocks and wishing the opiate would wash over her instead of the starfish. She cried into the dust as a group of travelers dragged his body up, and when a group of peasant women crouched down beside her to see how they could help, she silently stood, a tottering old woman, and followed them.

237

How long she walked, how far she walked, these are numbers for people with a sense of linearity, who are born with a certainty of time, but not for Luccia. At some point, the peasant women arrived at their houses and Luccia sat down on a rock at the junction of the village, the manuscripts now bulging in a sack beside her. She sat talking for so long that ferns grew up around her, spider webs hung between her sleeves and waistline, dogs stopped being wary and took to sleeping in her shadow in the afternoons. Women from the village brought her food and two men built a skin tarp over her, which made her realize that it had been raining. Children climbed on the rocks around her and listened to her babble but her stories frightened their mothers and the only way she could keep their company was to keep her stories to herself. So she rocked back and forth. Soon, young mothers would do needlework by her ever-moving side as the children climbed, and the older women would help her down to the stream to bathe.

One day, struggling up the slope from the creek, her dress draining rivers into the dirt around her, she found a young wayfarer, a 17-year-old man who had mistaken her tarp for a traveler's relief spot. He sat in a corner on a satchel, swabbing his brow and she moved back to her rock with her eyes averted and her shoulders pulled in. She didn't know where she was or how long she had been there but a crazy woman by the road is used for kindling soon enough. She sneaked glances of him from under her eyebrows but any time he caught her eye Luccia turned away violently.

Surprisingly, though, when he opened his satchel, he didn't take out a knife or a Bible or a shank of rope to string her up, he brought out brushes and pens, set an ink pot in front of him and, handling it with the deference it deserves, he slowly pulled out a blank book. The sight of the inkpot calmed her, the sound of the scratch of his pen on the paper made her close her eyes and forget the decade.

When Luccia opened her eyes he sat just inches from her face, his pen in hand, peering at her.

"Who are you?" Luccia asked him, not flinching over his close proximity.

"Pieter. Pieter Bruegel. I'm on my way to Italy."

"Scribe?" she questioned.

"Painter. You have the most chiseled face. Cragged. But you talk madness old woman."

"Seen madness, young man."

"Tell me," he said, turning his face to see her bone structure, to see if insanity had leaked onto her skin.

So Luccia told him. Of the Plague swallowing people whole like a building with a mouth that chewed them into charcoal, of a woman with a leather beak and an Irish brogue. She told him of women kept in cages on the hillside above a town, tortured by men who looked like ravens while the hill split open and spewed a harp woven by a spider. She told him of towns on fire and brooms stuffed with drugs to redeem Eve, of townspeople slaughtering their own to suck a Bishop and a little girl given to a pig farmer from the ashes of her home, of lovers in the crook of a river who then fell into lavender fields, of monkeys and clerics leading armies of pointy soldiers with tin heads. She told him of dunking stools and barbarous glass balls filled with the naked, and the pustules brought by the rats, a vessel of blood and everywhere the red hue of inferno, of death, of dismemberment for a sideshow. Of a man with a thin blonde beard in a shawl carrying the weight of a boat and a bubble and a scribe who devoured body parts with her eyes. A good man thrown off a cliff. Of a red shawl and assholes and the strange birds and fish of the Far East, and the legions of the sick crawling naked but never arriving, of a tree that bloomed with delicate leaves like love. She told him of petards and spears and the first sight of a mirror, of arrows honed like affection and the back doors, back woods, back alleys of frightened women. Of the leg swallowed by the fish beside the boat and the entourage of a beaten boy who became a beater and the monks outside town with the scratching of their quills. A bell that rang forever until it was more dangerous than the onslaught it announced. Of death from the sky, death from the rat, death from the greed of the holy, and her, Luccia told him of her, marching forward, in a drooping doublet and a ragged skirt, a bag of herbs, a basket with a cup and plate and a pan hiding a book, a finely-wrought box of poison under her arm, a soldier's breastplate over her dress, and always, a sword with a hollow pommel in her hand, saying there is medicine, there is sanity, there is a way but it is old, and one foot in a felt shoe in front of another it will persevere. He sketched, she spoke and when she was spent she pulled a vial from around her neck and smashed it on the stones.

"Dulle Griet" the young man said. "Mad Meg," but he had heard her, and his sketchbook was full.

Time is such an odd thing. Luccia had always thought it fast in joy and slow in pain. But her own death, finally, was too fast: it sped her towards a place where she became cold peat, a bag of bones, no wooden headstone. She had sent a girl to the well and in the past, her granddaughter came back with the bucket, but this time, she lay back across her rock and time took an even stranger bend: it rendered her mute and invisible, sped forward even faster than before, a blur of people and change.

They say a vine of the most astounding quality grew from her rock. She walked into the mists and from the distance, heard them talking of greenery that sprung out of a perfectly sound stone, cracking it in a hundred places, a vine of tenacity and brilliance sprouting all over the impenetrable, shooting out blossoms of a brilliant blue hue. Woad. The color of woad and bilberries. Despite the efforts of the villagers to yank it out there was no stopping it, no tracking in through the labyrinth of stone to pull it out by its deepest roots. It darted from the killer's hands, and appeared in the most unlikely places in the village, growing bushy and unstoppable, its leaves undaunted by the cold, by its own improbability, by the relentless pursuit of its demise. It raised its blossoms every evening, as did Luccia from the mists, resolutely waiting for the moon to rise.

Bibliography

Achterberg, Jeanne, *Woman as Healer*, Shambhala, 1990.

Allely, Baker, Comstock, Hamm, Hardcastle, Massey, Strunk, *The Traditional Bowyer's Bible*, Volume One, The Lyons Press, 2000.

Anderson, Bonnie and Zinsser, Judith, *A History of Their Own, Women in Europe from Prehistory to the Present, Volume 1*, Harper & Row, 1988.

Bayard, Tania, *A Medieval Home Companion: Housekeeping in the Fourteenth Century*, Harper Perennial, 1991.

Brooke, Elizabeth, *Women Healers Through History*, The Women's Press, 1993.

Connell, Evan S., *The Alchemist's Journal*, North Point Press, San Francisco, 1991

Cushman, Karen, The Midwife's Apprentice, Clarion Books, New York, 1995

Denman, Cherry, *The History Puzzle*, Turner Publishing, 1995.

Encyclopedia Britannica.com re: the invention of mirrors

Ehrenreich, Barbara and English, Deirdre, *Witches, Midwives and Nurses: A History of Women Healers*, The Feminist Press, 1973

Ellerbe, Helen, *The Dark Side of Christian History*, Morningstar Books, 1995.

Evans, Arthur, *Witchcraft and the Gay Counterculture*, Fag Rag Books, 1978.

Goodrich, Michael, *The Unmentionable Vice: Homosexuality in the Later Medieval Period*, Dorset Press, 1979.

Gies, Frances and Joseph, *Life in a Medieval Village*, Harper Perennial, 1990.

Kors, Alan C., Peters, Edward, *Witchcraft in Europe 1100-1700: A Documentary History*, University of Pennsylvania Press, 1972.

National Geographic Traveler, *France*, 1999.

Hall, Manly P., *The Mystical and Medical Philosophy of Paracelsus,* The Philosophical Research Society, Inc., 1964.

Mabey, Richard, *The New Age Herbalist*, Collier Books, 1988.

Molitor, Ulrich, *De lamiis et phitonicis mulieribus, Teutonice Vnholden vel Hexen*, or *The Archer Witch*, not before 1489 (Library of Congress LC Control Number 48040446)

Read, Donna, *The Burning Times*, (video), Direct Cinema Limited, Inc.

Roberts, Keith, *Bruegel*, Phaidon, 1971.

Salerno School of Medicine: History, images and manuscripts from 11th to 13th century, Quenn (sic) Mary and Westfield College, (pamphlet) 23rd April to 3rd May 1990.

Shaw, Henry, FSA, *Dress and Decoration of the Middle Ages*, First Glance Books, 1998.

Summers, Montague (edit.); Kramer, Heinrich and Sprenger, James, *The Malleus Maleficarum*, Dover Publications, Inc., 1971.

Susac, Andrew, *Paracelsus: Monarch of Medicine*, Doubleday, New York, 1969.

Thomas, Hugh, *A History of the World*, Harper & Row, Publishers, 1979.

Biography of the Author

Jess Wells is the author of 13 volumes of work including three novels, five books of short stories, and anthologies of fiction and social commentary. Her work is included in two-dozen literary anthologies and journals, university curricula and European publications. She is a two-time finalist for the Lambda Literary Awards.